Damaged

A Damages Spin-Off

D1518328

By

Natavia

SOUL Publications

Damaged: Damages Spinoff   Natavia

Jay

September 3rd 2017...

The Hartsfield-Jackson airport in Atlanta was too crowded for my liking, especially since it was a different atmosphere. My plane landed from the BWI airport in Maryland thirty minutes ago. I was waiting for my homegirl to come and scoop me up. It's been over ten years since I last seen her. Sadi was from Annapolis, Maryland, too, which was how I met her, but shorty moved to start over because of a drug addiction. I couldn't believe that I kept in touch with her for all those years because I wasn't the phone type of nigga. If it wasn't for my right-hand man, Bogo, smashing her friend, I would've lost contact with her. So, I decided to come to Atlanta to be her date to her friend's wedding. Basically, our friendship was long distance. I adjusted the volume to my headphones while listening to Kevin Gates. My phone beeped indicating that I had a text message. Someone tapped me on the shoulder while I was opening my messages. When I looked up, it was her. I stood up and pulled her into my arms to hug her. I stepped away from her and noticed she gained some weight. Sadi was slim years back, but the summer dress she wore hugged her curves. She used to wear short hairstyles but she grew her hair out, letting it come past her shoulders. The Georgia sun gave her a bronze complexion even though she was considered light-skinned. Shorty was always attractive but the woman standing in front of me was gorgeous.

"You look good."

"I thought I was funny looking," she replied.

Sadi used to be one of those bourgeois stuck-up broads and even when she was on drugs, she still had that same attitude. Long story short, I wasn't digging shorty before she left Maryland. She had that light-skinned privileged attitude back then. Sadi used to think her pretty hazel eyes and good grade of hair defined her until she got a taste of real life. But my views on her changed once I got to know the real her. She was young, spoiled and naïve to a lot of shit but now she was down-to-earth.

"Come on, shorty. I wasn't talking about your physical appearance. Your attitude made you ugly but we past that," I replied. She told me to follow her and I grabbed my luggage off the bench. When we left the airport, she pointed me in the direction of a black Ford Explorer. I remembered a time where she wasn't pushing nothing but foreign whips but that was when she was dating a drug dealer named Stacy. I put my luggage in the trunk then got in the passenger's seat. She was listening to Jhene Aiko on the radio so I changed it. Sadi popped my hand.

"Don't touch my shit," she said.

"I might have to jack your little ass up. I see your mouth got slicker," I replied.

"It comes from talking to you every day. I had to step my comeback game up," she laughed.

We argued on the way to her crib but that's how we clicked. Atlanta traffic wasn't a joke and it took an hour to get to her condo. My phone vibrated for the tenth time but I ignored it. I didn't know how to explain to my fiancée that I left town to go to a wedding with an old friend—a friend that I had feelings for. To be on the safe side, I put my shorty on *Do Not Disturb.* The heat was beating down on me and I wasn't the type of nigga who liked hot weather. I grabbed my luggage out the trunk seconds later after she parked. All I wanted to do was take a cold shower. My testicles were sweating and sticking to my leg, the shit felt nasty. When Sadi unlocked the door to her condo, I took my shirt off. I was also starving so I asked her what we were doing for food but shorty was staring at my chest.

"Sadi!"

"What?" she asked.

"You don't hear me talking to you? Are you cooking something or are we going out? I'm hungry."

She cleared her throat. "We can go out," she replied.

She pointed me to the hallway bathroom so I could take a shower. I looked down at my dick when I closed the door and my dick was hard. It wasn't as easy as I thought it was going to be. I figured our connection would change in person because I was looking for a flaw but there wasn't any.

****

"Take another shot," Sadi dared me.

"Naw. I don't drink like that." Shorty took me to a bar downtown Atlanta called Sky Lounge.

"I dare you, Jadiah," she said. She knew what she was doing calling me by my government name.

"Aight," I replied.

"I'm not drinking anymore. One drink is enough. I need to be alert at all times, shorty," I told her.

It was around two o'clock by the time we got back to her crib. I haven't done the partying thing in a minute. My girl always wanted me to go out with her and I declined but Sadi talked me into having a few shots when I wasn't a drinker. I had a weak spot for her. She laid across my lap when I sat on the couch. I rubbed my fingers through her hair and she closed her eyes. Her ass was poking out in her skirt. Maybe it was the liquor and the blunt I smoked on our way back to the condo because she had my dick hard again for the fourth time.

"Where did this come from? Is it fake?" I asked while squeezing her ass.

"No, it's not. It comes from being lazy and not doing anything. Don't touch my ass anymore," she said. Sadi was bluffing; she knew what she was doing by wearing a tight maxi dress. While searching for something to watch on TV, Sadi fell asleep. I dozed off myself a few minutes later.

****

I woke up when I felt something on my lips. When I opened my eyes, Sadi was straddling me.

"This ain't us, Sadi," I replied. I wanted it as bad as she did but I couldn't ignore how I was betraying my woman back home who was worried about me because I just up and bounced.

"I want to know what you feel like," she admitted. She kissed me again and I thought, *fuck it.* I slid her dress up to her hips to palm her ass. The heat from her pussy warmed my leg. She grinded on my dick print while she tongue-kissed me. I laid her down on the couch to pull her thong down. Sadi's pussy was wet, bald and fat just like I imagined. I pushed her legs back with her knees touching the arm of the couch. Her nails dug into my scalp when I kissed her pussy. Three seconds later, she screamed she was coming. She told me she was celibate for ten years and, honestly, I didn't believe it at first until she wasn't able to control herself. She pressed my face into her pussy and smeared her cream across my lips. My dick was ready to burst through my jeans. While my tongue was in her, I unzipped my pants then pushed them down. Once I freed myself, I pressed the tip of my head against her opening. It was uncomfortable trying to squeeze into her tight hole; a moan slipped from her lips once I slid all the way in. She pulled her dress over her head and I unhooked her bra so I could suck on her titties. While I was digging into her spot, she wrapped her legs around me and scratched at my back.

"Ohhhhhhh, Jayyyyyy! That's my spot, baby!" she screamed while I dug into her guts. She was crying about feeling me in her stomach when I went deeper.

"I LOVE YOU!" she screamed out when I slowed down the pace to make love to her.

"Fuckkkkk, I'm ready to nut," I groaned. I tried to pull out but she wrapped her legs tighter around me and told me don't stop because she was ready to come again. I should've pulled out but I didn't. I spilled my seeds into Sadi then collapsed on her sweaty chest.

What the fuck did I just do? She admitted to loving me but she doesn't know about my shorty, Isha.

I pulled out of Sadi and laid next to her. She snuggled against me and I could tell she wanted me to say something but I couldn't. Isha was heavily on my mind; she was too good for a nigga like me.

Twelve hours later….

After the wedding, we went to the wedding reception. Seeing her friends get married made me think about my own wedding. Was I supposed to confess my love to my fiancée knowing I had sex with another woman that she didn't know I was friends with? It made me feel worse about everything. I should've did more to stop Sadi from kissing on me, but when she did, Isha became a distant memory. Me and Sadi was chilling at the table while the bride and groom danced.

"What is your problem? We haven't talked much since this morning," Sadi said.

"I have a lot on my mind. I'm good, though. I don't mingle much with people I don't know."

"Then why did you come?" she asked.

"Because I heard the sadness in your voice when you told me you didn't have a date."

Sadi stood up and walked away with an attitude. She kept asking me the same question. She knew I wasn't the social type. I came to Atlanta because for two months all she talked about was not having someone to go to the wedding with her. I went into the men's bathroom and a big nigga walked in behind me.

"Hey, um. You Jay, right?" he asked.

This nigga running up on me like he knows me. Something told me to take the long drive down here so I could travel with my gun. But naw. A nigga just had to get on a plane for some bullshit ass wedding with muthafuckas I don't know.

"Yeah, that's me. Who is you, though?"

"I'm Kareem. A friend of Sadi, Shelley and her husband, Arnold. I'm only introducing myself. We should grab some drinks when I come out to Maryland. I have some folks out there," he said.

Kareem looked like the dude that played Biggie in the Notorious B.I.G movie. Something about him rubbed me the wrong way. I'm a street nigga, what the fuck do I look like meeting up with a nigga I don't know for some drinks? That's some police and bitch shit.

"Naw, fam. I'm not even from Maryland."

"Oh, my bad. Maybe I heard wrong," he said. I went into the stall to handle my business. After I was done, I washed my hands then left. Sadi was on the dancefloor and I just sat back and watched her have fun. She deserved it, especially since I was being rude to her. I didn't want her to think I regretted having sex with her because I enjoyed it more than she will ever know. I only regretted not being a single man because I wanted to explore our situation more.

****

Sadi was too drunk to drive home from the reception so I had to drive. I used the GPS on my phone to get us to her condo and we were an hour and twenty minutes away from Atlanta. She could barely walk so I carried her up the stairs and to her door. I unlocked the door then carried her into her condo and laid her on the couch.

"You owe me an apology," she said while I took her heels off.

"I know. I apologize for tonight."

"We talked on the phone for years about everything! Why wait until you get down here to shut me out? What did I do wrong?" she asked. I stared at her for what seemed like hours, pondering how I was going to tell her the truth. She must've known I was with the bullshit because her eyes watered.

"I'm engaged. I wanted to see you before I married my fiancée because I know after I marry her, we can't continue on like this." She stood up from the couch with tears falling down her face. Sadi slapped me and I deserved it.

"You should've told me!" she screamed at me. I reached out to hug her but she smacked my hand away.

"Do you love her?" she asked.

"I love the both of you. I realized it when I made love to you."

"Go home to her," she replied.

She went into the kitchen and I went into her bedroom to get my luggage. I stood in the entryway of the kitchen and she was sitting at a small bar table drinking out a bottle of wine.

"Shorty, I'm—"

Sadi cut me off and told me to go home. She didn't want to hear any more of my apologies.

"I love you," I told her before I left out the door. My flight wasn't until Monday and it was Saturday so I decided to call an Uber and have them take me to a hotel. I needed to get my mind right because I was hurting two women even though Isha didn't know it yet.

Tuchie

"What do you want, Chika?" I asked my cousin when she called my work phone. I was flipping through the stack of papers on my desk as I listened to her ramble on. I worked in the Human Resources department inside of a court house and it was going on my sixth year. The pay was more than great, but my job drained me. Often times, I thought about quitting and opening up my own business or something.

"I'm trying to decide what kind of cake I want for the wedding. Should I go with strawberry or coconut?" she asked.

"You know damn well our hood-ass family ain't eating a coconut cake. Get a layered marble cake or something. Matter-of-fact, tell your sister to help you out with that," I said. Chika's sister, Asayi, was a cook and had many restaurants, including a few bakeries. I didn't understand why she was asking me about that when Asayi knew more about this stuff.

We talked for five more minutes before I hung up. My cell-phone rang again, but that time it was my best friend, Isha. I met her through my cousin, Asayi. They went to culinary school together. I braided Isha's hair for years and we ended up becoming friends. She was down-to-earth and had a wonderful personality.

"Hey, Tuchie. Can you fix my hair tomorrow?" she asked.

"Oh, lord. Did Jay pull a braid out again?" I asked. Even though I had a full-time job, my side hustle was braiding hair. Isha had faux locs in her hair and she wanted me to re-do the front.

"Not this time. Jay is up to something. Do you know he hasn't been home in a few days? I called him and his phone was off," she said. Isha met Jay from hanging around me, Chika and Asayi. Asayi's husband and Jay were cool. Also, my daughter's father and Asayi's husband are cousins. Everyone was connected and we were all like family.

"He'll call. Jay just be busy doing what he does. You know that man loves you," I said. Three minutes into my conversation with Isha, my daughter's father called me. I'm always telling them to stop calling me like I don't have a job. I told Isha I was going to call her back before I clicked over.

"What do you want, Stacy?" I asked my daughter's father.

"Damn, hi to you, too. Yo, you always got an attitude. Yah nigga must not be hitting it right," he said.

"What me and Lucas do is none of your concern," I said.

"That clown-ass nigga. I had you gaining weight. That comes from good dick. That nigga got your ass flat," he said. Stacy was forever talking mess and always reminding me of how good his dick is, and lord knows it's more than good.

"Far from flat. I caught you staring at it the other night when you dropped Niji off," I said. I heard a woman's voice in the background and my blood boiled. I wasn't supposed to have feelings for him after I broke up with him almost eleven years ago. But what kept our feelings in sync was our daughter. We did everything like a family—

everything. It wasn't the healthiest thing to do because feelings were still there and it felt so right. Everyone thought we were in a relationship because we got along for the most part. The only time we argued was when he was dating someone and vice versa.

"Who is that?" I asked and he chuckled.

"My assistant, is that okay with you?" Stacy asked.

"Tamyra? That bitch still works for you? I thought you fired her," I replied.

"Naw, you wanted me to, but you don't run my record label, I do. Mind yo' business, baby," he replied.

"I was going to cook your favorite dinner tonight," I replied.

"I'll be there then," he said and hung up.

An hour later while I was going over payroll, my boyfriend walked into my office with food from a Jamaican carry-out across the street. We had been in a relationship for two months though we dated for ten. Lucas was six-foot-two and was the color of peanut butter. He had perfect white teeth and I loved the way his suits fit him. He was a lawyer and when he had a case at the court house, he'd come to my office to hang out with me. He locked the door behind him and took off his suit jacket.

"Do you have some time for me?" he asked. Lucas was thirty-five years old which was three years older than me. He had a strong jawline with a nice goatee. His cologne filled my office—there was something about a nice-looking man who always smelled good. He leaned into me and passionately kissed my lips.

"I have been thinking about you all day," Lucas said.

"Oh really?"

"Really. I was wondering if we could spend the weekend together," he said.

"I think Niji's father has something to do so I might not have anybody to watch her."

"It's been a year, Stacy. Why haven't I met her yet? Is there something wrong with me? I love you and you know that. Eventually, I'm going to want you to be my wife. We talked about this; we are not getting any younger," Lucas said.

Lucas wanted a wife and kids and I wanted the same thing. I just wasn't sure if I wanted it with him. I loved him, too, but I couldn't shake my daughter's father. Me and Stacy didn't start off on a good note. We hooked up from hustling together. When we were younger, a lot of things kept getting in the way of our complicated relationship, including his ex, Sadi. The bitch even set me up to get robbed, and in the process, I was shot multiple times and flatlined twice. But I never told Stacy she was the cause of it. After I went through that, he ended up cheating on me with her which was a slap in the face.

"Okay you can meet her at dinner tonight. I also want you to meet her father."

"That should be interesting," Lucas replied dryly.

Lucas didn't want to meet Stacy but he didn't have a choice. Lucas had to accept Stacy if he wanted to be serious with me because Stacy was a permanent fixture in my life.

"So, I was wondering if you have time for a little you know," Lucas said, eyeing my thighs.

"I have a meeting in twenty minutes, but tonight after dinner, we might can do a few things," I replied. We ate lunch together until it was time for us to get back to work.

****

Six hours later...

"But, Ma. I don't want to meet, Lucas," Niji said. She was sitting at the kitchen table doing her homework as I prepared dinner.

"We talked about this already," I said as I rinsed the lettuce off.

"Why can't my father live here with us? Or maybe we can move in his big house. Daddy is by himself in that house," she said.

"Me and your father are just friends," I said and she rolled her eyes.

"Roll them again, and I'm going to knock those muthafuckas out of your sockets," I said. At ten years old, Niji talked too much and thought she knew everything. She had me and her father in her when it came to her attitude.

The front door to my house opened then closed. Stacy walked down the hall looking like a snack. The man was finer than he was when I first met him. He used to have very long cornrows but he cut his hair off seven years ago. The beard on his face gave him extra points. He was a little thicker than he was when we were younger and he resembled a taller, lighter version of the actor Andra Fuller. Stacy wore a black fitted, long-sleeve shirt, dark jeans and black Givenchy sneakers. The tattoo of our daughter's name was written across his neck in thick cursive letters with roses around it. He kissed Niji's forehead before he sat next to her at the kitchen table. He winked at me and blew a kiss. I playfully rolled my eyes at him but I couldn't go a day without Stacy's flirting. I wished Lucas had the same sexiness to him. Lucas was fine as well but he didn't have that "yes, zaddy" swag like the girls be talking about in the beauty shop. Over the years, Stacy's pretty-boy persona was replaced with arrogance, and boy did I enjoy every bit of it.

"You see how Mommy is eyeing Daddy? Tell her to come home," Stacy said to Niji.

Bihhhhhhhhhhhhh! This nigga can get the business if he keeps talking like that. Ohhh, and I can see his print, too. Look at those lips and thick, curly waves on his head. Damn, he's pretty.

"Don't do that," I said.

"Whatever, what time is this nigga supposed to be here?" Stacy asked. Stacy gave me hell when I called him after I got off from work and told him it was time to meet Lucas. But despite his rants, he wasn't going to turn it down. He was very protective over Niji so Lucas coming around was a big deal to him.

"The language!" I said.

"You are a hypocrite, Tuchie. I heard you curse before I came in, and stop acting like your mother's name ain't Jonita," he said, and I laughed. I pulled the salmon out of the oven and sat it on top of the stove.

"Where is the snapper?" Stacy asked.

"I didn't have time to stop and get it," I replied.

"So, what am I going to eat? You know I don't like salmon," he said.

Oh, honey you ain't got to like the salmon. I got a strawberry cheesecake you can eat for dessert and it's right between my thighs.

The doorbell rang and I became nervous. Stacy got up to answer the door and I followed him. Lucas stepped into the foyer wearing a button-up and casual slacks after Stacy let him in. He had flowers in his hand and a stuffed polar bear for Niji. Stacy couldn't hide the scowl on his face if he wanted to. It was sort of a relief because I didn't like the feeling of sneaking around. I was practically hiding Lucas in fear of upsetting Stacy. They say you can't build a new house with old stones and that's exactly what I was doing. I was nowhere near over Stacy.

"Stacy, this is my boyfriend, Lucas. Lucas, this is Niji's father, Stacy," I said. Lucas held out his hand and Stacy shook it.

"Tuchie, you like daisies? I thought you liked pink roses," Stacy said when Lucas gave me the flowers.

"That was a long time ago," I lied. I wanted to slap the hell outta Stacy.

"Yeah, you right," he said. Niji came down the hall and Lucas kneeled in front of her.

"I heard you like stuffed animals. I'm Lucas and I heard a lot about you," Lucas said with his hand out. Niji looked at her father for permission to talk to Lucas and Stacy gestured to her that it was okay.

"Thank you, Mr. Lucas," Niji said.

My eyes locked with Stacy's and my heart sank to the pit of my stomach. He looked so sad but what was I supposed to do? My biggest fear was being cheated on. I realized the men I dealt with in my past were all hood. I wanted a different type of man who could show me something better. Stacy wasn't a drug dealer anymore but he still lived that lavish lifestyle. He lived in a mansion, drove expensive cars, wore flashy jewelry and he was handsome with a huge dick. He was surrounded by nothing but extremely thirsty women because of his success. He had one of the hottest record labels in the country and he invested some of his money into many of his cousin Trayon's businesses. Knowing Stacy all a woman needed was exotic looks and a model-sized body. Years ago, he was shallow and I was the exact opposite of what Stacy liked. At the time, I was chubby and wore short hairstyles. I lost weight in my stomach area but my thighs, butt and hips weren't going anywhere. I was confident in my skin but Stacy made me a little insecure. I honestly believed he didn't love me and only used me to get over his drug addicted ex-girlfriend, Sadi. I tried so hard to show Stacy what kind of woman I was and the man I needed him to be but I ended up hurting myself. I knew he cared about me but love me? I just didn't know. In the past, he didn't show me any real signs of true love.

"Something came up so I'm going to head out. I will catch you later, Lance," Stacy said.

"Lucas," he replied.

"Oh, right. I forgot," Stacy said. He told Niji to call him before she went to bed then he walked out of the door.

"Well, that went well. It smells delicious in here," Lucas said and I caught Niji rolling her eyes. She wasn't disrespectful towards adults, but at times she showed how she felt. She didn't like Lucas. I could see it on her face.

We sat at the dinner table and ate quietly. Niji played around with her broccoli and I listened to Lucas talk about his job. While he was talking, I was thinking about Stacy.

Jay

Two hours later...

The Uber pulled up to my house and it was eight o'clock at night. I wasn't thinking when I slept with shorty but it happened. Now I had to go into the crib and face my fiancée—my reality.

"Appreciate it, man," I said to the middle-aged Asian male driver. I grabbed my luggage out the trunk then walked up the sidewalk. My fiancée was blowing my phone up and I wasn't trying to cut her off but how was I going to explain I left home to see a female friend? Shorty would've taken my head off. I unlocked the door to the mini mansion we lived in and my wife's dog, Pepper, barked at me. I wasn't too crazy about the small dog but she grew on me. She ran around my legs in circles, so I picked her up.

"Heyyyyy, girl. You missed Daddy?" I asked and Pepper wagged her tail.

Isha came down the spiral staircase dressed in stretch jeans, an off-the-shoulder top with a pair of Red Bottoms. Her hair was styled in silky dreads that she wore down to her ass. My fiancée was bad. She was around a size twelve and had nice titties and wide hips but her ass wasn't as big. It didn't matter because her personality was gold. I met Isha through friends because we were around the same people. She also helped me take care of my daughter, Hadley. Hadley's mother died after she was shot in a drive-by shooting. She died after she had a C-section. I was only fifteen when I became a father but my mother helped me raise my daughter. Hadley's mother's side of the family was estranged but her aunt and a few of her cousins kept in touch with her over the years. Isha was the mother Hadley always wanted. Even though Isha was only twenty-seven, she was old-fashioned. I think her parents having her in their late forties had a lot to do with it. I tried to kiss my fiancée on the lips but she turned her face and snatched the dog from me.

"Where is Hadley?" I asked.

"I took her to the bowling alley a few hours ago. Brittany's mother is gonna bring her home soon. But fuck all that, where have you been? You have been gone for three damn days with not one fucking phone call!" she yelled.

"I had to take care of business," I said.

"Really, Jay? You expect me to believe that bullshit? Do I have 'fool' written across my forehead? What if I do that to you? I can't even hang out for a few hours with my friends without you complaining but you're allowed to do what you want, huh?" she asked.

"I said I was busy! Damn, yo. Get the fuck on!" I said and walked out of her face. Isha followed me upstairs, asking me thousands of questions. She was perfect but often times I had to ask myself if I was ready for marriage. I proposed to her because she kept saying how she didn't want to shack up with me without it being more than just a relationship. Hadley loved her so that was another reason why I did it but I couldn't help but think if I wanted to be with her for me or because my daughter had a close bond with her. Shit was all fucked up.

"Are you cheating on me?" Isha asked.

"What?" I replied, taking my shirt off.

"Nigga, did I fucking stutter? Are you fucking another woman? You handle business all the time and still pick up to call me and Hadley," she said.

"Listen to yourself," I replied and shook my head.

"The wedding planner is coming tomorrow. If you're not ready, just say it," she said. I began feeling guilty. I had a good woman but was fucking another one a few days ago like I was a single man. I cared for both women; a nigga was stuck. I wrapped my arms around her to get her to understand.

"Baby, you know I wanna marry you. Yo, why is you trippin'?" I asked, kissing her neck. My phone rang inside my pocket and Isha pulled away from me and walked out the bedroom. I should've put my phone on vibrate.

"Yooo," I answered.

"Jay," the voice said.

"What's up?" I asked.

"After you left I thought I could just walk away and let you forget about me, but I can't do this. I've talked to you for ten long-ass years and we can't end like this," Sadi said. I sat on the bed for a few seconds and we listened to each other breathe over the phone.

"I know and I apologize for doing this to you but I couldn't resist. I fucked up, shorty," I finally said.

"I can't stop thinking about you," she admitted.

"Oh yeah? I can't stop thinking about you, neither."

"This is so hard for me, you know that," she sniffled. The front door opened and I heard my daughter's voice coming from downstairs. I told Sadi I was going to call her back before we hung up. Hadley was in the kitchen with Isha when I found her. My daughter resembled her mother a lot. She had caramel skin and beautiful big brown eyes with a dimple in her chin. Hadley was also a straight A student and she was on the soccer team. She was a daddy's girl but I realized she became closer to Isha. I wasn't tripping about it because she was getting older and probably could talk to Isha about things she couldn't say to me.

"Hey, baby girl," I said and kissed her cheek.

"Hey, Daddy, I was just asking Isha if I could have a sleepover next weekend," Hadley said.

"And what did she say?" I asked, eyeing Isha. Shorty knew I didn't want a bunch of people in my crib.

"She said it was fine and she's going to take me shopping so I can get spa kits and some other things. It'll be fun," Hadley said. I wanted to tell her to cancel her plans but she seemed happy so I decided not to say anything. I waited until Hadley left the kitchen so I could talk to Isha about it.

"Yo, really? What is up wit' you getting into everything that concerns my daughter? Some shit you don't speak on. You know I don't want a bunch of muthafuckas in my crib!" I spat.

"You don't like how I raise, Hadley? Well, how about you stay your ass home and out the fucking streets so you won't have to worry about me doing what you're supposed to do. And you think those little girls gonna set you up or something? Leave that street mentality out of this house! Hadley is a teenager so get over her wanting to do teenage shit!" Isha yelled back. Honestly, I didn't know what was wrong with me because nothing she did mattered before. Maybe it was because of Sadi and me trying to justify why I cheated when I really didn't have a reason.

"I'm going over to Tuchie's house," Isha replied with sadness in her voice. She walked past me and I reached out to her but she snatched away from me.

"Yo, I apologize. I didn't mean it like that," I said. Isha ignored me, grabbed her purse and keys and headed out the door. Hadley was at the top of the stairs holding Pepper when I turned around.

"I heard what you said, Daddy. She's just trying to help," Hadley replied and walked away.

Damn, I'm fucking up already, I thought.

I went into the living room and pulled my phone out of my pocket. Instead of calling Sadi back, I called my fiancée. She sent my call straight to voicemail.

Isha

I sped down the road with tears falling from my eyes. Me and Jay had four great years together, but suddenly something changed. He left town without telling me and his phone was off! Then to top it all, the nigga had the nerve to come at me about Hadley. I couldn't help how much I loved his daughter. She was a perfect teenager. We were very close and she talked to me about everything. I never wanted Jay to feel left out but he was still roaming the streets, slinging dope. He had other businesses going on but he was knee-deep in the game. I loved Jay so much that I accepted all of him and never questioned him about anything. All I asked was that he respect me but I guess he was falling out of love with me. The thought of him seeing someone else sickened me to my stomach. It took almost an hour to get to Tuchie's house because I had to take a detour. As soon as she heard my car pull up in her driveway, she opened the front door.

"What's the matter with you?" she asked when I slammed my car door. I took the glass of wine out of her hand when I stepped into her house and she looked at me with a raised eyebrow.

"Jay's ass makes me want to kill him! The nigga been gone for three days and didn't answer my calls. So tonight he finally comes home and he had the nerve to catch an attitude with me. He got mad at me because I told Hadley she can have a sleepover," I said. Tuchie followed me into the kitchen and she had leftovers out on the counter. Suddenly, I began regretting coming over to her house. It was late and I remembered she had dinner with Lucas.

"I'm soooo sorry, Tuchie. I forgot about you and Lucas's dinner. How did it go and what happened with Stacy meeting him?" I asked. I was so busy rambling off that I didn't realize how stressed she looked. Lucas was a good man, but he wasn't Tuchie's type. Not because he didn't have a hood streak, but because he didn't know the real her. The way she acted around Lucas was too forced and I always told her to be herself.

"Don't worry about it. He couldn't stay long because he has a meeting tomorrow morning. But Stacy was cool with him. I can't believe I'm actually moving on with my life," Tuchie said. She fixed me a plate and put it in the microwave. It was ten o'clock at night and the house was extremely quiet because Niji was asleep. I never understood why Tuchie's house was so big when it was just her and Niji.

"Do you really want it to be over between you and Stacy?" I asked.

"I mean we have been over for ten years," she shrugged her shoulder. Tuchie was very hardheaded and stubborn but that was just her.

"But y'all were still a family. Like nobody knew y'all were broken up outside of our circle of friends. Do you still think Stacy is shallow?" I asked. She took my plate out the microwave and sat it in front of me then poured me a glass of Patrón on ice.

"I think Stacy will always be shallow. I really don't know if he's changed. What if we get back together and he cheats on me because someone is prettier than me? I hate to sound immature but men like Stacy don't know a woman's worth. I know he was young back then but now he's around all types of females every day. I don't feel like that with Lucas because I know he wants me for me and adores me," she said.

"Do what makes you happy," I replied.

"So, what's going on with you and Jay?" she asked.

"He feels like I'm overstepping his parenting. I mean he's always busy so instead of complaining, I stepped up to the plate and made sure Hadley had a parent around the clock. He's not a bad father but I can't pretend that he's always around. Jay is away from home all day and when he comes home, Hadley is asleep. When she wakes up for school, Jay is asleep. Anyways, maybe I should take a step back," I replied.

"You know that's your daughter, right? You don't have to give birth to a child to be a mother and don't let that nigga come between you and her. She loves you and it would crush her heart if you listen to Jay. Maybe you should stay gone for three days and see how it feels," Tuchie said.

"He'll have a fit," I replied.

"Tell him you had business to take care of," Tuchie replied.

"You want me to play dirty, huh?"

"Of course, let these niggas know that what doesn't break us will make us stronger. Trust me, if Jay is cheating on you, he's gonna regret every last bit of it. Men don't forget the good women they've done wrong," Tuchie said. Jay called my phone twice while I was eating and I turned my phone off. He could kiss my ass as far as I was concerned.

"Niji is asleep so we can watch some horror movies on Netflix," Tuchie said and I rolled my eyes.

"I don't like scary movies and you know this," I replied.

"Girl, grab your plate and come to the living room. That's what your ass gets for coming over here during my relaxation time," she spat. I grabbed my plate and drink and followed Tuchie to the living room.

Maybe I overreacted with Jay but I was definitely going to get down to the bottom of it.

****

It was four o'clock in the morning by the time I made it home. Me and Tuchie watched a few movies and had a few drinks. She didn't want me to drive home but I took a chance with it and snuck out after she fell asleep on the couch. I appreciated Tuchie but I didn't want to crowd her space. Besides, I wasn't the type to stay away from home under any circumstances. Pepper ran to me when I unlocked the front door. I went to the living room when I noticed the TV was on. Jay was lying on the couch with a bottle of Hennessy sitting on the table and an empty glass. His phone was next to the bottle and curiosity got the best of me. I had never had a reason to go through Jay's phone nor did I ever think I would have to. I trusted my fiancé and he never showed any signs of cheating in the past but something was off about him. I reached for his phone and he moved. By the time he opened his eyes, I grabbed his glass and liquor bottle off the table.

"Where are you coming from?" Jay sat up on the couch and scratched his chin.

"Tuchie's house. We had girl talk," I replied. Jay stood up and looked down at me. He tilted my chin up to kiss my lips.

"I apologize about earlier. I was way out of line. Do you forgive me?"

"Yes, I forgive you, but you can't do this again. You have never stayed away from home for days," I replied. Jay pulled away from me and I grabbed his face.

"I mean it. Don't disrespect me again because I won't hesitate to leave you. I'm in the house at a decent time and you always know where I'm at. I don't hide shit from you and I want the same in return. Tell me if you're not ready to get married. Don't make a fool out of me, Jadiah."

"I want to marry you and I'm not fucking around. I'm not trying to ruin my family, shorty," he replied.

Jay walked away from me and headed upstairs. For some reason, I still didn't believe him.

God please show me a sign if this man is making a fool outta me.

Sadi

Two months later...

"**P**regnant?" I asked the doctor.

I thought I had a stomach virus because I couldn't hold anything down. My friend, Shelley, took me to the doctor's after I finished my last client at the salon. Pregnant was something I didn't want to hear. Me and Jay were still talking on the phone but things were deeper between us. Every night, he snuck into the bathroom to Facetime me before he went to sleep. Part of me was feeling horrible because I was in love with another woman's man, but the other part of me knew where he belonged.

"That's what the test says. Get undressed and I'll be back in a few to see how many weeks you are."

The doctor left the room and Shelley came in.

"Is everything okay?" she asked.

"I'm pregnant. What am I going to do?"

"Oh, my lord. Did you tell Jay?"

"No, this is bad. I can't raise a baby by myself and Jay isn't moving to Atlanta. He doesn't like it here," I replied.

"You might have to move back home. It's only right. I'm here if you need me but I know you want him to be around. You can't do this all by yourself and definitely not long distance," she said.

"What about his fiancée?"

"Let him worry about that and you worry about this baby," she replied.

"I don't think I can go back home. I did too much shit. I'll deal with this here and if Jay wants to be a part of this, he'll have to move here," I replied.

Shelly grabbed my hand and squeezed it. She'd been my best friend since I moved to

Georgia. She knew everything about my past and not once did she judge me.

"I'll never lie to you but you need to go back and apologize to those people you hurt. I'm a firm believer in karma and sometimes it skips us and attacks our kids. Do it before this beautiful life comes into this world. You're still not clean although you left the drugs alone. Go home and apologize to your father, Asayi and Tuchie."

"Apologize to Tuchie? She was fucking my man and smiling in my face," I replied.

"Stacy wasn't your man when he got with Tuchie and you told me that. You also told me she only knew of you because you were best friends with her cousin, Asayi. Ten years passed, so you should apologize. She was shot because of you. We all make bad decisions but real growth comes from admitting your faults and asking for forgiveness."

"I don't want to go back home, Shelley."

Shelley shrugged her shoulders and walked out the room so I could undress for the sonogram. If my daughter by Stacy was alive, she would've been eleven years old. To go through pregnancy again while being sober scared me. I didn't know what to expect because I was numb during my last pregnancy. When I was getting high while pregnant with Aja, I didn't care about her well-being. It didn't dawn on me how much I was hurting her until after I gave birth to her; she was dead when she came out of my womb. The doctor came back into the room to give me a sonogram. I was eight weeks pregnant. Seeing the sonogram made me love Jay even more and it also made me realize I couldn't do it on my own. I wanted him to experience the feeling with me.

****

When I left the doctor's office, I called Jay but he didn't answer. I texted him and told him it was urgent and I needed to talk to him. He called me the next day, five o'clock in the morning.

"Hello."

"What's up, shorty? I was a little busy earlier. Isha had a lot of people in the house," Jay said.

"I'm pregnant." The line grew quiet and all I heard was the TV in the background.

"JAY!" I called out.

"My bad. Damn, Sadi. You sure?"

"Yes, I had an appointment yesterday. You would've known if you answered your phone. All I needed was two minutes. What are we going to do?"

"I don't believe in abortions under any circumstances so bear with me on this. You ain't planning on getting rid of it, are you?"

"No, Jay, I'm not but I can't do this by myself so some adjustments have to be made."

"Come back to Maryland. My businesses and shit are here and you know Atlanta ain't my style. I'll give you some money to open up your own hair salon. Matter of fact, I have an empty shop right now. I was going to use it for a landscaping business but I ain't got the time to start that shit right now," he said. The real reason Jay didn't want to leave Maryland was because he made his dirty money in the DMV. He would've probably started a drug war if he came to Atlanta and stole the hustlas' clientele.

"That's a big decision," I stated.

"I know but what do you want me to do, Sadi? My daughter loves Annapolis and it'll always be about her. I'm not moving to Atlanta, bottom line."

"Or is it because of your bitch?" I snapped. Nothing seemed fair to me because I waited for Jay all these years. I was celibate until he visited me a few months prior. So far, I sacrificed a lot and wasn't getting anything in return.

"Yo, are you fuckin' serious right now? The fuck you want me to do? Just leave my daughter and come down with you? No offense, baby girl, but I got too much shit going on. I know it ain't your fault but you know this wasn't done on purpose. Come back home and you'll have your own business. I'll make some calls later on and start getting the shop ready for you. Send me an idea of the layout and you got it."

"What if it doesn't work out? You know I left Maryland for a reason, Jay."

"The shop will be in Landover, Maryland. The chances of running into one of your old friends are slim to none. But, shorty, you can't let that shit control your life. You still have family here. Everybody fucks up," he replied.

"Let me think about this."

"No pressure. If you can't do it, I'll just fly out a few times out the month or whenever you need me to," he said.

Honestly, I thought Jay was going to be upset about the baby. I was caught off guard by his reaction. And he was right about everything. He couldn't just move because that's what I wanted. He had more at stake than I did. All I had in Atlanta was my aunt, best friend and my job. What Jay offered me was so much more.

"I miss you, shorty. Send me a picture of the sonogram," he said.

"Okay, I love you," I replied.

"Love you, too."

When I hung up the phone, I cried my eyes out because deep down inside I knew our situation wasn't going to change any time soon if I stayed in Atlanta. So, I did something I never thought I'd do.

I dialed a number and waited for someone to answer the phone.

"Hello," my mother said half asleep.

"Hey, Ma. I'm coming back home."

"Really, baby? I can't believe this! When are you coming back?"

"In a few weeks but don't tell Daddy. I want to surprise him."

"I can't believe this, Sadi. Are you coming back to our house?"

"No, but I'm going to be living forty minutes away."

"I prayed to God for years on sending you back home." My mother visited me once a year. She'd drive down and spend a week with me. Me and my father talked on the phone here and there but I knew he was still upset with me. I hurt my parents really bad when I was getting high and my father hadn't fully forgiven me yet. For years I stressed about the pain I caused him because I was a daddy's girl. It was hard to rebuild that trust with him long distance. I stayed on the phone with my mother for an hour before I went to bed.

****

I was feeling great after I got off the phone with my mother because everything was coming my way. My appointment wasn't coming into the hair shop until noon, but I decided to go early so I could help Shelley out. Shelley had more clients than me because she did bomb ass sew-ins. My specialty was braids, short hairstyles and I was also a barber. Most of my clients were men. Before I went to the salon, Elegant Styles, I stopped at Starbucks up the block and ordered the stylists some drinks. It was the least I could do since I was moving back home. When I walked into the salon, it was semi-crowded.

"Can you check Morgan to see if she's dry?" Shelley asked.

"See, this is why I came in early. I just knew you needed me," I replied. I sat the drinks on the counter at the front desk and the stylists came out of nowhere like bees. Coffee was like crack to us. Everyone thanked me as they headed back to their stations. I checked on Morgan's hair and it was still wet, so I added twenty more minutes to the dryer. The door opened to the shop and it was Kareem. I rolled my eyes because I was getting sick of him. He worked at the dealership across the street and was always coming in to check up on me.

I should've parked around the back instead of the front. This nigga is too pressed.

"Good morning, ladies," Kareem said to everyone.

"Heyyyy, Kareem," they replied.

The ladies in the shop loved Kareem. He was a gentleman but he wasn't my type. He was handsome but a little on the heavy side even though he wasn't sloppy. But then again, maybe I didn't see what everyone else saw because of Jay. Kareem wouldn't like me if he knew I used to be a drug addict with promiscuous ways. I feared dating other men because I didn't want a man to judge me about my past but I also felt like I shouldn't have to hide it, so to avoid any disappointments, I stuck with Jay because he knew all about me.

"Hey, Kareem," I said dryly.

"Good morning. You look beautiful by the way. Do you think we can talk in private?" he asked. The shop was being nosey because everyone was staring at us.

"I'm kinda busy."

"I haven't talked to you since the night you and Jay got into it. Was it something I did wrong?" Kareem asked.

"I'm at work, Kareem. Do I come to your job and disturb you? Give me the same respect. I will talk to you when I get off!" His nostrils flared. Kareem was trying to compose his anger so he just walked away and left the shop.

"That's a good man, Sadi. Hell, let us know if you don't want him. He graduated from Morehouse and he's single with no kids. Oh, and his record is clean. Girl, you fuckin' crazy," a stylist named Shameka said.

I need to leave sooner because Kareem is annoying the shit out of me!

Tuchie

I pulled up in the driveway of Asayi and her husband's mansion. Niji was in the back seat reading a children's book on her iPad.

"Ma, can we get a house like this? They have an indoor pool, a gym, movie theatre and Nevaeh has her own dance room," Niji said.

"Honey, Trayon and Asayi have wayyy more money than me. Your father has a big house."

"But he doesn't stay there much because it's too empty. I always stay at his condo downtown when he gets me. Maybe we should move into his house and tell Lucas to meet you somewhere else," Niji said.

"That's not nice. Lucas is a nice person."

"But Daddy loves your hair and clothes. Lucas doesn't say anything about that," she said and shrugged her shoulders. One thing about kids, they see things that many of us doesn't pay attention to.

Now I have to see if Lucas compliments my new hairstyle.

I rang the doorbell and Asayi came to the door. Niji hugged her and Asayi picked her up.

"Put her down. She isn't a baby. Girl, you look crazy holding her," I said.

"I know but she's so cute. Niji is gonna live with us for a month," Asayi joked.

"Yes, Mommy, pleasseeeee," Niji begged.

"No, because I'm not going to have anybody to get on my nerves," I laughed.

"That's what Stacy is for," Asayi said. Niji jumped out of her arms when she saw Hadley. Niji loved Hadley like they were sisters. Me, Isha, Niji and Hadley did a lot of things together like shopping and going on trips. Asayi brought her daughter one time with us and Nevaeh cried the whole time because she missed her father.

Semaj was walking down the hallway with a remote in his hand. In front of him was a guinea pig in some kind of ball with rollercoaster lights. Semaj was controlling the ball with the remote.

"Hey, Semaj? What is that?" I asked.

"It's my guinea pig's ball. It monitors its heart rate and detects when he needs water while he works out," he said.

"And you made it?" I asked.

"Yup," he said and the ball rolled over my shoe. The poor thing looked out of breath. Trayon spent mad money on Semaj's projects.

"Watch out, Semaj! Make sure it doesn't roll into one of my tables and knock a vase over!" Asayi called out to him as he jogged behind the ball.

"That boy is gonna be a genius. He's eight and has inventions already."

"I worry about him. He's so smart that he doesn't enjoy being a child. All he does is build things and enters every science fair in the county," Asayi replied.

"He's gonna be rich."

I told Asayi I was going to use the bathroom before I joined, her, Isha and Chika in the kitchen to help set up the table for dinner. Walking down the long hallway reminded me of a college university. The house was so neat that you didn't want to touch anything. Asayi's fancy decorations needed to be in a glass showcase. Asayi's oldest son bumped into me when I turned around the corner.

"Oh, my bad, cousin Tuchie. I ain't see you," he said with his phone in his hand. TJ was eleven years old and thought he was the king of the house.

"Boy, who are you talking to?" I asked and he hid his iPhone behind his back.

"I was calling AT&T customer service because my phone lost service," he lied. I reached behind him and took the phone from him.

"Who is this?" I asked.

"Asia," the little girl said.

"How old are you, Asia?" I replied.

"I'm thirteen," she said.

"You know how old TJ is?" I asked.

"Thirteen," she replied.

"Okay, sweetie. He'll call you back shortly," I said and hung up.

"What did your father tell you about talking to older girls?" I asked. TJ was a smart kid, too, but he was already into sports and girls. Even though he was eleven years old, he looked fourteen because of his height. He also had a temper problem like his father.

"Come on, cousin Tuchie. Don't tell nobody about Asia. I really like her," he said.

"Y'all go to school together or something?" I asked.

"Yeah, I told her I was in eighth grade, though. She doesn't know I'm in fourth. Don't tell my mother, I'm not supposed to be on the phone because I'm punished," he said. TJ went to a private school that had elementary, middle and high school kids.

"Punished for what?" I asked. TJ was always punished for something.

"Disrupting the class. The teacher lied to us and told us Martin Luther King Jr. died in 1966, I told her he was killed in 1968. She told me I didn't know and I told her she shouldn't be teaching Black History if she isn't black. She sent me to the office and the principal called my mother. I wasn't even wrong, though," he said. The door to the gym opened and TJ hauled ass down the hallway.

"Yo, was that my son?" Trayon asked when he came out the gym room. I peeked around him and saw Stacy playing basketball.

"Ummm, no."

"Yo, stop fuckin' lying. I know my kids. I'm gonna fuck his lil' ass up. I told him he couldn't come out his room for shit," Trayon said. He walked down the hallway and called out to TJ. Stacy was staring at me and it seemed awkward. We hadn't been talking much since he met Lucas. I couldn't hold it in much longer so I rushed to the bathroom. After I handled my business, I flushed the toilet then washed my hands. The door opened because I forgot to lock it and Stacy was standing behind me. Me and Stacy had been having sex for years. It started when Niji was two years old. But I stopped sleeping with him two months ago after me and Lucas became serious. Nobody else knew that we were messing around for all those years.

"What are you doing in here?"

"We usually sneak in here while everyone is eating. Why stop now?" he replied.

"Get out, Stacy."

He picked me up and sat me on the sink. I cursed myself for not locking the door.

"Why you actin' like you don't love a nigga?" he asked.

"I'm acting like a woman who is in a relationship."

"This shit is getting old, Tuchie."

"I know but I don't know what to do," I admitted.

"Why you with that niggga, Tuch? I want you and I think we should do the right thing. I never gave up because deep down I know you want me, too," he said. My cell-phone rang on the sink. It was Lucas calling me. I reached for my phone and Stacy dared me to answer. He grabbed my face and tongue kissed me. I moaned against his lips and he pushed my skirt up to my hips. I told Stacy I couldn't cheat on my man and what we were doing was wrong but he told me he was my man.

"Wait, Stacy! Stop!" His finger was already in my pussy so there was no turning back.

"Who made you wet like this, shorty?" he asked.

"Youuuuuu," I moaned while he slid his fingers in and out of me. He licked the nape of my neck and I wrapped my legs around him. Stacy pulled his joggers down to free that big piece of his. Seeing his dick and imagining what he was ready to do had me on edge. To keep anyone from hearing me I covered my mouth when I came. He pulled me to the edge of the sink then slid my thong down my legs. My legs spread for him so he could enter me. I was dripping wet and my nipples ached for attention so I unbuttoned my blouse. Stacy pulled my breast out of my bra and licked across my nipple. He knew my body better than any man I had been with. My nails scratched at his neck when he pressed the tip against my G-spot. Stacy covered my mouth when my moans were getting louder.

Nigga, what did you think was going to happen with you pounding my pussy like this?

"Mommy! Asayi said come and get your plate!" Niji banged on the door.

"I'm commminngggggg, Niji! I'm on the toilet!" I yelled out and Stacy went harder.

"Is Daddy in there with you?" she asked.

"Ummm, yeah! He's helping me fix my skirt!"

"It sounds like you're pooping!" Niji giggled. I yelled for her to go sit at the table.

"Shitttttttt, Stacy!" I moaned as he grabbed my breasts.

"Tell me you love me!" he demanded. He grabbed my chin and forced me to look at him.

"I LOVE YOU!"

Stacy let out a low groan when he came.

"Damn it, Stacy. Learn how to pull out."

"The fuck I need to pull out for? You already know what I'm tryna do," he replied.

"I can't stand you. Get out the bathroom and let me clean myself up. Niji might think we're crazy."

Stacy fixed his clothes and I took a small hoe bath. I walked out the bathroom before him so nobody could see us. When I sat at the dinner table next to Niji, everyone was looking at me.

"What?" I asked.

"Your skirt okay?" Asayi asked and Chika giggled.

"Yeah," I replied.

Stacy came out the bathroom moments later and sat next to me. He rested his hand on my thigh and I smiled at him. The man was hard to ignore but true love never stops.

****

"Wait a minute. You fucked Stacy in my hallway bathroom yesterday?" Asayi asked. We were talking about what happened at dinner the day before.

"Yes, and it was so good. I feel bad for cheating on Lucas."

We were in the mall shopping and I was trying to find a cute nude lip gloss. Keondra was in the MAC store and I rolled my eyes at her. She used to be Asayi's best friend but she fucked Asayi's ex-boyfriend years ago. Not only did she sleep with her ex, she watched him beat Asayi really badly where she could barely walk.

"Hey, Asayi," Keondra waved at her. Keondra was busted back in the day, but she started making money from stripping. Not only was she a stripper, but she was messing around with Jay's right-hand man, Bogo, who was a hustler.

"Hi," Asayi said dryly.

"I think it's time for us to all get along. I mean my man is friends with your husband. It's not fair that Bogo can't bring his woman around but everyone else can," Keondra said.

"She's good, luv," I replied.

"This is between me and Asayi!" Keondra spat.

"And? Asayi is my fucking blood and I'll never forget how her face looked after you watched that nigga beat her ass. You could've gotten help by calling the police. We good over here, plus our circle was never a rectangle."

Keondra rolled her eyes and went to the counter to pay for her make-up.

"See, I think I'm too nice. The thing with me and Woo happened like twelve years ago," Asayi said.

"It's okay, suga. Cousin Tuchie don't play."

"So, me and Trayon are working on having another baby," Asayi said.

"Awwww, how sweet! I can't wait. I love when you're pregnant because all you do is make desserts."

"Trayon wants to have six damn kids. I think my womb can only handle one more."

"Trayon loves the kids," I replied.

"He's only getting one more from me. I love him to death and I'll do what I can to keep him happy, but Navaeh had me on bed rest my entire pregnancy." She laughed. "I'm sitting up here complaining like I wouldn't give him three more," she said.

We went to six more stores before we left the mall. Niji was with her father so I could spend the weekend at Lucas's house since his family was flying in for his thirty-sixth birthday. It would be my first time meeting his parents.

"Have a fun weekend and let me know how it goes with the parents," Asayi said. I waved her goodbye in the parking lot as we got into our vehicles. On my way home, I thought about Stacy. My mother always preached to me that I should never cheat myself. I wanted a husband and I wasn't sure if Stacy could give me that. A while ago, Stacy said marriage was just a title. We had different views on relationships which was how I ended up dating a man who wanted the same thing I did. But it seemed impossible to shake Stacy. Shouldn't love outweigh different beliefs? Or should I be with a man who can give me what I want even though I couldn't love him the same? It was a constant battle of trying to figure out what I really needed. Often times I cried when I was alone for thinking about my terrible past with men. When I pulled up in my driveway, I wiped the tears from my eyes. I went into the house to grab my weekend bag. While I was in my closet, I opened the small safe where I kept my important papers. I pulled out a picture and got teary-eyed all over again. My life wasn't what it seemed. There were a lot of dark clouds over my head, reminding me that the person I was today didn't come into my life until I was thirteen years old. Tired of feeling bad for myself, I put the picture back then got undressed for the shower.

One hour later...

I pulled up in Lucas's driveway behind a white Range Rover. Two extra cars were in the driveway and I wondered how many people were inside his house. Stacy's mother made me hate meeting parents. The first time I met her, she wasn't that nice to me and even went as far as telling Stacy I wasn't his type because I was fat. Lucas came outside wearing khakis, a polo sweater and Sperry's.

"Am I under dressed?" I asked when I got out of my car. I was wearing a PINK black sweat suit with a black pair of high-top shell heads.

"No, baby, you look fine. But what happened with your straight hair? This makes you look younger," he said about my hair. My hair was styled with flexi rods with auburn tips. Everyone loved my hair, especially Stacy, but Lucas had a different opinion.

"Wait, I wore my hair like this before and you never said anything. But then again, you never compliment my hair so I don't know what you like." Lucas stated several times that I looked twenty years old so I assumed with the hair I looked too young.

"I know, baby. My parents are a little old-fashioned. How about you fix it for brunch tomorrow?" he asked.

Nigga, how about you take those tight-ass khakis off!

"Okay, I brought my flat-iron with me so I'll fix it," I said. He kissed my lips then grabbed my bags from the back seat. It was chilly outside but my palms were sweating. I was nervous. Lucas lived in a cabin-style home in the country. The windows were big enough to make the home look like it was made of glass. He squeezed my hand to assure me that everything was fine. When he opened the door, I heard a lot of laughter coming from the living room. Lucas sat my bag by the door and told me he'd take it to his room later. We walked into the family room and I counted five people. Four were sitting on couches and one woman was in a wheelchair.

"Mother and Father, this is my girlfriend, Stacy . Stacy these are my parents, Jack and Jill, and it's not a joke. On the other couch is my best friend, Thomas, and his beautiful wife, Catherine. Thomas is the friend I told you about that lives in New York," Lucas introduced us. Everyone greeted me except for Catherine. Thomas and Catherine were Caucasian. I noticed Lucas didn't introduce me to the woman in the wheel chair so I introduced myself.

"Hello, my name is Stacy. What's your name?"

"I'm Lynn," she said.

"She's Lucas's younger sister," Lucas's mother spoke up. I noticed everyone seemed annoyed by Lynn and I wanted to know why because she seemed to be a sweet person. Lynn was a pretty girl, she had a gorgeous pecan complexion with slanted eyes and full lips. Her hair was styled in braids and her clothes seemed a little dirty like she spilled something on herself and nobody wiped it off. Lucas's parents gave me a dirty look while I talked to Lynn. She was the only one in the room who seemed normal.

"She's tired, Stacy. So, tell me a little about yourself. Do you have any children?" she asked. I looked at Lucas and he played it off by laughing with Thomas.

"Yes, I have a daughter who will be turning eleven soon and her name is Niji. Lucas didn't tell you all that?"

"So, you're a single mother?" Catherine asked me.

"No, actually I'm not. Does that shock you?" I asked.

"Cut it out, Catherine," I heard Thomas whisper to her. Jill excused herself. She told everyone that she had to get Lynn ready for bed. It was only six o'clock in the evening.

"Make yourself comfortable, Stacy. We don't bite," Jack said. I sat in Jill's spot and Lucas poured me a glass of wine.

"Where are you from?" Thomas asked.

"Baltimore," I replied.

"So, you see a lot of dead bodies?" Catherine asked.

Calm down, bitch. Don't get gutta with these people before they have you locked up and fired from your job.

"Yes, I've seen a lot of dead bodies coming up, but they were all on TV. Do you watch a lot of movies, too? I love horror," I replied. Catherine smacked her teeth and excused herself to use the bathroom. Lucas was staring at me, apologizing with his eyes. Thomas and Jack were talking about politics and I found myself texting Stacy to see what Niji was doing. I could've texted Niji's phone but I wanted to talk to him.

What you want, Tuchie? We're bowling. I got Semaj and TJ with me so make it quick before TJ gets into something.

I miss you...

"Oh, honey we keep our cell-phones out the living room during family bonding time," Jill's funny looking ass said when she came back into the living room. Her and her husband weren't attractive but Lucas favored them in a handsome way. Lynn, on the other hand, didn't look like anyone.

"I'm talking to my daughter," I replied.

"Can you check up on her later? She's with her father so I'm sure she's fine," Lucas said.

"A mother's job is never done. Anyways, I'm going to step outside and make a phone call," I replied. I practically ran out of the living room with my purse. When I felt an anxiety attack coming on I smoked weed. Lucas stepped outside when I lit up my blunt.

"What are you doing? You can't smoke that while my parents are here!" Lucas said.

No he didn't just base on you, bitch! See, what you are not gonna do is talk to Tuchie like that! Don't let my degree fool you.

"Nigga, who in the fuck are you talking to?" Lucas's jaw dropped.

"What has gotten into you, Stacy? First, you show up dressed in hood attire with wild hair and now you're smoking pot?" he asked. I blew the smoke in his face and he dropped on the ground like someone was shooting at him. Lucas wasn't acting anything like the man I had been dating. Maybe it was because of his weird parents and their strict rules. He was trying to impress them.

"Don't raise your voice at me, and why didn't you stick up for me when Catherine was throwing her stereotypical questions of black women at me? That doesn't bother you?"

"Everyone is drunk. We have been drinking for a few hours. Her and Thomas crack black jokes all the time. I'll tell them to chill out and I'm sorry for acting like this but I was really nervous with my parents meeting you. Please forgive, baby," he said. He pecked my lips then waited until I was finished smoking my blunt. When we went back into the house, it was only Catherine, Jack and Jill in the family room.

"She's back. Don't mind us, honey. We joke a lot," Jill said.

These people have no personality whatsoever.

We ended up playing a game of chess at the kitchen table. More people were coming the next day and I wasn't sure if I was able to handle it. Jack and Jill's family wasn't anything like the black families I knew.

"Where is Thomas?" Catherine asked.

"He's out back chopping wood for the fireplace," Lucas said and Catherine shrugged her shoulders. The wine I was drinking ran through me so I went into the bathroom near the kitchen. While I was in the bathroom, I heard a noise coming from upstairs. It sounded like a loud thud. I flushed the toilet and washed my hands. The noise from upstairs got louder. When I went back to the table, Thomas was sitting next to Catherine but Lucas was missing.

"Where is Lucas?" I asked.

"He went outside to cut some wood," Thomas said. Jack and Jill were talking about eating red meat and how it wasn't healthy but I couldn't sit down. Something in my soul didn't feel right. I began having flashbacks of what happened to me when I was thirteen years old.

"Are you okay? You need some water, dear?" Jill asked me.

"No, thanks, I'm fine."

I sat at the kitchen table and watched them play the game. Ten minutes later, Lucas came into the kitchen sweating. It was chilly outside, so I didn't understand why he came in the house like that. His zipper to his pants wasn't zipped all the way. He sat next to me and I saw a scratch on his arm. Thomas whispered to Lucas about something then suddenly they burst into a fit of laughter. Catherine was eyeing Thomas with a scowl on her face. My phone vibrated in my pocket and it was a text from Stacy.

Yo, Tuchie. I know you with that fuck nigga but I want you back. Ditch that fool, shorty.

Okay.

Wait, fa real? That easy? You okay? You need me come scoop you up?

No, but I'll be at my house shortly. This family is weird and something isn't right with Lucas and his friend. We can talk more about this face-to-face.

"No, phones at the table," Jill said to me.

"Sorry, this is a family emergency. I'll be right back," I said. Lucas was asking me a question but I was already out the kitchen. I walked down the hallway then quietly headed upstairs. Maybe I was overreacting but I couldn't keep my nerves intact if I didn't figure out what was going on. Lucas's house only had two bedrooms upstairs but he had two more in the basement. The door at the end of the hall was closed, so it had to be the bedroom Lynn was in. I tiptoed to the door and put my ear against it. It was quiet—too quiet. It was eight o'clock and I figured she would at least have the TV on instead of lying in a pitch-dark room with the door closed.

Go home, Tuchie. You need to stop this foolishness. Not everyone is a victim of rape and not every man is guilty. Leave this girl alone because you don't know her!

I turned the doorknob and it was unlocked.

Turn around! They wouldn't leave the door unlocked if they were doing something. You are going to embarrass yourself!

My thoughts were running wild but I couldn't turn around. The moment I laid eyes on Lynn, I knew something wasn't right. Everyone was socializing when I walked in and she was sitting off to the side, looking straight ahead in a daze. Jill took her right upstairs after I introduced myself to her as if she was hiding something. I opened the door and the room was dark. I felt on the side of the door for a light switch. After I found it, I hit the switch. Lynn was lying in the bed with her back turned towards me and she was naked from the waist down. I closed the door and locked it before I went further into the room.

"Lynn!" I whispered walking around the bed.

"Lynn! Can you hear me?"

"Get out," she whispered.

Her face was covered in tears and she had a small cut on her lip.

"What happened?" I asked.

"I can't tell you," she said.

I kneeled in front of her and grabbed her hand. She burst into tears but she didn't make a sound.

"Did Lucas and Thomas come into your bedroom? I heard the noises when I was in the bathroom downstairs. You can talk to me. I can get you some help."

"Nobody is going to believe me."

"How old are you?" I asked.

"Twenty. I was adopted when I was fifteen years old. Nobody wanted a handicapped daughter, so the Browns brought me to their home." Lynn sat up in the bed, and I noticed her legs could move a little but not too much.

"I'm partially handicap. My parents were in a car accident while my mother was pregnant with me. It did something to my spine so I can't walk that good. I can come up the stairs with help and by pulling myself up with the rail," she said.

"Are Thomas and Lucas doing things to you?"

"Yes, they torment me every chance they get. They take my clothes off and sometimes pour cold water on me. Make me eat bugs and beat me with belts. Thomas came up just to push me out of bed and Lucas came up here to get me off the floor. After he laid me down, he stuck his fingers down my throat so I could vomit. Oh, and he jerked off on me. They are evil and I need to get out of here. Please help me because nobody believes me. My parents always say, 'Lucas and Thomas are great men. They'd never do anything like that.' I'll do anything, just get me out of here," she cried.

"They don't want me to tell their secret. When I was sixteen, I saw them through the basement window at my parents' house. I was outside watering the flowers when I saw it," she said.

"Saw what?"

"Thomas and Lucas. Thomas was on his knees sucking Lucas's dick. They stopped when Lucas saw me. I pretended I didn't see anything but they know I did. Lucas didn't want me to come here with my parents but they couldn't leave me alone in the house, so they brought me here. Lucas told them to put me upstairs as soon as you came so I wouldn't lie on him. They torture me to feel better about themselves," she said.

"I'm going to call the cops," I said.

"No, I tried that already. Lucas has connections so it was ignored. My parents made me believe I was seeing things and even put me on medication. I'm going to end up dead and nobody is going to help me. Please get me out of here," she said.

"I'm going to grab you some things and get you out of here," I replied. I was so hurt for what they were doing to a sweet person. She was helpless and those cowards were damn near killing her. She could've fallen and hit her head and those bastards had the nerve to laugh and joke about it. She pointed me to her suitcase in the corner and I helped her get dressed. It was going to be hard for me to sneak her out the house without being noticed. I held my breath when I called Stacy.

"Hey, beautiful. You ready come home?" he asked.

"I need your help. We have to kidnap someone," I replied.

"Kidnap? Shorty, you trippin! You want us to get locked up or sumthin?"

"Lucas and his best friend are abusing this girl and nobody believes her," I said.

"How old is she?" he asked and I could hear him shuffling around.

"Twenty years old."

"Shorty, give her a gun and bring yah ass home, Tuch," he said.

"She's handicap. Fine, I'll do it by myself."

"Wait, I'm over Trayon's crib. The kids gonna be here with Asayi so he's going to ride with me," he said.

"Nigga, have you lost your mind? Leave Trayon's scary ass home before we be on channel 13 news."

"We'll be there. Send me the address," he said then hung up.

"I'm going to go downstairs and act like everything is normal. When Stacy comes, he can distract them and I can sneak you out the back door."

"Okay," she said sadly. Lynn was let down so many times that she didn't believe in me.

"I promise, I'll try my best." She cracked a smile and I hugged her. I rushed out her bedroom and quietly closed the door. I heard footsteps coming up the stairs so I went into Lucas's room and laid across his bed to play it off.

"Stacy, are you up here? Why didn't you come back downstairs?" he shouted.

"I'm in here!" I called out. Lucas came into his room and smiled at me. He wasn't standing straight, he was rocking side to side.

"I was looking for you. Me and Thomas are going to run to the liquor store. Do you want anything?" he asked.

Great, I can sneak out when he goes to the store.

"No thanks. I want to lie down for a bit. I'm exhausted," I replied.

"You know what. I'm gonna stay right here with you. I have been neglecting you," he slurred. He closed his door and locked it. Stacy was only twenty minutes away but I prayed he was doing over the speed limit. Knowing what Lucas was about sickened my stomach. Not only was he a bully, he was part of a disgusting love triangle. Now I know why he was sticking up for Thomas and Catherine. All three of them needed to burn in hell. I'd known Lucas for a year and never saw him drunk, but then again, he was a whole different person around Thomas.

"Let's watch a movie then we can do a few things when everyone is asleep. I have this cute lingerie set in my bag." Lucas flopped on the bed beside me and tried to kiss me but I played it off.

"That might lead to something. Put a movie on," I said. He smacked his teeth when he pulled away from me.

"What do you want to watch?"

"*Brokeback Mountain*. I think it's a unique love story, plus it's sad," I replied. Lucas looked disgusted but I had to test him out.

"That movie is gay and goes against everything I stand for," he said.

"What is considered gay?"

"Two men having sex. Don't be so naïve, Stacy," he scolded.

"How about a man giving oral sex to another man? Do you think that's gay, too, because I have a few college friends that were curious?" Lucas rubbed his chin, probably thinking of how to answer the question.

The truth comes out when you're drunk.

"Oral sex is gay, too," Lucas said.

"Bro, come on before the store closes!" Thomas knocked on the door.

"I'm ready to watch a movie with my woman!" Lucas shouted.

Oh, so Thomas is the woman in the relationship, got it!

"Go away before it gets ugly!" Lucas said.

"Open the door before I kick it down, motherfucker!" Thomas yelled back, banging on the door.

Rich kid problems.

I would have never known they were messing around if I hadn't talked to Lynn. My phone beeped and it was Stacy letting me know he was outside. Just as I thought, he was there in fifteen minutes. The doorbell rang seconds later and my heart was ready to beat out of my chest.

"I'll be back. I think my cousins are here," Lucas said. He kissed my cheek and opened his bedroom door. Thomas peeked into the room and waved at me and I rolled my eyes. He shrugged his shoulders and walked away. I heard shouting coming from downstairs and it was Jew's voice. Jew was Stacy and Trayon's best friend. I thought it was just going to be two of them but I should've known better because Jew wanted to be in on everything with his bored behind. He was dating my aunt who was only forty-four and he was thirty-four, but she was married so to sum it all up, Jew was a side-nigga. We called him Jew because he was half Jewish and half black.

"Nigga, where she at? Y'all kidnapping bitches and shit?" Jew asked Lucas. I stood on the stairs with my fingers on the bridge of my nose.

"What are you talking about? You have the wrong house!" Catherine said. Jew looked at Trayon and Stacy.

"This the right house, ain't it?" Jew asked.

"Yeah it is," Stacy replied. I stormed down the stairs and stood between them.

"This is a big misunderstanding," I said and rolled my eyes at Jew.

Jew was ready to pull out a gun but Trayon shook his head at him.

"Why is your daughter's father and his thug friends in my damn house?" Lucas asked me. Stacy pulled me back and stepped in front of me.

"Who you talkin' to, nigga?" Stacy asked.

"All of y'all are going to jail!" Jill said.

"Stay out of this, honey. Let Lucas be a man," Jack said.

"Dad, really?" Lucas asked.

"I told you not to deal with a woman with a child and now look," Jack said.

"I'm going to get the shot gun!" Thomas said.

"Okay, wait a damn minute!" I screamed to get everyone's attention.

"Look, shorty. Just point us in the direction where the girl at so we can get her. I got to help TJ with his homework and y'all bullshitting," Trayon said.

"Upstairs, first door on the right," I replied. Jew and Trayon walked past Lucas as if they owned the house and went upstairs.

"What in the fuck is this about? And where are y'all taking Lynn?" Lucas asked.

"She asked me to help her. You and Thomas have been torturing her because she caught y'all sucking each other's dicks. Don't pretend like you don't know what this is about, Lucas."

"Wait a damn minute. Lynn is a liar and since she's tearing this family a part, get her stank ass out of this house! I'm tired of her spreading lies about my son! Sorry, Lucas, me and your father cannot take care of her anymore. That is your wife and you made this bed so lie in it!" Jill said.

"Wife?" I asked and Lucas dropped his head in embarrassment.

"Yes, she's my wife, but we're separated. Lynn does this every time a new woman comes around. The lies change every time. She pretends she's adopted and tells people she's younger than what she is. Lynn was riding a bike one morning and a car hit her. This happened two years ago. When it happened, we were headed for divorce. So I stayed in Virginia until she was released from the hospital and came here. I pay my mother to care for her and she wasn't supposed to come here today but she did. This is a big misunderstanding and I'm so sorry you found out like this," Lucas said.

"Oh, cut the bullshit, Lucas. You're still sleeping with her! She texted you and told you she fell out the bed. You went upstairs and helped her and came back with your zipper opened. The fucking cat is out of the bag, moron, so tell your girlfriend that you are still fucking your wife!" Catherine said.

"Stay out of this, Catherine!" Thomas yelled at her.

"Oh, fuck off! We all went to college together and you all started treating Lynn bad after her accident. No wonder she spreads lies to get attention. I bet Lucas didn't tell anyone else about the abortion he made her get three months ago. He's sick and I'm tired of pretending to like this damn family!" Catherine said.

"Bitch, shut up already!" Lucas yelled at Catherine.

"Don't talk to my wife like that! This is your fault!" Thomas yelled at Lucas. Everyone started arguing and I was pissed off at Lynn. Trayon and Jew helped her down the stairs and she had a smile on her face.

"Why did you lie to me, Lynn? That was pretty fucked up what you did. I thought they were going to kill you."

"Oh, bitch, please. You're a whore! I wanted you to stay away from him. Don't you think I get tired of hearing about you? I didn't think you were going to come in my room but you did, so I lied. Now I hope you stay away from my fucking husband!" Lynn said.

"I'm out," Trayon said and Jew followed suit. They both dropped Lynn on the floor and Catherine ran to her.

"Get her ass out of my house and never bring her back. I pay you a lot of money to keep your mouth shut until this divorce is final and you can't even do that!" Lucas yelled at Lynn.

"You did this to me! You always cheated on me. Tell everyone about the two kids you have living in Mexico. Fuck you, Lucas! I'm the one who got you that job because you failed the bar exam twice! You lived off me for years and I'm the one who helped your parents out of bankruptcy and this is what you all do to me? I'm going to make sure you all die!" Lynn screamed. I grabbed my things and rushed out the house.

"Yoooo, that was entertaining as a muthafucka. Better than *The Haves and Haves Nots*," Jew laughed.

"Yo, why you drop her like that?" Stacy asked Trayon.

"Shorty was heavy," Trayon lied.

"You riding with Tuchie? I'm ready to dip before they call 5-0," Trayon said.

"Yeah, good looking out," Stacy said. He dapped Jew and Trayon before they walked off the porch. One thing about the men in our circle was that they didn't hesitate when it came to the ones they cared about and that's why their women loved them to death.

"Trayon left so fast because he had guns in his trunk. We thought we had to kill them muthafuckas in there. I wanted to leave Lucas's little bitch ass stanking. I was trying to be cordial with the nigga but he was acting tough like that white boy was going to do something," Stacy said. I hit the unlock button to my truck and he got in the passenger's seat. When I got inside the truck, Lucas's front door opened. Lucas ran outside and banged on my truck.

"Get out, please! I love you and I'm sorry for not telling you about my wife, but now it's really over. I'm putting her in a home!" Lucas yelled. Stacy told me floor the gas and my truck went flying down the driveway. I looked in my rearview mirror and saw Lucas kicking at the ground in frustration.

"I should slap the fuck outta yah hot ass for being at this nigga's house anyway!" Stacy said with an attitude.

"Don't start. We are going to work it out. I'm tired of all of this."

"You thought that nigga was going to replace me because he's a lawyer? Naw, shorty, it doesn't work like that," Stacy said.

"I know and I'm sorry but you were dating other people. All I want to do is go home and cuddle," I replied. Stacy leaned over and kissed the side of my face.

"I love you, Tuch. We got a lot to talk about because from this day forward it's all about us. Fuck everybody else," he said.

Would you love me if you knew I was damaged goods?

I wanted to tell Stacy my secret because I knew I couldn't hold it in any longer. It had been affecting me for years and it was only going to get worse.

Jay

One week later...

"**J**ay, wake up," Isha said, kissing me on the lips. It was late and Isha was rubbing her breasts against my chest. We went from having sex almost every day to fucking once a week.

"Yo, I'm tired." Isha sat up in bed and snatched the comforter off my body. She opened her silk robe and her round breasts were pointing at me. Isha took her robe off and leaned in to suck on my lips. I gripped her hips when she deepened the kiss. She moaned when my erection pressed at her bud.

"Take it, shorty."

Most times I liked to relax while Isha rode my dick. Her ride game was so serious that it put me straight to sleep afterwards and made me tired the next day. She lifted her body and squatted over my dick. She slowly eased her pussy down my girth as her walls gripped me. I closed my eyes and bit my lip to keep myself from sounding like a bitch. Honestly, Isha's pussy was lethal. Enough to make a grown man get teary-eyed.

"Fucckkkkkk, shorty. Ride that muthafucka just like that!" She pressed her hands onto my chest and sped up the pace. The headboard banged against the wall as I gripped her ass to control her movements. Her beautiful breasts bounced and her nipples were like raisins; her body was perfect. I pulled her nipple between my lips while my free hand massaged the other. Her pussy walls gripped my dick; I couldn't let her outdo me. I flipped her over on her back with her nipple still in inside my mouth. My dick slammed into her G-spot and she wrapped her legs around me. She sexily moaned against my ear because she knew that shit made my dick harder. I pushed her legs up and drilled her spot as I thumbed her pink pearl. Her creamy essence coated my dick and her inner-thighs. Her nails dug into my ass and I hated that shit but I was focused on my nut. She pulled my face down to hers and sucked my lips. I had flashbacks of our first date. I damn near begged shorty to give me a chance because she wasn't into hood niggas. I saw her as my wife and the mother of my kids but somehow I got lost along the way and forgot how much I loved her.

"Jadiah, I'm ready to cum!"

"Cum, shorty. I'm gonna cum wit' you," I groaned. Isha's legs shook and I went deeper until she gushed onto the sheets. Seconds later, I was spilling my seeds into her. My cell-phone vibrated and Isha pushed me off her. She climbed out the bed and snatched her robe off the floor.

"The fuck is your problem?"

"It's two o'clock in the fucking morning! That's my problem!" Isha yelled.

"Yo, chill the fuck out before Hadley wakes up!"

"I'm the fiancée but lately I have been feeling like the side-chick. What is really going on? Tell me if you're seeing someone else so I can move on with my life. All we do now is argue and I'm sick of it," Isha sobbed.

"You nag me too damn much!" I shouted.

"Nigga, fuck you!" she shouted back.

"I just did and you still bitching. Take your dumb ass to sleep." Isha got in my face when I got out of bed to get my phone.

"Move, Isha!"

"Let me see your phone, Jay! I'm not moving until you prove to me that it isn't a bitch calling you," she said.

"I'm not proving shit!" I grabbed my baller shorts off the floor then stepped into them. All I wanted to do was go downstairs so she could cool off but she wasn't letting up. Isha followed me out of the bedroom. She ran in front of me, pushing me into the banister.

"Tell me what I want to know! You don't appreciate me? I'm not good enough for you anymore? Please tell me what I've done wrong! I want to fix this," she said with tears falling from her eyes.

"I'm not cheating on you, but accusing me of doing it is stressing me the fuck out."

"I'm moving out," she said.

SOUL Publications

"Bitch, you crazy. You ain't going nowhere so that's dead. You're the cause of this and don't even realize it."

I didn't mean to call shorty a bitch but she was talking crazy. A few times I told myself I wanted to leave her but it was easier said than done. I loved her but I loved someone else, too. It was complicated and stressful. Honestly, I wished I never went to Atlanta to see Sadi. My life hadn't been right since.

"Bitch?" she angrily asked. She smacked me in the face when I reached out to her. Hadley's bedroom door opened and she stepped into the hallway.

"What's going on, Daddy? Why is Isha crying?" Hadley asked.

"I'm fine, Hadley. I hit my foot on the wall," Isha replied.

"Why are y'all lying to me? You think I don't know what's going on? You and Daddy argue every day. Are you gonna move out?" Hadley asked Isha.

"It's a big misunderstanding. I'm just stressed a little," she replied. Hadley looked at me and I could see the disappointment on her face.

"I'm not a small child so I know what's going on. You're going to leave me," Hadley said. She went into her bedroom and slammed the door. I ran to her door and knocked.

"Open up! Let me talk to you!" The last thing I wanted to do was show my daughter how niggas can ruin a woman's spirit.

"Hadley, I need to talk to you!"

"Let her calm down first. We have been acting like idiots around her and she's upset with us," Isha said.

"It's your fault. You're tryna turn my daughter against me," I whispered so Hadley couldn't hear us. Isha walked away from me and went into our bedroom.

"So, now I'm turning Hadley against you? Why would I do something like that, Jadiah? You think I'm a bad person?"

"You provoke the fuck outta me, shorty! You want her to hear our business so I can look like the bad guy. She's my daughter and you keep coming between us." Isha didn't respond to me, she went into the bathroom and locked the door. My cell-phone rang again and it was Sadi. I ignored her call because I didn't want to make things worse than what they were. Sadi called again and I figured it was an emergency so I answered.

"What's up?"

"Hey, Jay. I'm in Maryland," she yawned into the phone.

"You're not supposed to be here until the shop is finished."

"I wanted to surprise you. I'm at my mother's house. You remember where she lives, right? But anyways, I hope to see you later. I just wanted you to know I'm back home," she said.

"Aight, bet," I replied and she hung up. I couldn't say much because Isha was probably listening even though I kept my voice down. Isha was still in the bathroom when I got back in bed. I was trapped in a fucked-up love triangle.

****

When I woke up, Isha wasn't lying next to me. I looked at the clock on the wall and it was eleven o'clock in the morning. Hadley was in school and Isha was at work. She usually brought me breakfast in bed but I couldn't blame shorty. I haven't been a good dude to her but I knew how I could brighten up her day. I used to send flowers to Isha's job every Monday because I knew how much she hated Mondays. I hadn't done that for her in six months.

"Damn, I'm slacking." I grabbed my phone and went to a website to order her flowers. Our wedding was only a few months away, but I had a feeling we weren't going through with it so I had to make the best of it while it lasted. After I showered and got dressed, I left the house to see what was up with Sadi.

Sadi's parents lived twelve minutes away from me but I got to her crib in fifteen minutes. I had flashbacks from years ago. Trayon had Sadi kidnapped and hid her away in the basement of an abandoned house so she could detox her body from cocaine. He did it out of the love he had for his cousin, Stacy, and his unborn daughter. I wasn't thinking about none of that shit when I was making love to her. I forgot about her past but her being home and pregnant with my seed was giving me thoughts I didn't want to have. It seemed like a good idea until reality hit me and I hoped she didn't go back to her old ways while she was pregnant. Twenty minutes passed without me realizing it because I was sitting in my whip thinking about the old Sadi. Someone knocked on my window, and when I looked up, it was her.

"Get out of the car," she said in excitement. I opened the door and stepped out of the whip. Shorty jumped into my arms and I hugged her.

"I missed you so much. I couldn't wait any longer."

"I missed you, too, beautiful," I replied when I pulled away from her. Her hair was brushed up into a ponytail and her face was clear of make-up. Her pretty greenish hazel eyes seemed to sparkle under the sun. The track suit she wore hugged her small curves and suddenly I forgot all about the shit that was on my mind. I pulled her into me and kissed her lips.

"Come on in. I want you to meet my parents."

"I don't know about that yet, shorty. It's still some shit I have to straighten up before I can do that if you know what I mean. It just won't feel right," I replied.

"Okay, I'll go inside and get my purse. Maybe we can grab something to eat."

"Bet, I'll be out here," I replied. She kissed me before she jogged into the house with the screen door slamming behind her. Seconds later, she came out the house and I got in the passenger seat so she could drive. I was tired from messing around with Isha earlier. We drove past one of Asayi's brunch spots and Sadi wanted to go there.

"I'm gonna turn around so we can eat at Southern Brunch. I know they have good food," Sadi said.

"Naw, don't go there. Asayi owns that spot. Matter of fact, she owns a lot of restaurants in this area." Sadi smacked her teeth and rolled her eyes at me.

"What in the fuck does she have to do with us, Jay?" she asked.

"My fiancée is friends with her and she's one of her head chefs. Most of those recipes belong to Isha. It'll be disrespectful as fuck. Bad enough I have been treating her like shit since we..."

"Since, what? Why do I feel like you want to blame your infidelities on me? After years of friendship you couldn't be man enough to tell me you had a fiancée? Then you talked me into coming back home knowing that people are going to eventually find out about us. Oh, you must think I'm going to lie about this pregnancy!" Sadi yelled.

"Yo, this conversation is dead. All I'm saying is I'm not trying to disrespect Isha more than I have been. It ain't your fault but don't act green to the shit! I'm still with Isha, Sadi. She's my daughter's mother and it ain't easy to just cut some shit off because I knocked you up. I can't even pretend that Isha deserves this shit anymore. Look, just bear with me. I wanted you close so I can be there for my seed regardless of how it happened. No matter what, we can't change that."

"So, you're saying it's just about the baby and not about me? I moved from my condo in Atlanta and quit my job for you!" Sadi screamed and the car almost swerved off the road.

"What's wrong with that if it's about the baby? I didn't want you down there pregnant and alone. You wanted me to move there without thinking about my life here. Everything can't be about you and I remember telling you that shit years ago. I love you and I do want to be with you. Some days I want to leave Isha but I love her, too. Yo, this shit is hard," I said.

"I'm not going to remain a side chick until you figure it out. I gave up a lot for you and I want the same shit in return!"

"And losing my family ain't a lot to you? Matter of fact, we can talk about this later," I replied.

Sadi was hot! She cursed me out and mushed my head against the window. I wanted to choke her until she couldn't breathe but I couldn't. A while back, me and my niggas was talking about cheating because Lim stepped out on Chika a few times. Trayon said, "A man can't truly be in love with two women because there wouldn't be a second woman if he was already in love." Bottom line is, one of them I wasn't in love with but figuring it out was stressful. I grabbed Sadi's hand and kissed the back of it.

"I promise you that I won't string you along. Just be patient with me," I said.

"Only for now, Jay. Only for now."

****

Seven hours later….

Me and Sadi spent all day together. She wanted to look at a crib next to her hair salon. She fell in love with a four-story brick townhouse in Ardmore, Maryland. It was a good area close to the Woodmore Towne center. I told her she didn't have to worry about paying any bills so she wouldn't stress with the baby. It was almost ten o'clock at night when I dropped Sadi off at her parents' house. She caught another attitude with me because she wanted me to come in with her. I explained to her a million times that I didn't feel right meeting them until I figured out my situation with Isha. Thirty minutes later, I went to holla at my right-hand man, Bogo. I pulled up to his crib and blew the horn. He walked out the house with two trash bags in his hands.

"Ay, yo! Pop the trunk!" Bogo said. I popped the trunk and shook my head at that nigga. Him and his bitch, Keondra, was always beefing about something. Bogo was on and off with shorty for years. They started out just fucking but then the nigga wifed her while she was still stripping. She didn't quit until he knocked a tooth out of her mouth. Keondra was a slut and I hated that Sadi still kept in touch with shorty. Keondra was nothing but trouble but Bogo loved the hell out of that hoe. She ran out the house only wearing a bra and thong. It was chilly outside but shorty was wildin'.

"Bring your black ass here, Eden. Who was that bitch texting your phone?" she screamed. Keondra was a beautiful broad and her body was bomb. She had a body that women were paying for. Shorty also had natural long hair. But as beautiful as she was, the only nigga who wanted her was Bogo.

"Get your hoe ass in the house! Weak-teeth bitch. Baby corn-ass teeth," Bogo said. I wasn't trying to laugh but that nigga was a fool. Before Keondra got her teeth fixed, they were messed up terribly, almost like she drank acid.

"Fuck you! I got my teeth fixed!" she screamed.

"Okay, Cardi. Get your ass in the house before I pistol-whip you. Keep fucking with me while I'm taking a nap with yah dirty ass," Bogo said. Keondra kicked Bogo in his leg and he pushed her onto the ground. She threw a rock at him but missed and the rock shattered the back-seat window.

"Yoooo, get your girl!" I shouted at Bogo. Keondra was throwing rocks at my new whip. Bogo picked up a rock and threw it back at her before he got into the passenger's seat. I backed out of the driveway before she bust another window out of my whip.

"Leave that broad alone," I said.

"Leave Sadi alone, nigga. At least Keondra wasn't on crack. Bruh, Sadi was getting high and turning tricks for it. Don't speak on my bitch, nigga," Bogo said.

"She was sniffing coke, muthafucka."

"Nigga, all that shit is almost the same thing. Crack is a broke man's habit. Bottom line is that you have a good shorty at home. Shid, I know my woman ain't shit so you ain't gotta bring it up. Me and her go well together because I ain't shit, neither. But you a good nigga. Always been about your daughter and was never out here doing dumb shit. Get your mind right, bruh," Bogo said.

"Sadi is back in town and she's pregnant," I admitted. Bogo was the last person I wanted to tell because he would clown me forever about it.

"Yo, hold up, bro. You knocked her up when you went to Atlanta a few months ago? My nigga, you couldn't use a rubber?" he asked.

"It happened fast and I wasn't thinking. I was caught up and we ended up fucking."

"How do you know if that's your seed, bruh?" he asked.

"I'm the only one she's been with in ten years."

"But that was before she found out you had a fiancée. You don't know if she was fucking other niggas after you left! Nigga, she wasn't a virgin when you smashed so it ain't impossible. Damn, nigga. How did you get caught up like this? You don't remember when Trayon had her locked up in the basement so she could get clean? She was pregnant! At the end of the day, shorty ain't wifey or mother material," Bogo said. I slammed on the brakes and his head hit the dashboard.

"Nigga, I'll body your bitch-ass for speaking ill on some shit you don't know about. Shorty used to get high but that was a long time ago, nigga. What she did to Stacy ain't got shit to with me and her."

"But she was fucking her nigga's right-hand man and that was before she was getting high, so what's the excuse for that? All you had to do was smash her and leave her ass in Atlanta but you brought her back. How can you say she changed by talking to her on the phone? Listen to yourself, nigga! You're the same nigga who told me to leave Keondra alone but you went and knocked up a broad who betrayed everyone she was cool with before she left. She ain't leave on good terms, neither, my nigga. Shorty left because she couldn't take the heat from all the bullshit she did. Damn, my nigga."

"Yo, I know for a fact I'm the only nigga in her life so we can end this conversation. Now, shut your bitch-ass up and ride. We got some things to take care," I said. Bogo waved me off then pulled a bag of kush out of his pocket. Me and that nigga always argued but he was like my brother. I acted like I wasn't listening but I heard him. The thing is I know how Sadi was but shorty changed and that's the person I fell in love with. I just hoped shorty wasn't playing with me because she'd end up dead.

"You can drop me off at a hotel room when we finish handling business. Keondra ain't gonna see me for a month." Bogo was talking about having two girlfriends while I was texting Isha. I wanted to know if she got the flowers I sent to her job, but she didn't respond. For some reason I was still trying to hold on when I didn't want to.

Tuchie

The weekend was over and I was back at work. When I walked into my office, it was filled with flowers. I also had teddy bears and balloons. All it was missing was some people yelling out, "surprise" because I was feeling like it was my birthday.

"What in the fuck is this?" I dropped my purse on the floor and went to the front desk. My secretary was on the phone running off with her mouth about some fight she was in at the club over some nigga.

"Myisha," I called out to her. She placed the phone on hold and looked at me as if I was bothering her. Myisha was twenty years old and sometimes she acted a little childish but she was a good worker and rarely called out.

"Sorry about that, Stacy. I sat the payroll papers on your desk."

"Thank you, but I didn't come over here to talk about that. Did Lucas come into my office this morning? If so, he shouldn't be in there without my permission."

"No, he sat everything on my desk and I put them in there for you. Y'all are so cute," Myisha beamed.

"Next time, keep them for yourself. And if he calls, I'm always in a meeting," I said.

"Will do," Myisha said. She picked the phone back up to finish her story.

I went into my office and placed all of Lucas's things together so they could go out in the trash. What happened over the weekend really bothered me. Lynn pretended to be a victim and Lucas didn't tell me he was married. Even though I cheated on him with Stacy, the way I saw it, we were both using each other to get over someone. I got comfortable in my chair at the desk to check my emails.

"They are cutting up already."

My cell-phone was ringing inside my purse despite me telling everyone not to call me until lunch time. I thought about ignoring the call but it could've been an emergency.

"Hello."

"Yes, hi. May I speak with Stacy Cook."

"May I ask who is calling?"

"My name is Thomasine Davis. I met her in South Carolina when she was a little girl. She was staying with her father's sister."

"You have the wrong number," I replied and hung up. She called my phone again but I couldn't answer. Thomasine Davis, how could I forget her name? I met her at the worst time of my life. There was a time where I wanted to die because things were too complicated for my young mind to understand.

"Is she sleeping?" I heard a boy's voice in the background. I was drinking a lot of liquor with friends from my school. My head was spinning and I tried to talk but I couldn't because vomit threatened to come up my throat.

"Yeah, nigga. She's asleep. Hurry the fuck up. I want my money, too, after you're finished," a boy said. I heard a door open then more voices. The last thing I could remember was hands touching on me and my pants coming down...

Tears fell from my eyes, causing my mascara to run onto my blazer. My first boyfriend set me up to get raped so he could join some crazy gang in Baltimore city. Every man that came into my life found a way to hurt me. What happened to me when I was younger made me vicious. I fought a lot, shot at niggas and bitches, and even hustled. It mentally tormented me but my princess Niji healed all the wounds that were left open from my past. Thomasine Davis was a name I wanted to forget. After I was raped, I moved to South Carolina with my father's sister because the gang was threatening me. They told me they would kill me if I told anyone what happened. My father's sister died a few years later so I had to move back to Baltimore. That's when I hooked up with my ex-boyfriend, Rock. He was older than me but he made sure I didn't have to worry about that gang again. Long story short, Rock turned out to be a snake. He had a wife that I didn't know anything about. My first year of college, his wife and cousins jumped me and I almost died. I had a miscarriage and suffered from broken ribs, a concussion, a broken arm and one of them stabbed me in the chest but thankfully I didn't die. I went through so much and I didn't talk about it to anyone because sympathy wasn't going to help me. So far, I escaped death three times and the way I saw it, there wasn't any use in me complaining because I was still alive.

****

I went to Stacy's studio as soon as I got off from work. He wanted me to bring him dinner so I stopped at a Jamaican restaurant and got him fried red snapper, cabbage and peas and rice. Stacy would eat red snapper every day if he could. His building was located in a high security place downtown, Annapolis. A few rappers were robbed and even shot at coming out of the studio late at night so the security around the area was deep. Weed smoke hit me as a security guard let me inside the building. There were six guys inside the spacious recording room lounging around on the couch. Stacy was on the computer adjusting the bass in the beat.

"What's good, baby mama," he said when I approached him. He stood up and wrapped his arms around me.

"Where my plate at, Tuchie?" a rapper by the name of Fendi asked me. Fendi was around eighteen years old but he was a talented kid. I found myself listening to his music because they told stories about the struggle of poverty.

"I'm tired but next time I got you," I replied.

"Hook me up with Jay's daughter, Hadley. Then we'll be even," Fendi said.

"Sit yah lil' ass down, boy. Jay will kill you," Stacy said while stuffing cabbage in his mouth.

"Yeah, aight," Fendi said.

A female walked into the room but for some reason she didn't seem too happy to see me. Stacy gave me a list of names of all the women he fucked who were in the industry and I wondered if she was one of them. She was thick, probably around a size eight. She was wearing a green lace front wig which stopped at her hips. She was dressed in skin tight jeans and a sweater. She was a pretty girl but something about her lips and nose seemed a little odd like she had surgery. She was definitely following the "Barbie" trend.

"What you want, Bailey?" someone called out to her.

"Nothing, is this a bad time or something?" she asked Stacy.

"We busy right now. Come back tomorrow," he said without looking up from his food.

"But you told me you would sample my music today. Me and Fendi had a song we want you to listen to," she replied.

"Aight, you can sit down." Bailey sat on the couch with an attitude but she couldn't keep her eyes off me. I wanted to ask her if she had a problem but it wasn't the time nor place. It wouldn't have been a good look for him.

"I'll see you at home," I told him.

"Hold on, I'll walk you out." He grabbed his jacket and followed me out the recording room.

"Who is that Bailey bitch? She looks familiar. Was she in Fendi's video?" I asked.

"Yeah, a few months ago, but she wants me to listen to her music," he said.

"Why was she looking at me like that?"

"That's just how she is. Don't start that bullshit, Tuchie," he said.

"I was just asking. Anyways, I gotta pick up Niji from Isha's house then go to the grocery store."

"Are you aight? Something don't seem right with you today. You look sad, shorty," he said.

"Just exhausted." I was still shaken up about that phone call from Thomasine.

"Yo, Tuch. You can't be out here lying to me, shorty. We been around each other too long. I know when something is bothering you, so what's up?"

"We can talk about it when you get home. Can you see if Niji can stay with your mother?"

"I'm ready wrap this up and I'll be on my way. I'll call her right now," Stacy said. He was worried about me, I could hear it in his voice. We had to do it right the second time around so it was a must that I laid everything down on the table. He kissed me before he walked into the building.

****

Two hours later...

When I stepped out the shower, I grabbed a towel off the rack. My body felt heavy and my head was throbbing. I could feel an anxiety attack coming on. I had them when I was extremely stressed. Sometimes I thought I was having a heart attack. Tears wouldn't stop falling from my eyes and a knot formed in my stomach. I sat on the toilet seat and fanned myself because I was sweating bullets. I heard a buzz coming from the front door downstairs. It meant someone came in the house and I knew it was Stacy.

"Tuchie!" he called out. I splashed cold water on my face and took deep breaths to calm myself down.

"Tuchie!"

"I'm in the bathroom!"

He came into the bedroom and took his shoes off. His back was turned towards me when he took his shirt off. He had a picture of Niji tattooed on his back; she was four years old at the time. I dried off then put on my Winnie the Pooh pajama shirt.

"Niji is staying with my mother for a few days since she hasn't stayed in a while," Stacy said.

"Thank you. My mother parties too much to keep up with Niji." I pulled the covers back on the bed and slid underneath the sheets. Stacy was staring at me, waiting for me to tell him what was going on.

"Yo, I'm nervous. I was driving here in a daze thinking about what we have to talk about when we already talked about bettering our relationship a few days ago. All I could come up with was that nigga Lucas knocking you up. I don't think I can deal with that one even though we weren't together. That would kill our future."

"No, I'm not pregnant. Me and Lucas used protection. What I have to say has nothing to do with him. It's about me," I replied. Stacy turned off the TV so I could have his full attention. My stomach was cramping up and the room was spinning again. It had been years since I talked about what happened to me.

"I have a son," I whispered.

"The fuck you just say!" Stacy yelled at me.

"I have a nineteen-year-old son!"

"Yo, Tuch. I ain't never lay hands on you but honest to God I wanna rock you in yah shit right now. The fuck you mean you have a grown-ass son and when did this happen? Why you ain't tell me this shit years ago! Niji had a brother all this time? Who is that lil' nigga's father?" Stacy fussed.

"I don't know his father." I dropped my head down in embarrassment and covered my face.

"Oh, so you were a baby thot and was letting niggas bust you down?"

"I WAS RAPED!" I screamed at him. Stacy sat next to me and stared at the wall.

"I know I should've told you a long time ago but it was something I wanted to forget. For years

I never had closure from that and I don't think I ever will. This boy I liked at my school set it up for some type of gang initiation. We went together for a month then he invited me to his brother's party. I had so much to drink that I passed out and nobody gave a shit. I didn't know I was pregnant until my stomach started growing. I was trying to hide it but my mother caught on. I was six months pregnant when she took me to the abortion clinic. She told me I had to wait until the baby was born because I was too far out. Anyways, a girl I knew was in the clinic and she told the guys that raped me I was pregnant so they were harassing me in school. My mother sent me to South Carolina with my father's sister. I had my son and gave him to my aunt's neighbor. She adopted him because she couldn't have children. Every day I used to sneak into Thomasine's house to see him. All I wanted to do was hold him and tell him I was sorry for everything and how much I loved him. Thomasine called the police on me and they told me I could get in trouble since I didn't have rights to him. She gave me a warning and told me I had to move or else she was going to file charges. So, my aunt moved and one day I came home from school and she was lying on the bathroom floor. She had an aneurism. I came back to Baltimore when I was seventeen and my mentality wasn't the same anymore. I was cold-hearted and angry with everyone. I called Thomasine and begged her to let me sing to my son for his fourth birthday. She told me I wasn't a mother and I needed to forget about *her* son. I realized she was right and I stopped reaching out to her. She called me earlier today after all these years. She hurt me deeply when she took him away from me. I didn't want to interfere with her parenting, she could've called me his cousin. She knew it wasn't solely my fault that I became a teen mom and because I was young, my mother signed the rights over to her. My mother didn't have the money to take care of him and she was scared that one of the boys would try to harm me. Thomasine thought I didn't feel anything for my son because of my age, but I cried for years about him. I have a picture of him in my safe that I look at throughout the day. My history with men hasn't been great because of that. Every man I trust, hurts me. It's a cycle that constantly repeats itself."

Stacy's eyes watered. I didn't know if it was because he was upset or if he felt sorry for me.

"Do you hate me?" I sobbed. Stacy hugged me so tight I couldn't breathe.

"I'm sorry, shorty. It might be too late but tell me who those niggas are and they are dead."

"They had their karma. I'm just trying to move on with my life and be better for my family. It made me insecure for a very long time so when you cheated on me, it wasn't just about Sadi, it proved my theory of men to be true. But I know you love me and my insecurities made me miss out on the years I could've spent with you and expanding our family," I replied.

"Call that woman back, Tuch. Your son might be in danger. Something had to happen for her to reach out to you after all this time," he said.

"I'm scared. What if he hates me? He'll feel like I loved Niji over him when the circumstances were different. I know how adopted kids think and no matter what I do, it won't make up for the years I missed."

"It doesn't matter. It's better late than never. You won't know until you call her back," he said. I climbed out of bed and went into my purse to get my cell-phone. My palms were slippery and my hand trembled as I clicked on Thomasine's number. The phone rang five times before she answered.

"Hello."

"Hey, Thomasine. This is Stacy. Sorry about what happened earlier, I was surprised you called me after all these years. Is Rush okay?"

"That's why I called. I'm getting old, I'll be sixty soon. I can't keep up with him and nobody in my family wants to deal with him. He's a troubled teen. Every week it's something. But the final straw was when someone shot at my house and killed my husband. I can't deal with his street war and bury my husband at the same time. Come and get him, please. I know I haven't been nice to you but I thought I could raise him better. I'm paying for it now, and as God is my witness, I'm very sorry. I love Rush so much but I'm scared one day a police officer is going to knock on my door and tell me he's dead." Tears wouldn't stop falling from my eyes. I was afraid of the outcome but I knew I was the only person my son had left.

"Do you still live in the same house?" I asked.

"No, we had to move last year because of finances. I'm just tired," she said.

"Text me your address. I'll leave now," I replied. Thomasine cried and thanked me before she hung up. Stacy put his shoes and shirt back on. I hurriedly got dressed in a sweat suit. It was a seven-hour drive but that was the least of my concern.

"I'll drive while you get some rest," Stacy said.

"Are you sure you're up to this? I don't want to force my problems on you."

"Bring yah fine ass on, Tuch. He's family and what concerns you concerns me, too. We'll get through this," he said. It was eight o'clock at night so traffic wasn't going to be in our way.

****

Six and a half hours later...

We pulled up to a small house surrounded by tall grass. It was a cute country cottage. South Carolina had a bunch of long, back country roads with a lot of farm land. It was a comfortable place to live but there was something about the city life that I adored. Stacy parked his Navigator behind a two-door white sports BMV. There was also a van in the driveway. The porch light was on and the quiet made me nervous. I looked at the clock and it was a quarter to three o'clock in the morning.

"This is it," Stacy said.

"I'm shaking," I replied.

"I'll knock on the door and you can stand behind me," he said. We got out the truck and Stacy walked in front of me. I stood at the bottom of the steps while he rang the doorbell. My legs almost gave out as I walked up the steps. In all my thirty-two years, I had never been this frightened of rejection. I was afraid of my own child. The door opened and it was Thomasine. I almost didn't recognize her. Her hair wasn't combed and her eyes drooped. She looked eighty years old. Her housecoat hung off her shoulder. Maybe it used to fit at one point in time.

"Hi, Thomasine," I said when I stepped around Stacy. She wrapped her frail arms around me and pulled me in for a hug.

"I didn't think you were gonna come after I told you what was happening, but I should've known better. Come on in," she said and stepped to the side. The living room was a mess and there was dried-up blood on the carpet.

"Sorry about my home. The coroners had to move things around to get my husband's body out the living room. Who do we have here?" she asked, looking at Stacy.

"I'm her fiancé, Stacy."

"You two have the same name. It's nice meeting you, Stacy," she said and shook his hand.

"Where is he?" I asked.

"Upstairs, probably playing that damn game. He's been quiet since James was killed. They were very close," she said.

She called for Rush and told him to hurry downstairs because it was important. I heard a door open and I squeezed Stacy's hand. Tears threatened to fall from my eyes when he came downstairs. Rush was almost Stacy's height, probably an inch shorter. His dark skin was so pretty that it looked like he had on foundation. His hair was a curly fro with pretty black coils and tapered on the sides. Rush's eyes were a dark gray which he probably got from his father. He had my full lips and nose. As handsome as he was, he hid it behind a scowl. I was expecting a teenager but Rush looked to be twenty-three.

"Who are these people, Ma?" he asked Thomasine. Rush had a set of gold fronts in his mouth. I also noticed the Rolex he was wearing and wondered what he was really into. I figured the BMV in the driveway belonged to him.

"Remember when I told you that you were adopted? Well, this is your mother, Stacy and her fiancé," Thomasine said. Rush looked at me with confusion.

"My mother? She looks too young, and besides you told me my mother was dead," he said. Thomasine held her head down, ashamed of the lie she'd told him about me.

"She had you when she was thirteen and I adopted you. I told you she was dead because I didn't think you were going to ever see her, but I called her because I can't have you here anymore. I'm getting old and I'm developing arthritis in my knees. I can't keep running around looking for you when you don't come home for days. You don't have any respect for me! I begged you to leave the drugs alone and what did you do? You bring that shit in my house and now James is dead! You gotta get out of my house, Rush. I'd rather you move away from here and start over instead of putting you out on the streets to get killed. I can't protect you and you can't protect yourself, neither. So, please, do this for me. I'm begging you to move away from here and start over. You won't have to look over your shoulders every time you step out of the house," Thomasine said.

"You went behind my back to call a woman I don't even know? You don't know them, neither. What makes you think she can protect me when she didn't even raise me? She doesn't know shit about me! The only reason why I stay here is to make sure you're straight. I can get my own crib if you want me gone," Rush stated.

"Get to know her because she's your mother and I'm done with you! I want you out of my house and out of South Carolina," Thomasine said. Rush's face softened when Thomasine wiped her tears away.

"Ma, I'm sorry. I told you I'll get those niggas back for killing Pops. Why you trippin'?" he asked.

"Get them back by leaving with your mother. Do it for me. If you're sorry for what you put me through, leave my house. Go to Maryland and start over. You're a smart boy who has a bright future ahead of you, but if you stay here, I won't forgive you," she said. Rush looked at me and Stacy and it saddened me that he was caught up in the streets like that.

"What about my whip?" Rush asked.

"I can have someone ship it to Maryland," Stacy said.

"I'll grab my stuff, but I'm only doing this for you, Ma," Rush said to Thomasine. He went upstairs and slammed his bedroom door. Thomasine told us to come in the kitchen so she could make us coffee.

"You two have a seat," she said. We sat at the dinner table and she grabbed a few coffee mugs off the counter. She poured coffee into the cups then placed them in front of us.

"Rush had gotten some older girl pregnant months ago, but she lost it. I don't even think she was ever pregnant. He cared about her a lot and I told him she wasn't no good. She didn't have any manners and dressed like a slut. Apparently, she was creeping with some boy who had it out for Rush. When he broke up with the girl, the problems got worse. Rush and her boyfriend got into a big fight at a party and Rush was stabbed in the leg. I'm tired of this shit," Thomasine said.

"How old is the girl?" I asked.

"Twenty-four. These older women think he's older than what he really is," Thomasine said. After she brought us cream and sugar for our coffee, she sat across from us.

"He's a sweet boy. It's just that he wanted things me and James couldn't afford. James was an alcoholic and couldn't keep a job. The bills were piling up and I couldn't pay all of them with my retirement check. Rush started hanging out in the streets," Thomasine said.

"How old was Rush when you married James? You were single when you adopted him," I replied.

"Rush was three when I married James but I didn't realize he had a habit until Rush was six years old. We have been struggling for years."

I wanted to ask her why she didn't contact me sooner but I thought better of it because she didn't have to raise him, but it would've helped if she didn't shut me out. I would've found a way to come back for him because I didn't want to give him up in the first place.

"How did you get my cell-phone number? Have you been keeping in touch with someone I know?" I asked.

"No, I typed in your name and your hair shop came up," she said.

"That was before I finished college. I'm glad I kept the same number."

Stacy was quiet. I guess he didn't know what to say. I'm sure he didn't expect Rush to look as grown as he did. We talked for a few hours while Rush packed his things. I excused myself to use the bathroom. Thomasine said it was located upstairs across from Rush's bedroom. There were pictures on the wall of Rush when he was a baby. I heard moving around and knocked on his bedroom door. The door opened and he had that scowl on his face again.

"Can I come in?" I asked. He stepped to the side and I walked into his bedroom. His room looked apart from the house. He had a king-size bed, a flat-screen TV on the wall and a shoe shelf on his wall with all expensive shoes. Rush's room was very neat.

"You can sit down if you want to. We don't have roaches or no shit like that. That Stacy dude is Fendi's producer so I know y'all live in a big house on a hill. This shack makes you uncomfortable?" he said.

"Naw, I'm from Baltimore. We had rats but continue on," I replied, walking around his room. Rush had my attitude but I couldn't dwell on that. He didn't know me and he was going through a lot but eventually I was going to talk to him about us being cordial. He went into his closet and opened his safe. He had jewelry, stacks of money and a gun.

"You ain't taking that gun to my house," I said.

"I wasn't going to, but I do need my money. I'm not looking for no handouts so when I get out there I can get my own spot."

"Maryland is very expensive. A one-bedroom will cost you over a stack. I have a nice size house and you will be comfortable there," I replied. Rush sat on the bed next to his duffel bags and stared at the wall.

"Who is my real father?" he asked.

"I don't know. I was raped at a house party," I replied.

"Sorry that happened to you," he said, loosening up.

"I know it's hard but your safety is important. You have your whole life ahead of you. Thomasine can visit any time she wants, so don't think she's not going to be in your life anymore."

"I'm doing this for her, not for me. I'm ready when you are," he said.

"I'm ready as soon as I use the bathroom."

Once I was finished, I headed downstairs. Rush was in the living room and Stacy was helping him with his bags. I picked up a bag and Rush grabbed it from me.

"I got it. It's too heavy," he said.

Me and Thomasine stood in the doorway and watched Stacy and Rush load the truck.

"I'm going to miss him," Thomasine said.

"You're more than welcome to visit."

"Thank you so much," she replied.

Stacy called out to me and told me he was finished loading the truck. Rush came on the porch and hugged Thomasine.

"Be good for your mother and call me as soon as you get settled in," she said. He kissed her cheek then hugged her again. She went into her house and locked the door. I felt sorry for her even though she never cared about how I used to feel. Rush got in the back seat of the truck then put his Beats headphones on. I told Stacy I'd drive back so he could get some rest. He grabbed the back of my hand and kissed it. I wondered how excited Niji would be once she found out she had an older brother.

Damn! How the hell am I going to explain this to everyone?

****

It was one o'clock in the afternoon when we arrived home. I called out from work and told them I had a family emergency and needed to take a few days off. Rush and Stacy were asleep when I pulled up in the driveway.

"We're home!"

They woke up and Rush stepped out of the truck. He was hesitant about walking in after I unlocked the front door and turned off the alarm.

"Come on," I called out to him.

"Go ahead. I know you ain't tryna stay out here," Stacy said to him. Rush stepped into the house and looked around.

"Come on, I'll show you around." He followed me upstairs and I took him to the guest bedroom that had a small bathroom inside. The bed was a queen and there was a TV on the wall but it wasn't as big as the one he had at his old home.

"This is your bedroom. You can fix it up however you want to. There is a big bathroom in the hallway in case you want to take a bath because the bathroom in here only has a shower. What grade did you stop going to school?" I asked.

"Twelfth."

"Okay, that's not bad. You can enroll in night school. Do you have a driver's license?" I asked.

"Yeah, I got it."

Rush sat on the bed and kicked off his shoes. He seemed to have a lot on his mind. I wanted to hug him, kiss his face and tell him I didn't mean to hurt him but that was just wishful thinking.

"Get some rest. We can get your bags out the truck later," I said.

"Thanks," he said and turned his back towards me. I closed his bedroom door and went into my bedroom. All I could do was sit there and cry my eyes out. Regardless of the circumstances, it was hard for a mother to interact with their child like strangers. I gave birth to him but that's all I did—

all I could do. Stacy walked into the bedroom and hugged me.

"Get some rest, Tuchie."

"I can't rest. There is so much I have to do. Nobody knows about him, not even Asayi. She thought I went to South Carolina because my mother had issues with her finances. It's just so much but I'm glad he's here. It's like the weight of the world has been lifted off my shoulders," I replied. My cell-phone rang inside my pocket and it was Asayi.

"Hello," I answered.

"We had a lunch date remember? I went to your job and they told me you called out. Is everything okay?"

"Not really. I had to go to South Carolina to get my son."

"Your son? What are you talking about, Tuchie? You only have Niji," she said.

"It's a long story but I had him when I was thirteen. Remember when I went to South Carolina? Well, that's why. I gave him up to my

Auntie's next-door neighbor. She is older now and can't deal with him because he's involved in the streets so me and Stacy left last night to pick him up."

"Can we see him? Or is he not up for visitors? I'm so emotional right now," her voice trembled.

"How about tomorrow? We're tired from traveling."

"Listen, don't you cook a thing. I'm going to bring food to your house so we can have a family dinner. I'll take care of it but can you sneak me a picture? Do I know his father? How does Stacy feel?"

"I'm going to send you a text in a few," I replied.

"Okay, love you. If you need anything don't hesitate to call me. I don't care what time it is, Tuch."

"Love you, too."

I hung up the phone and Stacy was knocked out. Sleep was calling me so I took off my shoes and climbed in the bed next to Stacy. I kissed his lips and thanked him because he helped me through it. He would make a perfect husband— my husband.

Isha

Me, Jay and Hadley were on our way to Tuchie's house. I dropped my phone and cracked the screen the day before when Asayi told me Tuchie had a nineteen-year-old son. Instead of calling her, I decided to wait until I saw her so we could talk because I knew she was overwhelmed. Besides, Asayi told me what happened. Me and Tuchie talked about everything but she never said anything about being raped. I wasn't in my feelings over it because it was something a lot of people were ashamed to admit. Jay was driving and I was sitting in the passenger's seat. Hadley was in the back texting on her phone. Me and Jay hadn't been talking much since we had that huge argument. It originally was just going to be me and Hadley but Jay wanted to come. Usually he hooked his phone up to the Bluetooth inside of his car for his music, but I noticed he wasn't doing that. Maybe he didn't want me to recognize the numbers when they came up on the screen. Jay showed a lot of signs of cheating but I still needed more proof. I couldn't leave until I found out who he was fucking. The driveway was full when we pulled up to Tuchie's house so we parked on the street behind more cars.

"They must be having a party," Jay said.

"I'm sure there's a lot of her family in there."

We got out of the car and walked up the driveway to Tuchie's home. The door was unlocked so we walked in. The house was crowded with people I hadn't seen before. Something told me the women were in the kitchen so that's where I went. Asayi, Tuchie, Chika and their mothers were sitting at the kitchen island drinking wine.

"Come have a seat right next to me," Tuchie said, patting the stool. I hugged everyone before I sat next to Tuchie. Tuchie's mother, Jonita, was tipsy which was always.

"Where is your son?" I asked Tuchie.
"He's somewhere around here. I didn't think my whole family was coming but then again, they're nosey. They are gonna talk about this for years," Tuchie replied.

"I can't wait to meet him," I clasped my hands in excitement.

"Well, he's not in a good mood. The only one he really talks to is Stacy and Niji. She has been following him around the house all day and I tried to tell her to give him some space but she wasn't hearing it. My biggest fear is that he'll hate me," she said.

"Think positive."

Asayi's daughter, Navaeh, came into the kitchen and I picked her up. She was so adorable and it was difficult to not spoil her. She gave me a kiss on the cheek and everyone was in awe.

"Can I keep her for three days?" I asked Asayi.

"Ask Trayon."

"Umph, never mind," I replied.

"Trayon acts like someone is gonna hurt his kids. I'm her aunt and I can't even keep her," Chika said.

"That's 'cause you smoke too much weed and can't cook. You know Trayon gotta make sure his baby girl eats those good meals her mama makes," Tuchie said.

"Lim loves my cooking," Chika said while holding her six-month-old daughter. Navaeh mistakenly squirted her juice box on my shirt.

"Ohhhh nooo. I'm sorry about that," Asayi said, grabbing paper towels. She picked up Navaeh then handed me the paper towels. I excused myself so I could clean my shirt in the bathroom.

"This isn't coming out." I was scrubbing my shirt on the way to the bathroom, not paying attention, when I bumped into someone.

"Oh, I'm so sorry," I said to the stranger. His gray eyes were so pretty that I couldn't stop myself from staring at him. He even had pretty dark skin which brought his eyes out. He was tall, about six-foot-one or two. The man was gorgeous!

"You good," he said with a smirk.

"Um, okay. I'm just gonna squeeze past you."

"Yo, Rush! Come here for a second. I gotta show you sumthin," Stacy said, walking towards us.

"Hey, Stacy," I said and he hugged me.

"What's good witchu? I saw Jay but I didn't see you come in," he replied.

"I went straight to the kitchen. Where is Tuchie's son? I wanna meet him. I hope we're not scaring him off."

"He's standing next to you," Stacy said. Tuchie's son was staring at my chest and I felt so dirty for looking at him the way I did. He looked to be twenty-three. I wasn't expecting someone so tall to be her son. Matter of fact, so much was going on that I forgot his name.

"Nice to meet you. I'm your mother's best friend, Isha," I said and held my hand out to him. He didn't shake my hand but gave me a head nod instead.

"Nice to meet you, too, Isha," he said then walked off with Stacy.

Awkward!

A few hours later, the crowd was dying down. Tuchie's relatives left so it was just the crew who stayed behind. I had a little buzz because Jonita made moonshine. The kids were upstairs with Hadley and the adults were downstairs. Tuchie was in and out with her feelings. One minute she was happy then the next she'd get emotional, but I couldn't keep my eyes off Jay. He stayed on his phone the majority of the time, texting. It pissed me off so much that I hadn't said a word to him since we arrived. While he was texting, he had a smirk on his face. That bitch was definitely keeping him happy and I wondered if he ever smiled that way when I texted him. Matter of fact, I doubted if Jay was ever happy with me. All I wanted was love, family and a healthy relationship. Lately, Hadley was the only one who kept me smiling when I wanted to break down and cry. Most days, I felt myself dying on the inside.

"Are you alright? Who do I have to slap?" Chika asked me.

"I'm fine. Jonita's moonshine got me trippin'."

"That's because she put some weed oil in it," Chika laughed. Jay got up when his phone vibrated. He must've thought I didn't see a number calling him. I waited a few seconds before I got up to follow him. He was in the hallway bathroom so I listened by the door.

"I'll be over there in a few hours, I'm chilling with my family," he whispered.

"Yo, Sadi. You're starting to get on my nerves, shorty! I'm doing the best that I can and you keep calling me after I told you I'd call you when I leave my peoples' crib," he said. I turned the doorknob and it was unlocked. Jay dropped his phone on the floor when I walked into the bathroom. I hurriedly picked it up then bolted out of the bathroom and up the stairs. I had enough! I found a bedroom and locked the door behind me.

The caller was still on the phone.

"Who is this?" I asked. The woman wasn't saying anything but I could hear her breathing.

"Bitch, I know you hear me talking to you! You like being the side chick, huh? How does it feel to sleep with someone's man? How does it feel begging for his time when you know he's with his FAMILY?" I asked and she hung up. Going through his messages almost sent me to an early grave. She sent him a picture of a sonogram. I wasn't done yet, though. I went through his photo album and there were more pictures. He had a lot of nude pictures from the same person but none of them were of me and I sent him plenty. He must've deleted them. I dropped down to the floor and cried my eyes out, almost screaming. Jay wasn't just cheating, he was in another relationship and she was carrying his child.

"Isha, open the door! I gotta talk to you!" he knocked.

"Baby, please! It's not what you think," he said. A door inside the bedroom opened and Tuchie's son came out with a towel wrapped around his waist.

"Yo, what the fuck are you doing in my room?" he asked.

"Open the door!" Jay yelled out.

I opened the door and closed it behind me so Rush wouldn't be exposed to our drama. Jay reached for his phone but I put it behind me.

"How long, Jay? Is this baby the reason why you have been treating me like shit? We're supposed to get married soon and you do me like this? How long have you been talking to this bitch?"

"Can we please talk about this at home? The shit is embarrassing," he said.

"Was it embarrassing when you knocked her up? Who is this bitch?"

"You don't know her!" he said.

"Nigga, I don't give a fuck! Who is she?"

"Me and her have been cool for a very long time, but a few months ago I went down to Atlanta and shit happened. We had sex and I knocked her up, is that what you want to hear? I have been cheating on you for the past three months. It was hard for me to tell you because you're too good of a person to be let down like this," he said. I walked out of his face and headed downstairs. Jay followed me, begging me to forgive him. I grabbed my purse off the coffee table and stormed out of the house. Jay ran outside and grabbed my arm.

"Baby, wait!" he called out. I turned around and punched him in the eye.

"FUCK YOU!" I screamed and jumped on him. Jay wrapped his hand around my throat to restrain me but I couldn't stop swinging. I kicked and punched him to ease the pain but it made it worse. He made me waste four years after knowing I wasn't what he wanted.

"I loved you!" I screamed. Tears fell from his eyes, but I didn't think it was tears of regret. Jay wanted me to feel sorry for him even though I was the one hurting.

"Baby, I'm sorry. Let's go home and talk about this," he pleaded. Somebody's car alarm went off when our bodies fell against it. Chika came outside then called for help when she saw us fighting. Seconds later, everyone was outside. Stacy pulled Jay away from me and Chika's fiancé, Lim, tried to talk me out of hitting Jay again.

"You're gonna regret this, bitch! I'm gonna fuck any nigga I want to because you're dead to me, Jay! You and that bitch can rot in hell! I was everything you wanted!" I cried. Tuchie and Asayi were talking to me but I wasn't hearing them. Everyone wanted me to stop yelling at Jay because they didn't know the whole story. Jay was calling me all types of hoes because I told him I was going to see other men.

"You were probably fucking other niggas anyway! I knew you was too good to be true. I'm gonna kill you if you come back to the house!" Jay yelled at me.

"What is going on?" Asayi asked.

"That nigga got some bitch knocked up!" I said. Jay's shirt was ripped to shreds and he had scratches on his face. I wanted to take his eyes out.

"You foul as fuck, Jay!" Chika yelled at him. She tried to go at him but Lim grabbed her.

"Get him away from my house, Stacy! I want him gone now!" Tuchie said.

"Aight, I'm leaving. Someone tell Hadley come on," Jay said. Asayi went inside to get Hadley and she came out moments later. She looked at her father's face and wanted to know what happened and, of course, he lied to her. He told her that we had a little too much to drink and was playing around. Hadley was old enough to see through our bullshit.

"Are you coming, Isha?" she asked.

"You can stay here," Tuchie said to me.

"I'm gonna go home and get my things. I'll be fine. Sorry for disturbing the party. I just couldn't take the disrespect anymore," I replied.

"We all act a fool sometimes. Call me when you get home and don't hesitate to shoot him if he tries to hurt you. You still keep mace in your purse, right?" she asked and I nodded my head. Jay got into the car and Hadley got in the back seat. Jay's phone was on the ground buzzing and I picked it up. It was that bitch, Sadi, calling again.

"Jay is busy!" I answered then hung up. I put the phone into my purse and walked over to his car. Everyone was looking at us, probably wondering if I was going to fight Jay again. I slammed the door after I got into Jay's car. The nigga had the nerve to grab my hand and kiss it when he pulled off.

"I'm gonna fix this, Isha."

I pulled away from him. If he thought having a baby by another woman was something to be fixed, he was a bigger fool than I thought.

"I want to know what happened to the old Jadiah. The one I fell in love with."

"He's still here. I'm human and we make mistakes. Just know that I love you," he said and I wiped the tears from my eyes. Hadley was quiet—too quiet.

Forty minutes later, we were pulling up to our home. I remembered a time when I couldn't wait to come home. After a long day of work, my handsome and lovable boyfriend would wait for me in the living room to ask about my day. Those days seemed so long ago. We got out of the car and Jay unlocked the front door. Hadley went upstairs to her bedroom and closed the door. Jay wrapped his arms around me, squeezing me and begging me not to leave him. I stood still not knowing what to do. At that very moment, I hated myself because even after knowing he was cheating, I couldn't find it in my heart to leave him. It was my first time experiencing a real heartbreak. I told myself that I was leaving as soon as I found out he was cheating, but it was easier said than done. He pulled away from me and wiped the tears from my eyes.

"I didn't mean the shit I said but I can't lose you. I love you so much and I'm sorry," he pleaded. I pulled away from him then headed upstairs to our bedroom with mixed emotions running through my mind. I caught a glimpse of myself in our bedroom mirror and stared at myself, feeling unattractive. What changed about me for Jay to fall out of love with me? Was it my appearance? My hair was always done, I didn't gain any weight and I kept my fashion game up. I sucked his dick the way he wanted me to and cooked his favorite meals. Our house was always spotless and I didn't ask him for money. I paid my own bills, too. What in the hell was wrong with me for him to fall in love with another woman? I knew he loved her. Jay was never the type of man to have sex without a condom so therefore he trusted the bitch. Jay came into the bathroom and ran my bath water. He helped me undress and we didn't say a word to each other. I sat in the tub and stared at the wall. Jay lathered my bath sponge with my favorite Dove Deep Moisture body wash.

"I know I'm a fuck nigga now and nothing I say can make you feel better, but I swear I didn't mean for shorty to get pregnant," he said.

"Get out and let me take a bath." I snatched the sponge from him and he stood up looking down at me.

"I don't want to lose you," he said. His eyes were bloodshot red and he had desperation in his voice. Back in the day, I never understood why women took cheating men back. But here I was, still loving and wanting to be with a no-good ass nigga. His pleas seemed sincere and those tears in his eyes were convincing me that he really couldn't live without me.

"Get out, Jay."

"Yo, are you gonna leave me while I'm asleep? Matter of fact, don't even worry about that. I'm going to sit up and watch you sleep like I used to do."

"Leave me alone if you're concerned about my feelings. I want to sit here and think but you are interrupting me. Get the fuck out of the bathroom!" I yelled at him.

"I'll get your nightclothes for you," he said. He left the bathroom and closed the door behind him. Something was telling me to run and never look back but love told me to believe him and stay to work it out.

Sadi

Two weeks later...

Jay hasn't called or visited me much since his fiancée found out about us. I had bigger things to worry about, though, and that was getting my shop up and running. There were only a few things that needed to be fixed before the grand opening, but in the meantime, I was on the computer designing a business page for my salon. My cell-phone rang on my desk and it was my friend, Shelley, from Atlanta.

"Hey, girl."

"Ugh, when are you coming back home? I'm so damn bored," Shelley replied.

"I'll visit after I get my shop up and running. It was more than I thought it would be. Jay was helping me at first but now he's trying to be the perfect man for his bitch. He gave me the impression he wasn't happy with her. They don't have any kids together, so why is it so hard for him to leave her? What if I'm making a mistake?"

"We all make mistakes but be patient. You only know what he tells you, but there might be more to the story. Even if it doesn't work out, at least you are back home. You gotta remember Jay wanted you to move out there because of the baby. What if he doesn't want a relationship with you? Eventually, you'll have to decide what's best for you. I know you don't want to hear this, but I wouldn't be a friend if I didn't tell you the possibilities of this relationship. What if he really loves that woman? I used to be with a man who had a woman. I waited for three years for him to leave her but he didn't. She went from his girlfriend, to wife then they had a baby. He kept making excuses as to why he couldn't leave when he had the opportunity before he proposed to her. All he wanted to do was sleep with me and make up for the small things his wife lacked. So, at the end of the day, this is about the baby and not about you and him. Build your clientele there then open up a shop in Atlanta. Look at it as a business move, too," Shelley said.

"So, you're telling me to use him?"

"Why not, Sadi? Use him until you can't anymore! The man has a fiancée, which means he's going to possibly marry her. He offered you a business, so make as much as you can and open up a shop down here. Then you can open up several more. Hell, you secured the bag. He's using you, too, so it's only right," Shelley replied.

There was a knock on my door and I told Shelley I'd call her back. I hung up the phone and got up from my desk to answer the door. After I looked through the peephole, I opened it. My mother and Stacy's mother, Deborah, stepped into the foyer. Ms. Deborah and my mother had been friends for years; they even lived next door to each other. That was how I fell for Stacy. He was my next-door neighbor and used to be my best friend. We developed feelings for each other when we hit our teens but we didn't date until our early adult years. Things just weren't how I thought they would be between us.

"Deborah wanted to see you," my mother said and I hugged Deborah.

"You look so beautiful. Oh, my heavens. You were twenty-two the last time I saw you. I can't believe this!" Deborah said and hugged me. I was caught off guard by her visit because the last time she saw me was when I had Aja. Deborah tried to help me get clean but I betrayed her. I stole her car to look for drugs while I was pregnant with my daughter and that was enough for her to hate me.

"I know and I'm very sorry for all the trouble I caused," I replied.

"The important thing is kicking that addiction and now look at you. I can't believe this and I hear you're expecting."

"Yes, I'm three months pregnant. Come on, let's go to the kitchen and pour a glass of wine," I replied. My mother was at my home every day so she knew her way around the house. Jay put me in a luxurious townhouse and I absolutely loved it. It was very spacious. My condo in Atlanta seemed like a shoebox compared to my home in Maryland. While my mother took Deborah on a tour, I poured them a glass of wine. My mother came into the kitchen while Deborah was using the bathroom.

"Ma, where is Daddy?" I asked.

"Well, he's at work."

My father wasn't home the day I came back. My mother told him I was on my way and suddenly he got called into work. My father was still upset with me. Even though I was clean, he was still mad that I used to be on drugs which made me steal from my parents. My mother never lost faith in me, but it crushed him the most since I was a daddy's girl.

"Ma, he's not at work," I replied. She sat at the kitchen island and looked at me with worried eyes. My mother was in her mid-fifties and still had a youthful look to her. She could pass for thirty-five. She wore her hair in a silk wrap with a part in the middle. There wasn't one strand of gray hair on her head.

"He didn't want to come. Your father won't let it go, maybe because you left and was gone for years. You two didn't have a chance to physically heal together. I know it's old but you really hurt him. You stole the money he was saving for us. Stacy paid us back but what if he wasn't able to? We would have had to start all over and it took us years to save that small amount. Anyways, I'm very proud of you and I can't wait to become a grandmother. I put it all in God's hands and now look at you. You're shining more than ever," she said.

Deborah came into the kitchen and sat at the island. I gave her a glass of wine and she thanked me.

"Where is this excellent man your mom keeps telling me about?" Deborah asked.

"Well, he's busy working but hopefully y'all can meet him soon," I replied. My mother didn't know Jadiah had a woman. Every time she asked about him, I had to make up excuses. All she knew was that I had a man and we moved back to Maryland for business purposes. She thought he came from Atlanta with me.

"I still wished you and Stacy worked out. Y'all were so cute when y'all were younger. I still remember it like it was yesterday. Whenever you spent the night, he slept on the couch so you could sleep in his bed. That was the good ole' days. He was so in love with you," Deborah said.

"Well, now he has Tuchie," I replied.

"Yeah, Tuchie and her grown-ass son. Stacy is just finding out about her having a teenage child down in South Carolina. Her excuse is that she was raped by a gang and they threatened to kill her if she had the baby. I don't know what to believe. What if she has more kids out here? That girl came from Baltimore's filthy streets so anything is possible," Deborah said.

"Tuchie, the angel, has an older kid?" I asked.

"And the reason he's here is because the lady who adopted him didn't want him around her anymore. He was selling drugs and all kinds of stuff. I don't trust him around Niji. Stacy deserves better. Tuchie is a respectful woman but she comes with a lot of baggage," Deborah said.

"Wait a minute, Deborah. Stacy wasn't always innocent, neither. He used to sell dope years ago. Maybe her son is going through a phase. Stacy can teach him a lot of things since he's been there before. He's still a kid," my mother said.

"Stacy never brought drama to my house and teenagers these days are different. He's a bad influence on my granddaughter and I have a problem with that. Tuchie knows nothing about that boy to have him around her Niji," Deborah said.

"It sounds like he's just like his mother. Tuchie sold drugs and pulled a gun out on me. The apple doesn't fall too far from the tree," I replied.

"Amen to that," Deborah said.

My cell-phone rang from an unfamiliar number. I answered it thinking it was Jay because he switched numbers a lot.

"Hello."

"Yeah, Sadi. We need to talk and I mean now!" the caller said.

"Kareem?"

"Who else would it be? We need to talk," he spat.

"We don't have shit to talk about. How did you even get my number? I told Shelley that I wasn't interested in you because you're not my type, but you won't give up! You're a creep." Kareem was practically in love with me, perhaps obsessed. I explained to him on more than one occasion that I didn't want to be with him.

"What's your type then? Drug dealers? Gang bangers? What is it? I'm not good enough for you because my background is clean? Tell me what it is!" he yelled into the phone. I hung up and added his number to the block list so he wouldn't call or text me.

"Who was that?" my mother asked.

"Some guy in Atlanta. He's a stalker and he's another reason why I left."

"I'm hungry. Me and Deborah were going out to eat. Do you want to come?" my mother asked.

"No, I'm fine. I have to finish this website."

"Let me know if you need any help. I don't have nothing to do during the week," Deborah said. We sat in the kitchen, talking for two hours until it was time for them to leave. As soon as they left, I called Jay's phone. It was time that he met my mother and I didn't want to hear shit else about it.

"Yo, I'm around the corner. I'll be in there soon," he said and hung up. I stared at the phone in disbelief. He's been quiet lately but all of a sudden he decided to do a pop-up. I sat the wine glasses in the dishwasher and wiped off the kitchen island. The front door opened then closed. My back was towards the entrance of the kitchen but I knew he was behind me because I could smell his Tom Ford cologne. Jay always smelled good and it made my clit throb every time. It had been a few weeks since we made love and I needed him. While I was cleaning the sink, he wrapped his arms around my waist. His hands rested on my mid-section while his soft lips graced the nape of my neck.

"I missed you," he whispered.

"You have a funny way of showing it. I came here for you and look how you have been treating me." He held a key out in front of my face and I pulled away from him.

"I don't have time for your games, Jay!"

He leaned against the counter and crossed his arms. Jay was looking so good that I almost forgot about being mad at him. He was wearing a pair of gray Nike joggers with the matching jacket. On his feet were a pair of black Lebrons. The only jewelry he wore was a gold diamond Audemars Piguet watch with a diamond gold necklace. His beard was trimmed nicely and his sandy brown hair was freshly cut. Jay was very light skinned with small freckles on his face that made him look like a white man sometimes. His pretty hazel eyes were always low from smoking hella weed. Both of Jay's parents were Creole. They moved from New Orleans to Maryland when Jay was two years old. His father left and went back to New Orleans when Jay was six and he hadn't seen him since.

"I got you something. Come outside and look," he said, grabbing my hand. He pulled me out the kitchen and down the hallway to the front door. There was a 2018 white Lexus GX truck parked in my driveway.

"Is that mine?" I asked in excitement.

"Yeah, I got it for you today. Ain't nothing wrong with having two whips."

"You can't keep spoiling me like this. I want to spend time with you instead of your money," I replied.

"I feel you but this is all I can offer right now. Shit has been hectic at home now that Isha knows about the baby. I wasn't expecting her to find out the way she did. She ain't the same anymore and it's my fault. I crushed her," he said. There wasn't a doubt in my mind that Jay didn't care for his woman. It was all fun in the beginning until he got caught.

"And you're telling me this because of what? I'm supposed to put her feelings before mine and my child's? I didn't ask for this shit! Eventually you gotta choose. I'm here now so all these second thoughts are dead!"

"Yo, what are you talking about? We go through this every time we're together. I promised you everything before you came back home and I gave it to you!" he said.

"Thanks for the truck, now you can go home," I said.

"I am home. Let's go in the house so I can fix us something to eat. I know your bougie ass ain't cook nothing," he replied.

We went back into the house and Jay headed towards the kitchen. I had a few things in the fridge but not too much. Jay took his T-shirt and jacket off. He wasn't bulky or even thick. Jay was on the lean side and he was also tall. He probably weighted one-hundred and eighty pounds. He pulled out a tray of flounder fish and broccoli.

"Damn, shorty. The fridge is empty as shit. I gave you a thousand dollars to go grocery shopping and it looks like you only spent fifty," he complained.

"I'm not into grocery shopping," I replied.

"Shorty, you gotta fix that. I like home-cooked meals," he said. I sat at the island and watched him rinse the fish off before he dipped them into an egg batter then a seasoned flour batter. After the grease got hot, he dropped the fish into the pan and it sizzled.

"You really know how to cook, huh. Who taught you?" I asked.

"My mother. She worked while I sat home with my daughter so I had to feed us. Isha taught me how to cook a lot of other shit, though." I didn't want to hear anything else about Isha. She had the nerve to cuss me out from Jay's phone. I didn't know they were engaged until after I slept with Jay. Matter of fact, I had to get my number changed so she wouldn't know it was me calling his phone. Jay was single since he wasn't married yet so I owed her nothing!

Jay dropped broccoli into a pot filled with a little water. The kitchen was smelling good and my stomach growled since I hadn't eaten all day. He was the only man who opened me up to a lot of things I wasn't used to. He cooked for me, spoiled me and gave me the best sex I ever had. I couldn't stop blushing thinking about the life growing inside me. Soon, it was going to be, me, Jay and our bundle of joy. His daughter was better off with Isha because I knew she wouldn't accept me, so it was pointless to build a bond with her. I was once a teenager and nothing people said could get through to me.

"Why doesn't Isha have any kids?" I asked.

"She's waiting for marriage. Isha is a little old-fashioned. She didn't want to move in with me and Hadley until we were married but we begged her," he said.

"So, she's perfect?"

"Yeah, she is. I can't say one bad thing about her."

I was waiting for him to tell me something. There was no way in hell he was going to leave her if he thought she was this perfect angel. The bitch had to be flawed somehow—we all are.

"How about the sex life?" Jay turned around and grilled me.

"Why in the fuck are you asking me all these questions about her?"

"Most men have a reason to cheat, or at least they think they do. So it has to be sumthin," I replied.

"I guess for the same reason an attractive woman like yourself is willing to have a baby by a nigga who is with someone else. Stop asking me shit that I can't ask you," he spat.

"I'm in love with you so I went against everything I believe in."

"Me, too," he said dryly.

Jay's phone rang and he walked out the kitchen to answer it. I already knew who it was, his insecure bitch! Jay probably thought I was overstepping my boundaries but I no longer cared. We knew each other before she came in the picture. I was tired of being alone and not coming home to a man after a long work day. Isha cooked, fucked him good and took care of his daughter. All I could offer him was pussy and a baby. Tears threatened to fall, perhaps it was the hormones. I was getting too emotional over everything. Nothing felt right anymore and a part of me missed my old best friend, Asayi, because she had the answer to everything. Jay came into the kitchen and saw me crying.

"What's up witchu?"

"I'm stressed out. Every day I tell myself that I deserve better and look at me. Being in Maryland doesn't feel right anymore. I'm forty minutes away from Annapolis, my mother wants to meet you and I'm trying to get this house together. I feel like I'm having an out-of-body experience," I replied. Jay went over to the stove and turned it off.

"What are you doing?"

"Get up," he replied. He picked me up and sat me on top of the kitchen island. He pulled down my leggings along with my panties.

"I know what you need," he said. He slid me to the edge of the counter and wrapped my legs around his neck.

"Ohhhhh, Jay!"

His tongue entered me and I was on the verge of exploding on the tip of his tongue. He buried his fingertips into my thighs while his head thrashed around between my legs. Jay's tongue reminded me of a baby snake as it darted in and out of my hole. My essence dripped from my slit and drizzled between my buttocks. I pushed his face further into my center and rubbed my pussy across his lips.

"Ummmmmm," he moaned.

"Ohhhh, Jay! I'm about to cum!" I yelled out. His went underneath my shirt and cupped my round breasts. My body was on fire and my pussy was throbbing uncontrollably. A gasp escaped my lips and my upper body lifted off the counter as I exploded. Jay pulled down his joggers and briefs, showing me that pretty thick dick of his. He helped me off the counter then turned me around to face the sink. He gripped a handful of my hair and with his free hand he spread my pussy lips. Jay rubbed the tip of his head against my moist slit, making me beg for it. My back was arched and my feet were planted firmly against the marble floor. The head of his shaft squeezed through my tight opening. I bit my lip to keep myself from making inhumane noises. Jay's strokes were long and deep. He took his time exploring my G-spot. He pressed himself further into me and the pressure went into my spine, causing my body to tense up. My nails scratched at the counter as his body slowly slammed into mine. A yelp slipped from my lips followed by a hoarse cry.

"You feel soooooo gooooodddddd!" I moaned. Jay's dick jabbed at my sensitive spot, my cum was spilling out from my pussy as he pumped in and out of me. A stream of wetness ran down my inner-thighs as Jay continued to stroke me. He squeezed my ass and grabbed the back of my neck when he sped up. Jay went from making love to fucking me senseless.

"I'm cumminnnggggggggggg!" I cried out. It was my third orgasm and my body was drained, but Jay was nowhere near finished. He turned my body around so I could face him and picked me up. I wrapped my legs around him and held onto him tightly while he gripped my ass and slammed me onto his dick. He told me to take off my shirt and bra. They came off in ten seconds. He took my breath away when he pulled my nipple into his mouth. Jay's dick was harder and he throbbed inside of me. He groaned my name as he gripped my ass cheeks, spreading me so I could take every inch of his nine-and-a-half-inch dick. He let out a deep groan when he spilled his seeds into me.

"We can eat later. Let's take this shit to the shower," Jay said. He placed me over his shoulder and walked up the stairs. He was tickling my side and biting my ass cheek. I was happy all over again. Jay was my new addiction. I was depressed when he wasn't around, but my mood changed the moment I saw his handsome face. He sat me on the toilet seat then ran the shower water. After the temperature was right, we got into the shower and went for another round. That time, Jay showed no mercy on my pussy. I thought he was going to split my back in half.

Two hours later, we were lying across the couch with empty plates in front of us on the coffee table. My head was resting on Jay's chest as he rubbed his fingers through my hair. His cell-phone rang on the coffee table but he ignored it.

"Answer the phone."

"Naw, it ain't nobody but Isha. These past few weeks been crazy at home. We argue so much that Hadley been staying over her best friend's house. My home life fell apart," he said. Isha called three times before Jay silenced the phone. Isha was the woman who had to deal with Jay staying away from home. As far as I was concerned, Jadiah Amir LeRoux was all mine.

Jay

Me and Sadi fell asleep on the couch. I was trying to work it out with Isha for the few past weeks but she was complicated. I couldn't touch her, talk to her or even look at her without her cursing me out. A muthafucka ain't got to tell me I was fucking up because I knew. Isha was wife material so it looked crazy on my part but she had too many rules. I wanted to have a baby with her but she wanted to wait until she was thirty-five years old and after being married for a few years even though we were already fucking. The thing is I wanted more but that shit was on hold. Life was too short for that bullshit, especially since a nigga was still hustling. Sadi wrapped her arm around me when I slid from underneath her.

"Where are you going?" she asked.

"To use the bathroom." She pulled away from me then pulled the blanket over her. I grabbed my cell-phone and had over a hundred missed calls. Most of them were from Isha and the rest were from my homeboys. My stomach formed into a knot because I had a feeling something happened. It was five o'clock in the morning but I knew Isha was probably up. I called her back and she answered on the third ring.

"Jay! Where the fuck are you?" she sobbed into the phone.

"Tell me what's the matter!"

"Hadley is in the hospital! Her and some friends snuck off to a party and Brittany was driving drunk. They crashed head-on into a tree and everyone died except for Hadley but she's in bad shape. I hope that bitch's pussy was worth it!" Isha screamed into the phone.

"I'm on my way!"

I hung up the phone and looked around for my clothes. I remembered Sadi threw them in the washing machine but didn't dry them.

"Jay, what happened?" Sadi asked when she got up from off the couch. I ignored her and went into the laundry room.

"Those clothes are wet," she said, standing in the doorway. She watched me put on wet clothes in confusion.

"My daughter was in a car accident."

"You shouldn't drive like this. Annapolis is a ways from here. Let me drive you," she replied. She went upstairs and came back two minutes later wearing a sweat suit and a pair of slippers. She grabbed the car keys and I followed her out the door. My nerves were fucked up and my hands couldn't stop trembling. All I had to do was answer the phone but I thought Isha was calling to clock my moves. The first time she called was like six hours ago. My daughter was fighting for her life and I didn't know shit about it.

"Tell me what happened," Sadi said as she sped down the small road.

"Hadley was riding in a car with her drunk friends," I replied.

"Isha let her out of the house that late?"

"She snuck out. Isha goes to bed early because she has to be up by six in the morning," I replied.

While Sadi was driving, I hit up my nigga Bogo because he called me a few times, too.

"Yooooo, where you at? We at the hospital," Bogo answered.

"On my way. What are the doctors saying?"

"I don't know, bruh. Isha and your mother are the only ones back there with her. Everyone else is in the waiting room. All I know is Hadley lost a lot of blood so they had to give her a few blood transfusions," he said. I clutched my phone in my hand, angry at my myself for failing Hadley. My baby girl was hurt. I lost her mother and couldn't lose her, too. Shit in life wouldn't matter to me if my daughter didn't make it. I wanted to give her everything she wanted, including Isha...

Four years ago...

We were at Trayon's crib on Thanksgiving. The house was crowded with close friends and family.

Everyone was sitting at the table having fun and cracking jokes. Hadley was sitting across from me, next to Isha. My daughter didn't talk much around a lot of people because she was shy, but somehow Isha got her to warm up.

"I want to get my hair done like yours," Hadley said to Isha.

"You don't need extensions. You have pretty hair, but I think Tuchie can braid it similar to mine."

"Daddy, do you like Isha's hair?" Hadley asked. I was texting Sadi because she sent me a "Happy Thanksgiving" text. I wasn't looking at Isha in that way to notice her hair. I saw her when I came around the crew but we didn't talk much.

"Yeah, it's nice," I replied.

"Thank you," Isha said, blushing.

After we finished eating dinner, I went into the living room where it was quiet so I could talk to Sadi on the phone. Lately, I was thinking about her heavy. Even though she was far away, it didn't seem like it. Tired of playing games, I was ready to hit her up to see if she could come visit me for a few weeks but Hadley walked into the living room.

"Daddy, can I stay over Isha's house?" she asked.

"Isha is too old to be your friend, baby girl."

"I know but we can do girly things together. Grandma be too busy now and you're boring. Can she take me to get my nails polished tomorrow?" she asked.

"How about I take you," I replied.

"But you're always busy and forget a lot. Pleeeassseeeeee, Daddy?" she begged. I couldn't tell my daughter "no" so I went along with it.

"Aight, she can come with us but you can't go with her by yourself. I don't know here like that." Hadley hugged me then ran out the living room to tell Isha.

The next day...

We met Isha at the nail salon. I tapped on her car window and she put her phone in her purse. She got out of the car and Hadley hugged her.

"I couldn't say 'no' to her with those cute eyes. I'm a sucka for sad faces. You can wait in the car if you want to. I know men don't like sitting in nail places," she said.

"Aight, cool. Be good for Isha, Hadley, or you can't go on anymore nail dates."

"I promise I'll be good, Daddy," she replied. I gave Isha six twenties and told her it was for her, too. She wanted to give the money back but I declined it. Hadley grabbed Isha's hand and pulled her into the nail place. I sat in my car and waited, thinking about asking Sadi to come to Annapolis but my pride kept getting in the way. After thinking about it for a while, I sucked it up and called her but she didn't answer. The first time Hadley interrupted the call and the second time I didn't get an answer. Maybe it was a sign or something because the thought of me wanting to pursue her went away. When she called back, I didn't mention anything about her coming back to Maryland. I told myself if it was meant to be then it would be. We talked on the phone for ten

minutes until she had to start her next client's hair.

An hour later, Isha came out the nail salon with Hadley. She opened the back door of my whip and Hadley climbed in to show me her nails. They were pink and designed with flowers.

"They straight, baby girl," I chuckled.

"Say 'cute,' Daddy," she replied.

"Naw, that ain't my style," I laughed.

"Okay, Hadley, I'll see you later," Isha said to her.

"Thanks, Isha," Hadley replied. Isha closed the door and I nodded my head at her, thanking her. I didn't pull off until Isha safely got into her car. On our way home, Hadley kept talking about Isha.

"Daddy, all my friends have mothers and I don't have one. They go get their nails done, go shopping and get their hair done, too. Can you date Isha?"

"That's not how that works and maybe she's taken," I replied.

"No she isn't because I asked her. She's very nice and I like her clothes, hair and nails. I want to be pretty like Isha," she said. The rest of the ride home was quiet. What Hadley said weighed heavily on my mind. She was getting older and needed a positive female in her life.

The next day, I went over to Trayon's crib to talk to Asayi. I wanted to know more about Isha. Asayi didn't tell me much other than I should find out for myself. I wasn't the type of nigga to ask a woman out on a date. Honestly, a nigga was a little shy so I told Tuchie and Asayi to put in a word for me. They told Isha I was interested in her but shorty said she wasn't going nowhere with me if I couldn't ask her myself. A month later, I asked Isha out and she told me she'd think about it. Let's just say, shorty made me work for that date and I had been working for everything since...

"JAY!" Sadi called out, bringing me back to reality. I looked to the side of me and we were at the hospital. I thanked her and got out her whip. She called out to me but I ignored her. The emergency room was crowded. Tuchie, Asayi and Chika was giving a nigga a dirty look, but Tuchie looked like she wanted to kill me. I went to the front desk and told them I was Hadley's father so they escorted me to the back. There was a small waiting area with three chairs in the hallway. My mother was consoling Isha as she cried. I found myself getting choked up because I kept hurting my family. Catching feelings for Isha wasn't my intentions in the beginning of our relationship because she wasn't necessarily the type of shorty I wanted. I only got with her to make Hadley happy.

"She's still in surgery," my mother stated.

My mother, Adele, was fifty-five years old and walked with a cane. She had hip surgery from falling down the stairs and never fully recovered. She sucked her teeth when I sat next to her.

"You have something on your neck, son," she said in disgust. Isha glanced at my neck and cried harder. I didn't have to look in the mirror to know that I had a passion mark. Sadi was always sucking on my neck, especially when I was hitting her spot. I knew shorty was doing it on purpose to get back at Isha for arguing with her.

"I hope this whore is worth it. I taught you better than this! I raised you to respect and cherish women. You wouldn't want a man to do to Hadley what you're doing to Isha, would you? Have some fucking decency!"

"Not now, Ma," I replied.

"Why not? You think I'm gonna sit here and console you or care about your feelings? This is the devil's work! Shit like this only happens when you stick your dick into evil beings," she said.

We sat for another hour before the doctor came out and told us Hadley was sedated. She suffered from two broken legs, a fractured arm and eye socket. She also had internal bleeding. With all that he mentioned, I assumed he was finished telling us what was going on with her, but he wasn't. Hadley had lost some of her left breast because a sharp piece cut across her chest and was embedded into her skin. My angel went through a lot and her protector failed her.

"Can we see her?" Isha asked while wiping her eyes.

"Yes, follow me," the doctor replied.

We followed him down the hall to a set of double doors. He swiped his badge across a pad on the wall and the doors opened. The sounds of machines beeping and the coldness of the ICU wing reminded me of death. Hadley's room was the last room down the hall.

"My little baby," my mother cried. Hadley was in a whole body cast it seemed. I counted almost eight tubes connected to her body. She also had a tube down her throat to help her breathe.

"She had a gash on her forehead which is why you see a little blood on the gauze pad. I'm assuming her head hit the window from impact and the glass shattered on her chest. She's a strong a girl to survive such a tragic accident. But she was also the only passenger who had her seat belt on. We found a trace of MDMA and marijuana in her system. A lot of teens are trying what they call 'Mollys' now and Percocet. A nurse will come in soon to check her vitals, and make sure you buzz me if you need me," the doctor said.

"Thank you so much, Dr. Conrad," Isha said and hugged him. He nodded his head at us before he left the room. I pulled a chair close to Hadley's bed. When I grabbed her hand, a sense of relief came over me from her warm skin. I was watching the monitor with her heart rate, praying that I wouldn't see a flat line. My baby girl didn't look too good. Her face was swollen to the point where her nose seemed so small, almost the size of a penny. Her lips were bruised and scraped pretty badly. My mother rubbed my back as I held onto Hadley's hand, telling her how much I loved her. Isha sat on the opposite of Hadley praying and that shit ticked me off.

"She's not dead, shorty. Kill all that," I said.

"We can still pray for her healing process," Isha replied.

"How in the fuck did my daughter sneak out the house, Isha? I guess you was so busy calling me that you missed it. Look at her! This shit is your fault. Matter of fact, take your funny-built ass home," I seethed.

"I was asleep! Hadley was in bed doing her homework the last time I checked on her. You should've been home but instead you wanted to chase that tramp. I love her and she's the only reason why I decided to stay with your sorry, ungrateful, cheating ass so don't make it seem as if I don't care about her! I'm not going anywhere, so deal with it. I'm gonna be here every day, all day until she can come home. Besides, your mother has custody of Hadley. You forgot you were a teen dad and couldn't take care of her so your mother had custody of her. Adele will never tell me to leave so shut the fuck up and pray for your daughter before I get real fucking nasty and you don't want to see that side of me. I have been patient with you but right now I'm disgusted that I even shared a bed with you," she said.

I don't know how my mother being Hadley's legal guardian slipped my mind. When Hadley's mother died, they wouldn't let her go home with me because I was young and in school. Hadley's grandmother was a fiend and her family was filled with crackheads and alcoholics. Hadley was in a foster home for a month before she was allowed to come home with me. The system doesn't favor men when it comes to their seeds. They'd rather send a child to an estranged family member before the father. I probably wouldn't have been able to get Hadley until I was eighteen and I still couldn't see them letting me have custody of my own daughter because I didn't have a job. When I got older, I was hustling and had a criminal background so I let it go and never filed for custody. My mother left the hospital room to give our friends and family an update on Hadley's condition. Isha's eyes were puffy and red from crying. Honestly, she didn't look the same and it was my fault. I couldn't blame her for Hadley sneaking out of the house. I should've been there but my guilt was clouding my better judgment. I wanted to believe that me going over Sadi's crib didn't play a part in Hadley's accident even though it did.

"Why didn't your bitch come and see about your daughter?" Isha said.

"Shut the fuck up, damn. It's not the time for this right now."

"When a woman loves a man, she loves his children, too, or maybe all women aren't cut from the same cloth. I'll give you your space. I gotta go home and pack my things but I'll be back," Isha said. She kissed Hadley's cheek and told her she loved her before she left the room. My mother came in a few minutes later and sat across from me in Isha's chair.

"Hadley can't have visitors until they move her to a different room. I told everyone that it could be a while, but they decided to wait anyway," my mother said.

"I'm lost, Ma."

"I know you are. I can see it in your eyes. You don't love Isha, so let her go."

"I love her very much, but I have been confused lately," I replied.

"You're not confused. You just want your cake and eat it, too, but there are some things you don't know about me and your father. Your father was a married man when I got pregnant with you. His wife kicked him out after she found out he had a son so he decided to come to Maryland with me. At the time, I thought I won but noooo, baby. Your father was still in love with his wife. He kept in touch with her for four years after we moved from New Orleans. So one day I came home from work and his things were gone. I called him and practically begged him to send me some money because I needed help taking care of you. He told me that his wife didn't want him to, so he didn't. Long story short, your father didn't love me. He loved how I made him feel in bed and he loved my curvy figure. A man could love everything about a woman and not love her. Your father used to look at me like I was the only woman on this Earth, but it didn't mean a thing. Sadly, his wife lost her battle to breast cancer when you were ten years old. He tried to come back to me, but I couldn't do it. I haven't heard from him since. So, my karma was raising a child by myself with a broken heart because I had no business sleeping with a married man unprotected," she said.

"I love Isha, but I've been feeling this woman before Isha came into the picture. Hadley wanted me to date her so I thought I was being a good father by giving Hadley what she wanted. All I wanted to do was make my baby girl happy. Isha wasn't a part of my plan, Ma. But it's my fault because I should've told Sadi my feelings sooner."

"Be careful, Jadiah. A damaged heart can ruin lives," she said.

****

I stayed at the hospital for three days. Me and Isha weren't talking to each other. It was almost like we didn't spend four years together. Bogo stopped past my crib to bring me some clothes because a nigga was musty. I would've asked Isha but that would've started an argument. While I was dozing off, Isha walked into the room with flowers and a stuffed bear. I looked at the clock on the wall and it was almost four o'clock. Sadi said she was stopping by to bring me something to eat because the food in the hospital was bullshit.

"I thought you told the nurse you were coming back at six."

"I was but I got finished moving my things out sooner than I thought. How is she feeling?" Isha asked. It was the most we had said to each other in the past few days.

"She woke up for a few minutes but the medication got her a little confused. They said she'll be like this for another week or so because she's still in a lot of pain," I replied. Isha sat next to her and grabbed her hand.

"Don't worry, baby. Mama is going to get you all dolled up as soon as we get you out here," Isha said to Hadley.

At that moment, I looked at Isha as Hadley's real mother. I said things out of anger but I was lucky to have a woman in my life that loved my daughter as her own. The nurse walked Sadi in two minutes later and I regretted telling her to bring me something to eat. Sadi was decked out in all designer shit and she dyed her hair blonde. Isha looked a little uncomfortable because she had on an old sweat suit and dirty shoes from moving. The nurse must've felt the tension in the room because she rushed out. Isha's eyes darted to Sadi's midsection. Sadi's stomach was slightly noticeable because of the stretch long-sleeve shirt she was wearing. They were probably wondering what I saw in them as they stared at each other because they were completely opposite.

"Is this a bad time?" Sadi asked.

"Yes, it is. Are you family?" Isha asked.

"I'm a friend of Jay's," Sadi replied.

"You mean his baby mama?" Isha asked.

"Look, I didn't come here to start anything. Jay was hungry so I brought him something to eat," Sadi said. Isha snatched the bag of food out of her hand then dumped it into the trash can. I wasn't hungry anymore anyway.

"I thought you were coming at six, Ish," I said.

"Get this bitch out of my face, Jay. You couldn't meet her ass downstairs in the lobby? You sneak around any other time," Isha said.

"To my understanding, you and Jay are no longer together so there wasn't a need for me to meet him in the lobby," Sadi replied.

"And to my understanding, side chicks don't get family privileges. Don't you think you did enough?" Isha asked.

"I actually don't think I did anything wrong. I've known him before he knew you and I didn't know of you until after he came to Atlanta but you know this already. I'm sorry you had to go through this and I didn't mean to hurt you. Jay made the decision to be with me and you should understand that," Sadi said.

"Yoooo, Sadi. Chill out with all that," I said.

"Made the decision? Honey, I left that nigga. Looks like you're the rebound yet again. Trust me, you'd still be seeing him after-hours if I hadn't left," Isha stated.

"It doesn't matter. I get to enjoy the two vehicles he bought me and the four-level brownstone he moved me in. Oh, and let's not forget about the hair salon he fixed up for me, too. This man knows where he wants to be which is why he's setting up a foundation for us. What business did he help you with?" Sadi asked. Isha looked at me and I could see all the hate shorty had for me in her heart. The only reason I gave Sadi that shit was because I knew I fucked up and wanted to show her how sorry I was for putting her in an awkward situation. Isha stormed out of the hospital room and I followed her.

"Baby, wait!" I called out to her. She pressed a button on the elevator and I pulled her back.

"Get away from me!" she whispered.

"Yo, it wasn't like that," I replied.

"It doesn't matter. Give her this since you gave her my life!"

Isha threw her ring at my chest and I caught it. The elevator opened and she stepped on. I watched the tears fall from her eyes as the doors closed. Seeing Isha cry tugged at my heart because I knew she was probably the one who could satisfy me if I hadn't knocked up Sadi. Sadi was sitting in my chair when I walked back into Hadley's room.

"Yo, why did you have to tell her all of that?"

"You didn't hear how she was talking to me? I was trying to be nice but she kept blaming me for your cheating ass. I'm just as fed up as she is," Sadi said.

"Fed up? Muthafucka you got everything! A baby, cars, a house and a fucking hair salon. What you should've did was shut the fuck up or left the room. My daughter is lying in a hospital bed and all you could do was be happy about stealing someone's man? Isha is hurting right now. That's her daughter, too, so she had every right to be angry with you being here. All you had to do was leave when you saw her out of respect."

"Wait, you're mad 'cause I made her cry? And what do you mean I have everything? And I didn't know the bitch was gonna be here!" Sadi gritted.

"I didn't know, either, but I'm sure you had a feeling who she was before you came into the room. The curtains are open. You can see everything in here before coming in."

"Well, I'm sorry I came in. I wasn't expecting your fiancée to look so busted. Hell, I thought she was a crackhead," Sadi said.

"But you looked worse than that when you were on that shit. Humble yourself, shorty."

"Fuck you, Jay!" Sadi snatched her purse off the floor then walked out the hospital room. When I turned around, Hadley was looking at me; I rushed to her.

"Hey, baby girl. You need me to call the nurse?" I grabbed her good hand and kissed the back of it but she pulled away from me.

What in the fuck just happened?

Tuchie

Isha sat at my kitchen table crying her eyes out while drinking out of Stacy's Hennessey bottle. I rubbed her back and handed her some tissue. Jay was a straight up fuck-nigga. I wanted to hit up some of my old friends from B'more so they could put a bullet in Jay's ass but Trayon wouldn't let that slide. Jay was like Trayon's baby brother. I liked Jay before he all of a sudden switched up.

"Why do good people get hurt all the time? I have been doing everything I could possibly do to make Jay happy, but after all this, he was in love with another woman. How is this even fair to me? Every time I turn around, I see a whore winning! This bitch was on drugs, lost her baby behind it, fucked her man's best friend and stole from her parents? On top of that, she was responsible behind you getting robbed and shot. That bitch doesn't deserve shit! How can someone like her be desirable to anybody? What does she have to offer besides a pretty face?" Isha ranted. I told Isha everything about Sadi after I found out who Jay was seeing. I didn't know they knew each other like that, but then again, Keondra was messing with Jay's best friend and Sadi and Keondra had been friends for years. I wondered if Stacy knew his ex-girlfriend, Shady Sadi, was back in Maryland.

"It's time for me to live for myself and get out of this shell. I wanna be a thot. I wanna get drunk at a club and wake up next to some nigga I don't know. What if I start smoking weed again? It's time for Isha to do whatever she wants to fucking do! Hell, I might join a gang bang or be a porn star. My pussy is good enough," she slurred. I took the bottle from her and sat it on the counter. Rush came into the kitchen and went into the fridge. He was warming up to us but some days he had his moods. I think he was missing his old home. He was very close with Stacy and was even going with him to the studio. I desperately wanted that kind of bond with him but he was still rejecting me.

"Men love hoes," Rush said.

"Boyyy, if you don't stay outta this business," I replied and he smirked. I almost jumped for joy because I was able to make him smile.

"I'm just saying. I heard her from upstairs. Niggas like hoes because they don't come with a lot of expectations. It's convenient. But when a man doesn't mind working for it, he'll get a good girl. It's common sense," Rush said.

"I think he has a point," Isha said then clapped her hands. She got off the stool then strutted across the floor, throwing her hips from side to side. I looked at her sideways and wondered why she was making herself pigeon-toed.

"Yeah, just like that, baby girl," Rush laughed.

"What you think, Tuchie? Do I seem whorish?" Isha said.

"You want me tell her the truth?" Rush asked me.

"I want you to stay out of grown folk's business," I replied.

"What's grown about this, though? Females get their hearts broken at all ages. I'm giving her my point of view from a man's perspective."

"You're only nineteen years old," I replied.

"I'll be twenty in four months, Tuch."

I hated when Rush called me Tuch. He was doing it to provoke me. No mother wants their child calling them by their nickname out of respect. I wasn't expecting him to call me, "Ma," but I'd rather him call me Stacy.

"Call me Stacy."

"But your nigga's name is Stacy, too," he said. He sat on Isha's stool and watched her while drinking a grape soda.

"Something is missing. I think you need a little more backside," Rush said to Isha.

"I think you need an ass whipping and your PlayStation privileges taken away," she replied.

I called Stacy's phone to see if he was on his way home. When he answered, I heard loud music playing in the background.

"Where you at?" I asked.

"At the studio. I'll be home in a few hours," he yelled into the phone. I heard a woman's voice and asked Stacy who was in the background. He said it was his artist, Bailey. I didn't trust her at all but I wouldn't tell Stacy that because producers worked with male and female artists. It was his job and I didn't want to trip because of my insecurities. Isha was back to drinking out of Stacy's bottle when I hung up the phone.

"Put that down! You're drunk enough," I said and took the bottle from her. Deborah called my phone and I answered. I was so wrapped up in Isha that I forgot I had to pick Niji up from her house. I was an hour late.

"I'm on my way," I said and Deborah hung up on me. I wanted to know what her problem was with me. We had been cordial over the years but I knew she wasn't too crazy about me. Years ago, I heard her tell Stacy I wasn't his type and that he liked slimmer women. Something was telling me it was about Rush because her attitude had been very funky since he came to Maryland.

"Put your shoes on, Rush, so you can ride with me to pick up Niji."

"I can stay here," he said, eyeing Isha's breasts.

"No, you can't, now let's go so Isha can take a nap."

I went inside Isha's purse and grabbed her car keys so she wouldn't drive drunk. She laid on the couch and I tossed a blanket over her. Rush went upstairs and grabbed his jacket and tennis shoes. I was feeling bad for him because he didn't have anything to do and couldn't start night school until the following school year because we were late for enrollment. I gave him the key and told him to drive.

"Put your seat belt on."

"I forgot. I'm used to driving without one in South Carolina," he replied. Rush reclined the seat back and I never understood why men drove leaned back so far. Sometimes it looked like Stacy was taking a nap when he was behind the wheel.

"What's your favorite color?" I asked.

"Black."

"Tell me about Thomasine and her husband," I replied.

"They were straight. James didn't help out with the bills so I stepped up and did what I had to do. Didn't think she was going to disown me for it," he said.

"She loves you but you brought a street beef to her home."

"I was her son for nineteen years until she realized I wasn't perfect. She returned me to you like I was a pair of shoes she didn't want. Everything I did was for her! Her nigga wasn't doing shit! Why she ain't kick that nigga out instead?" he asked. He was hurt and tried to mask it but I could see right through him because we had the same attitude and most times, we were misunderstood.

"I think this is God's way of telling me that it's not too late for me to be your mother. I really hate that this happened to you but the important thing is that you were raised by a woman who really cared about you."

"I don't know how to be your son. It's weird because you're young and feel more like my sister," he said. I knew that was going to be an issue but he was finally holding a conversation with me and I was satisfied with that.

"What else were you doing besides hustling?"

"You might clown me if I told you what I did. It was before I started hustling, though," Rush said.

"No judgements here. Tell me and I'll tell you whatever you want to know," I replied.

"I did a few porn videos. I got like thirty g's from it. It was right after I turned eighteen," he said. It was chilly outside but I had to put the window down. I was on the verge of having an anxiety attack.

"What made you do that?"

"I was chilling with this girl one night. We were smoking and drinking so she told me record her sucking my di—I mean giving me head. One thing led to another and I ended up recording the whole thing. She got mad at me and uploaded the video to Pornhub. My twitter and IG blew up and that's when this company contacted me about doing a few videos for them. So, they had me doing threesomes with milfs. I fell for this girl so I chilled out with it," Rush said. My son was a porn star and a drug dealer! Me and Thomasine failed him.

"Is there a way you can delete those videos?"

"Naw, I still get royalties from them. My first professional video has over twenty million views, so I know they ain't taking that down," he chuckled.

"Change the subject," I said.

"Do you have an idea which one of those niggas is my father? Like do I look like one of those niggas?"

"You look like my boyfriend who set me up but then again, he looked like his brother. His brother had pretty eyes and curly hair, but they're dead so we don't have to worry about it."

"We ain't gotta talk about this anymore after today. I wish I didn't know I'm a product of rape," Rush replied. He turned the radio up when Fendi's song, "Laid Up," came on. It was his way of telling me that he was done talking. We arrived at Stacy's mother's house and I noticed the brand-new Lexus truck in the driveway. I knew it didn't belong to Deborah because Stacy just copped her a Bentley coupe for her birthday the year before. I got out of the truck and Rush got out with me.

"You think she'll let me use her bathroom?" he asked.

"Let's see."

I rang the doorbell and I heard giggling on the other side of the door before it opened. It was Sadi and the little heifer had the nerve to smile at me.

"Hi, Tuchie. It's been a long time. Me and Niji were just playing tic-tac-toe. Deborah is in the kitchen making dinner for Stacy. Are you and your boyfriend eating with us?" Sadi asked. I pushed my way into the house and Rush stepped in behind me. Deborah knew she was foul for having her around my daughter. I walked into the kitchen and Deborah was taking a tray of macaroni and cheese out the oven.

"You didn't tell me Sadi was going to be here around my daughter," I said.

"I told you to pick her up over an hour ago but you were late. Since you're here, why not stay for dinner? Stacy should be on his way soon," Deborah said.

"Stacy wanted me to cook dinner."

"A man never passes up his mother's cooking. You know that," Deborah said. Sadi came into the kitchen with Niji and they were laughing about something.

"Mommy, Sadi is funny! She should come over to our house," Niji said.

"Mommy has a lot of expensive things in her home that might end up missing so we can't have people in our house that we don't know," I replied.

"Sadi told me she's Daddy's best friend and her daughter, Aja, would've been a year older than me," Niji said. I wanted to slap that wicked bitch's face.

"Go in the living room so I can talk to Sadi and Deborah," I said and Niji skipped out the kitchen.

"Bitch, you have lost your fucking mind!" I yelled at Sadi.

"She needs to know she had a sister. Loosen up, Tuchie, but then again you always acted extra ghetto for no reason. Do you have any more kids Stacy doesn't know about? I didn't know that boy sitting in the living room was your son. Wow, we all have a past," Sadi said.

"You told this bitch my business?" I asked Deborah.

"Don't disrespect my house, Tuchie. Everyone knows you were raped and had a secret baby," she said.

"You're going to regret coming back to Maryland. The next time I pull a gun out on you, I might just use it. You got some big balls showing your face after what you did to me, Asayi and Chika. You think Jay can defend you?" I asked Sadi.

"I'm carrying his child, so why not? You don't scare me. Lay a hand on me and you'll lose that fancy job of yours. I'm too old to be out here fighting but I will press charges on that ass. Try me, fatty," Sadi spat.

Sadi knew exactly what she was doing because nobody was going to touch her while she was pregnant. She also knew that Jay wouldn't let nobody bring harm to his baby. But what she didn't know was that Jay could be touched, too. Jay had the audacity to bring that hoe into our lives again. He didn't know everything about her but he knew enough to know that she was a bad habit. Too bad Isha got caught up in that web but she had loyal friends and we were going to make sure she shined above it all.

"I'm fat because I'm drug-free bitch. Addicts lose weight instead of gaining it. I hope you don't kill this baby with your dirty nose, goose pussy," I said and Deborah gasped.

"But your son is a thug and you didn't raise him. Who are you speaking to about parenting?" Sadi asked.

"Your baby father is a thug, too, little bitch! And regardless of how Rush was born, I still cared about him to make sure he had a decent home to go to. Don't make me beat your triflin' ass up in this house! You have no excuse as to why you failed your child! Nobody put a gun to your head and made you betray your family and friends! So don't pretend to be this uppity bitch like you wasn't out here setting up your best friend to get robbed for cocaine. Oh, honey, I have receipts. The only reason why you came back is because I didn't tell anyone what you did and that was to spare Asayi and Chika's feelings because they were almost raped! All of that was because of YOU! So, respect me when you see me because I saved your worthless life. Stay your triflin' ass away from my man, too. Think I'm playing? Try me, powder nose," I said. Sadi was quiet but Deborah came to her rescue like she always did and told me to take that loud mess away from her home.

"I'm leaving your house now, Deborah, but just know I see through you, too. You still want your son to be with her, huh? Is this what this private dinner was all about? You, Stacy and Sadi? I bet he doesn't even know she's here. Next time you need your hair braided, get that bitch to do it."

"Bye, Tuchie and don't come back. Having class is free," Deborah said and Sadi giggled.

"You don't ever have to worry about me stepping foot in your house again," I replied.

Rush came into the kitchen to see what was going on. I didn't want to make it hard on Stacy but his mother disrespected me so many times and I dealt with it because I loved her son. I wanted to be close to her to avoid conflict but she has never given me a chance. There were other things for me to worry about and that was my kids.

"Aye, Ma. You ready to go?" Rush asked.

"Yeah, let's go."

Niji stepped into her boots and kissed her grandmother goodbye. Not even a second after we walked out the door, Niji asked why me and her and grandmother was fussing.

"It was a big misunderstanding. Don't worry about it, okay?" I replied.

"Yeah, but I'm sad about my sister. I would've had someone around my age to play with," she said.

"I'm sad about her, too, baby but she's in a good place," I replied. Rush got into the driver's seat and I sat in the passenger's. Niji was on her iPad watching a movie and Rush was bopping his head to the music on the radio. I, on the other hand, was livid!

"Thank you for that," I broke the silence.

"I couldn't call you Tuchie in front of them. I heard everything they said about us but I'm not trippin. It is what it is," he shrugged his shoulders.

Forty-five minutes later, we were pulling up in our driveway. The front door of to my house was halfway open. I got out and ran into the house. Isha was asleep when we left but there was no sign of her. Her purse was in the middle of the kitchen with the contents sprawled out across the floor. Me, Niji and Rush searched the house for her. She even left her cell-phone. She had a lot of missed calls from Jay and text messages but she didn't respond to them so he probably didn't know where she was, either. I panicked and called Asayi.

"Did you talk to Isha? She left my house and the door wasn't shut. Her purse, shoes and phone are still here."

"No, I was trying to call her and she didn't answer. Isha hasn't been herself lately and I'm worried about her. Trayon is home so I'm coming right now," she said and hung up. Shit just kept happening back-to-back. I walked out of my back door and the yard was clear. I even checked the shed in the back of the house. My house sat alone and was surrounded by nothing but trees. I should've taken her with me but I was a little relieved I didn't because she would've saw Sadi and snapped.

"I'll walk down the road to see if I see her," Rush said. I wanted to call Jay and yell at him for ruining my friend but it wasn't the right time because he was dealing with Hadley. Sadi was back in town and Jay was in for a rude awakening.

Isha

I stood by a rail on the bridge having thoughts of jumping to end it all. Nobody understood my pain. I was sick of crying and having the feeling of someone jabbing me in the chest with a knife. The image of Sadi's beautiful face and cute round stomach was haunting me. She looked so happy and I stood there like a coward by letting her and Jay flaunt their affair in my face. How dare he send a bitch an invitation to our relationship. I wanted the pain to go away and death was my final solution to ease it. The hurt I was feeling clouded the good times I had with Jay—actually, I didn't remember any. My memories were replaced with tears, sleepless nights and that sonogram picture I saw in his phone.

Jump, Isha! Jump! Do it to make Jay feel the pain he caused you. He'll live the rest of his life in guilt for everything he did to you!

I climbed over the rail asking God to forgive me for not being able to live through it anymore. Hell seemed like paradise compared to thinking about Jay and Sadi. I used to wonder why people cheat themselves by committing suicide, but then I realized some things can't be fixed while you're alive so what's the point of living in misery? Instantly, my pain was fading away because I knew it was going to be over soon. The feeling was serene. I opened my arms and felt myself falling over, but somehow my body crashed onto the ground. I opened my eyes and it was Tuchie's son lying on top of me while cursing me out.

"The fuck is you doing? You got people out here looking for you and your crazy ass is about to jump over a small ass bridge? You weren't going to do shit but break some bones. That water ain't deep!" he yelled at me. My vision was a little blurry but the bridge looked high while I was intoxicated.

"Would you leave me the fuck alone?" I asked then pushed him off. He helped me up and I shoved him into the rail of the bridge.

"Mind yah business!"

"Aight, jump then. I'm going to put you on live video right now so people can see how dumb you look jumping off an overpass. Go ahead before my battery die." My foot was hurting really bad so I sat on the ground to take a look at it. There was a rock embedded in my skin and it was bleeding.

"Please, just leave me alone and let me think," I begged.

"Yo, you cannot be this dumb in real life. Fuck that nigga! Tuchie and Niji are going crazy looking for you and you out here acting crazy. One nigga don't care about you so you about to say fuck everybody else? I know how neglect feels but that shit should make you stronger. Man, I need to smoke a blunt. Y'all folks got too much shit with y'all out here in Maryland," Rush said. He sat next to me on the ground to roll up a blunt.

"You're just like your mother. Always know what to say," I replied.

"Yeah, but always do the wrong shit. I'm tryna go back home but I know Tuchie will be disappointed. It's hard trying to adapt to this place. I miss the country life and even the boardwalk. Me and my niggas used to spend the whole day at Myrtle Beach. Chilling, smoking, drinking and meeting some bad-ass broads. All Maryland has to offer is the city life and good seafood. The cribs out here are mad expensive, though, unless you live in Baltimore," he said. After he rolled up the blunt, he passed it to me.

"You smoked before?" he asked.

"A long time ago." I put my lips on the blunt and took a long pull. The heat burned my nose and chest. Spit seeped from the side of my mouth and Rush took the blunt from me.

"You might have to smoke regular before you put your lips on this kush," he laughed. I rested my head against the rail to stop it from spinning. Dark liquor caused me to act out which is why I only stuck with tequila.

"I'll help you sober up." Rush helped me up and walked me to a big hill next to the over pass. I almost slipped but he caught me. He took me to the stream and that's when I realized it was probably only three to five feet. He pulled me into the water and it was freezing.

"Ohhhhhhhhhh, it's cold!" I screamed.

"You up now, ain't you?" He handed me his jacket; my toes felt like they were about to fall off.

"Please don't tell anyone about this. Just say you saw me walking. I'm so embarrassed right now. I can't believe I'm venting to a teenager," I said. Rush shook his head and walked out the water.

"How old are you?" he asked.

"Twenty-seven. I'll be twenty-eight in a few months."

"I'll be twenty but eight is a low number. You ain't old enough to be my mother so don't pretend like I don't know shit 'cause of our age difference. We can walk back as soon as I finish smoking this blunt," Rush said. I was shivering as I stepped onto the grass. My teeth were chattering so Rush told me to hit the blunt again to warm me up. I sat next to Rush on a rock and hugged myself. My body wasn't freezing like it was moments ago, but my toes were numb.

"Did you have a little girlfriend at home?" I asked. Rush grilled me so I decided to chill out with the young remarks.

"Naw, but my ex-girl was only a few years younger than you," he said.

"No offense but what can a young man offer an older woman?"

"Everything an older nigga can, unless she wants a nigga with degrees. You got something against young niggas?" he asked.

"No, but teenagers don't know what they want. Hell, can young men be faithful? Or even be satisfied with one woman? Can y'all be deeply in love without thinking about pussy all the time?" I replied.

"What's the difference between a nigga my age and your nigga? Weren't you just crying about him cheating and shit? So, what age got to do with it, Isha?" he asked. I scooted away from him and he pulled me back.

"You ain't gotta do all that. I'm just speaking facts," he said. He passed me his blunt and I hit it again.

"I feel so old. I think because I was only twenty-three when I started dating Jay and his daughter was eleven. It's almost like I lost sight of living for me because I put them first. I don't regret her, though, I just wish I stayed in touch with what Isha wants. I feel lost now."

"You need some fun in your life, old head," he joked. I giggled which I hadn't done in so long. To my surprise, Rush was right. I had to live my life the way I wanted to. It was still possible to care for Hadley and myself. But I had to let Jay go. It would probably take years for me to stop loving him but he wasn't good for my soul.

"I do need to have some fun. Perhaps, I should go clubbing and take vacations. Maybe I can work on publishing my own cookbook. I always wanted to be the next female Bobby Flay. It's so much I want to do."

"Do it then," he said.

"What do you want to do?" I asked.

"Mannnn, you'll clown a nigga if I told you."

"Tell me, I'll keep it a secret," I replied.

"I wanted to be a singer. My mother had me in a church choir when I was younger and shit but I stopped going when I was like sixteen. That's when I started acting out but I don't think about that shit anymore."

"Tuchie can sing, too. Asayi and Chika as well, more so Tuchie, though. She has that beautiful strong voice. She sang for a church when she was younger. Baltimore has the best choir singers," I replied.

"I heard her singing the other day while she was cooking dinner. She did sound nice. But, yo, this is between us," he chuckled. Rush's teeth reminded me of pure white snow. A chocolate brother with pretty teeth was a beautiful combination.

It gotta be the weed and alcohol because this boy is so damn fine! Wait, that's Tuchie's son. I can't be looking at him like that but he's legal. Ohhh nooooo, what am I thinking? This is so bad. I need to pray tonight because I shouldn't be having these thoughts.

Rush finished his blunt and I wanted to tell him that we shouldn't go back yet because he made everything so much better. But I kept my mouth shut as he helped me up the hill.

"Can you walk? Want to get on my back?" he asked, looking down at me.

"Uhhhh, I'm good."

"Let me guess. Young niggas ain't strong enough?" he asked.

"Would it make you feel better if I climbed on it?"

That didn't sound good at all! He might think I'm trying to come on to him.

"Would it make your feet feel better is the real question. You don't have any shoes on and the road has a lot of rocks. It's your call," he said. I thought better of it because it was a ten-minute walk back to Tuchie's house, probably longer. My feet were sore and one of them was bleeding. So I told Rush I'd get on his back. He kneeled so I could climb on. I thought he was going to drop me but he didn't.

"Am I heavy?" I asked.

"Naw, I'm a country nigga anyway. My stepfather had me lifting logs and shit when I was seven years old. You're a lightweight," he said.

****

Police was in front of Tuchie's house and I wondered what happened. Rush put me down on the ground and I winced in pain from the wound on my foot. Tuchie and Asayi ran out the house.

"What the hell, Isha! I just filed a missing person's report," Tuchie said.

"I wasn't gone for twenty-four hours," I replied.

"You were drunk so we thought someone found you and took advantage of you," Asayi said. Tuchie went to the police car and told the officer I had returned safely. Asayi hurriedly pulled me into the house so I could take off my wet clothes.

"I'm fine, Asayi," I said.

"You need to take a bath! You smell like pond water, alcohol and weed. Come on," she spat and pulled me down the hallway. I turned around, looking for Rush but he was already upstairs. Asayi helped me out of my clothes in the hallway bathroom.

"I hope nothing changes between us after I tell you this but I can't be your chef anymore. I decided to start my own business and focus on what I really want out of life." Asayi leaned against the sink with a smirk on her face. Asayi was beautiful. She had peanut butter-colored skin with slanted eyes and full lips. She was also a plus-size curvy girl. She was probably around a size eighteen. Her and Tuchie resembled a lot; Tuchie was just a little darker. They reminded me of Jill Scott and Kelis.

"So, you finally decided to go out on your own, huh?" Asayi asked.

"I didn't want you to be mad at me," I replied.

"You were the only seventeen-year-old in our Culinary Arts school so I've always known how serious you were about being a cook. I'm ecstatic that you're finally living out your dream. Besides, we're family so you'll always have my support. I can't tell you who to be with but I hope you can move on from Jay. You don't deserve to have Sadi's bullshit mixed into your life," Asayi said.

"Thank you for everything you've done for me. I'm going to sit in the tub for a while and maybe take a nap."

Asayi took my clothes out of the bathroom and closed the door behind her. The tub was relaxing and sleep took over me. I was drained from moving out of Jay's house and visiting Hadley. With my eyes closed, all I could think about was chocolate skin, white teeth and pretty gray eyes. I had officially lost my mind.

****

The next day, I went to see Hadley. Jay was on the couch in her hospital room asleep, but he woke up when he heard me scoot a chair closer to her bed. Tuchie did my hair before I came to the hospital. We didn't have time for braids so she used flexi rods on my natural, shoulder-length hair. My hair was thick, full and bouncy—full of life. I was wearing ripped stretch jeans, a tunic tan sweater with a pair of fur Gucci loafers. Jay was staring at me for a while, probably wondering where my hair came from, but I was focused on Hadley.

"I like your hair like that," Jay said.

"Thanks."

"She was up for a little while a few hours ago and she asked for you. I called you like ten times yesterday after you left," he said.

"I was busy."

"Yo, Ish. I'm really sorry about everything. I don't want to beef with you because at the end of the day, you held this family together. I'm gonna always love you and I deposited half of my money into our savings account before I took my name off it. I want you to have everything so it's about a million dollars in there and it belongs to you. And before you ask, it's not drug money. It came from my businesses so you ain't gotta worry about the IRS. I know how paranoid you get," he said.

"I don't want your money. Have I ever wanted your money? You think that's going to fix everything you did to me? To us?"

"I know that but I want you to be straight for a long time. Either way, I owe you that. I wouldn't have legit money coming in if it wasn't for you. Shorty, you taught me all that," he said.

"All I did was prepare you for someone else. But it's a new day and I don't want to talk about that anymore. It's in the past now."

"I'll leave you alone so you can have some privacy," Jay replied. He kissed my cheek before he left the room and the touch of his lips brought back so many memories of us making love. Jay had a way with his lips, tongue and fingers. My body experienced a lot of orgasms from him without penetration—he was a great lover. Hadley's eyes opened and they were bloodshot red.

"I'm so glad to see you awake," my voice trembled.

"I been awake. I pretend to be sleep most of the time or ask for pain medication so I can zone out. I heard him talking to Sadi on the phone this morning. He's selling our house to move in with her. Where am I going to go?" she cried. Hadley's voice was raspy, probably from the tube she had down her throat after her surgery. She was still hooked up to a lot of machines and the swelling went down on her face but it was badly bruised; her face was very dark. She was still unrecognizable.

"Let's not talk about that right now because I don't want you stressing about our issues. My only concern is you. I'm glad you're here with us and I'm so sorry I went to sleep that night. You're still a child and I was supposed to watch over you."

"I'm sorry, Isha. I wasn't thinking. Brittany texted me and told me to come to this party with her because Adrian was going to be there. Adrian is this boy that goes to my school and I like him. Anyways, him and his friends were drinking, smoking and popping pills. I thought it would've been cool if I did it so I followed what everyone else was doing. I woke up in the hospital and found out my friends are dead, you moved out and Daddy got another lady pregnant. That's why I want to stay sleep," Hadley said.

"Just because I moved out doesn't mean I'm going to leave you. Me and your father haven't been happy for a while but we still love you. Now you'll be a big sister so you'll have someone to look after."

"I gotta tell you a secret," Hadley said. Hearing those words made my stomach turn because I was an emotional wreck and couldn't bear to find out anything else.

"My father wanted you because of me. I begged him to give me a mother because I wanted to have what all of my friends had. I'm so sorrryyyyy, this is my fault. My father didn't want to be with you but I kept pressuring him and now I regret it," she cried.

Tears fell from my eyes after I promised myself I wasn't going to cry anymore. A part of me believed that Jay loved me at one point but finding out he never did was the icing on the cake. It was all making sense, he just wanted a mother figure for his daughter and like a fool I gave it to him just for him to have a family behind my back. He used me and made me believe he wanted a life with me. The nigga even proposed to me in front of our friends and family but it was only to keep me close for Hadley.

"It doesn't matter anymore, but get some rest and I'll check up on you tomorrow." I kissed Hadley's forehead before I left her room. It wasn't her fault because she didn't force Jay to do anything. She was a little girl who wanted a mother which was a natural thing to want, but Jay should've handled it better. He should've hooked up with Sadi instead of me since he had so-called known her longer. But I knew his karma was going to bite him in the ass and quite frankly I didn't give a fuck.

Rush

Four days later...

"How much you said this crib was a month?" I asked, looking around the condo.

"Nineteen-hundred," the property manager replied.

"I can get with it."

"Great, you'll love it here. There is a lounging area on the roof and a pool. There's a lot to do during the summer time," she replied. Tuchie was looking out for me but I didn't feel right staying at her crib all the time. I was beginning to like Maryland. The fashion was different from South Carolina and so was the slang. To sum it all up, Maryland was what I needed to start over. I was getting into all kinds of shit back home, like merking niggas and fucking hella broads, especially the ones who went to my mother's church. The first time I had sex was when I was twelve and it was with my mother's best friend's seventeen-year-old daughter. We were on a camping trip and she snuck into my tent. I had a growth spurt around that time so a nigga was looking sixteen instead. Sex wasn't my main focus, though, chilling with Stacy at the studio made me want to go back to singing and writing songs. That was another reason why I wanted my own crib because I liked silence. Tuchie's cousins were always coming over and my little sister couldn't stay out of my room. Niji was mad cool but I didn't want her around my business.

"How soon can I get the keys?" I asked the property manager.

"Today if you have the security deposit and first month's rent. Since you don't have any credit, your security deposit is going to be a little high so we're looking at three thousand dollars today to move in," she said.

"Okay cool."

I had a backpack full of money saved up before I left South Carolina. My plan was to leave anyway but not so soon because I wasn't finished stacking my chips.

"Great, now all we have to do is sign a few papers then you'll have your keys," she said. The property manager looked around thirty years old. She was slim thick and had nice legs but she had too much weave in her head. I was probably the only young nigga this day and age who liked natural haired women, especially women with dreadlocks. I followed her to the leasing office to sign the papers and after I was finished, I gave her the money.

"I'll see you soon and don't hesitate to call me if you need anything. My personal number is on the back of the card inside your folder," she said. I didn't even catch her name. She was checking me out but I ignored it. It had been a while since I smashed a broad but I wasn't interested in any of them. I thanked her before I walked out of her office. My cell-phone rang in my pocket and it was Tuchie calling me.

"Yo."

"Hey, Rush. Can you do me a favor? I'll pay you for it. Isha needs someone to help her move her furniture around. I told her I'd help but I have to stay at work late and Stacy is at Niji's dance rehearsal," she said.

"Aight I'll do it. I'm good on the money, though. Send me her address."

"Thank you so much," she said and we hung up. Tuchie sent me the address and I used my Maps to see how far it was from me.

She only lives in the next community. Damn...

****

"Come in," Isha said after I rang the doorbell. I stepped into her crib and looked around. She had a lot of shit and I wasn't expecting it to be that much, but I'd do whatever I could to make her smile. There was something about her that made her angelic. She wasn't one of those pretty, stuck-up, smart-mouthed kind of broads. Isha was beautiful as fuck to me. I joked about her not having much of an ass but her hips made up for it and so did her breasts. What I liked most about her face was her long eye lashes and almond-shaped eyes. Her skin was the color mahogany and she had a pretty smile. She wasn't a dime, more like a twenty-plus. Her ex-nigga was crazy for the moves he made, but fuck that nigga. Every man was for himself, plus I didn't know him like that. Isha was wearing a pair of gray leggings and a sweatshirt. Her hair was pulled up into a kinky ponytail and I thought that shit was so sexy. I caught an erection from observing her.

"It's a lot and you don't have to help me if you don't want to," she said. I took my jacket and shirt off and hung them on the rail of the stairs. Isha covered her eyes because of my bare chest.

"Yo, chill out with that. I don't like moving around with a lot of clothes on, it makes me hot." I pulled her hands away from her eyes and she took a step back.

"Go sit down and I'll get this straight for you."

"I don't want to take advantage of you. How much do I have to pay you?" she asked.

"How about you talk to me while I get this done for you?" I replied and she smiled.

"Talk, huh?" she asked.

"Yeah, what else do you have to do?"

"I'm going to help you. You have to let me help you because this is too much," she said.

"Naw, let me handle this real-nigga work. Go sit down and talk to me."

Isha sat on one of the boxes while I moved the heavy furniture around her living room.

"Are you dating?" she asked while I unwrapped her ottoman.

"Naw, I'm just chilling and getting to know the area a little better. I realized D.C. is much more fun than places around here. You would've thought it was hours away from here instead of thirty minutes."

"That's where I want to open my catering business," she replied.

We talked for hours while I unpacked and broke the boxes down for her. I spent nine hours at Isha's crib, but I wasn't complaining because we talked about everything. Not only was she beautiful, she was very smart. Honestly, I'd never met a woman of her caliber before. The older women I smashed in the past were thots and all they wanted was a young nigga with a big dick and stamina. It was three o'clock in the morning when I laid across her couch. My muscles ached and I was exhausted. Isha came into the living room and handed me a beer.

"Don't tell anyone I gave you that," she said as she sat across from me.

"Yo, when are we going to stop with the young jokes?"

"You bother me," she admitted.

"How?"

"Because I don't know if this is normal, you know with us talking about things. It makes me uncomfortable but it's also soothing," she giggled."What are you shy about? Be honest," she said.

"Nothing. Being shy prevents you from being yourself. What about you?"

"I don't know if I should tell you this," she said.

"Here we go with this bullshit again. Yo, you just gave me a beer but you can't tell me nothing because you think I'm too young to understand? But you ain't got a choice but to tell me anyway."

"And if I don't?" she asked.

"I'm gonna hold you down and feel those sexy-ass lips."

"Fine, I'll tell you, geesh. Anyways, I don't like pleasing myself in front of anyone. Jay wanted to watch me please myself but I couldn't. It feels too personal," she said.

"Yo, get the fuck out of here with that. You childish fa real," I chuckled. Isha smacked her teeth and told me to leave because I was teasing her but I wasn't going anywhere.

"I'm chilling. I unpacked almost all your shit for you and now you're trying to put me out?"

"It's really not funny, though."

"Why you smiling then?" I asked and she covered her mouth. Isha was blushing, she couldn't stay mad at me.

"Come here, Ish," I said in a serious tone and she shook her head "no."

"Naw, I'm dead-ass serious, come over here. I know you want to."

"But I'm not over Jay and I think I should stay away from men for a while," she replied.

"Is that nigga here?" I asked.

"No."

"Walk your ass over here then," I replied.

She sat her beer down on the coffee table then walked over to me. I told her to sit on my lap with her back towards me. She looked puzzled for a few seconds until I pulled her onto my lap.

"What are you doing?" she nervously asked. Isha wasn't really denying me. I knew she was curious about me when I met her. She bumped into me in the hallway at Tuchie's crib and I saw it in her eyes. I grabbed her hand and placed it inside her panties.

"Wait!" she called out.

"Ssshhhh, I'm going to help you play with it," I replied. She was trembling on my lap, probably nervous because I was straight forward. I gripped her ponytail and pulled her head back so she could rest on my chest while guiding her hand between her slit.

"How does that feel?"

"It feels sooooo good," she panted. I pulled my hand away from hers so she could please herself.

"Use your middle finger and rest your other fingers on the side of your lips. Pretend you're using a computer mouse. Yeah, just like that," I coached her. Isha's legs were hanging off my lap while her back was arched against my chest. To get her in the mood, I kissed the nape of her neck and pulled at her hair. Her breathing deepened and her moans were hoarse. She moved her hips in a circular motion causing my dick to poke at her backside. I pulled her hand out of panties and replaced it with mine.

"Goddamn!"

Isha was wetter than a broken fire hydrant. I slipped a finger into her hole and her pussy gripped my finger. My free hand squeezed at her breasts.

"Ruuusshhhhhh, wait! Nooo this isn't right!" I wasn't trying to hear that shit. I wanted to make her cum. I entered another finger and her legs trembled.

"You want me to make you come?" I asked.

"Noooooo," she whined. Her cries were getting louder and her body jerked when I sped up the pace. Her little pussy squeezed the hell out of my fingers and then a big splash spilled into her panties. I pulled my fingers out of her and they were coated in her cream.

"Go home, Rush," she said. She slid off my lap and I stood up to grab my shirt and jacket off the rail on the stairs.

"Can I call you?" I asked when she walked me to the front door.

"Ummm, okay, sure," she replied.

"Goodnight."

SOUL Publications

"Goodnight, Rush."

I left her crib and got into my whip. Her scent was still on my fingers and it made me hard all over again.

Two days later...

I was inside Stacy's studio listening to Fendi's new single. It was a bop, but a few of his bars wasn't catching me.

"What do you think?" Stacy asked while Fendi was in the recording booth.

"That nigga shouldn't be using auto tune for the chorus part. It's messing up the song and, besides, he ain't a singer. Maybe you need to get someone to do the chorus," I replied. Stacy told Fendi to get out the booth. Fendi snatched his headphones off then stormed out with an attitude.

"Come the fuck on, Stacy. I'm tired of repeating this song, bruh," Fendi complained.

"Rush has a suggestion," Stacy said and I grilled him.

"Wait, I gave you my opinion and that was it," I said and Fendi crossed his arms.

"Let me hear it then because this nigga got me out here working extra hard," Fendi complained.

"The auto tune sucks, bruh. You are a street rapper so that singing shit is dead. Change the hook or get someone else to sing it for you." Fendi looked at Stacy and Stacy shrugged his shoulders.

"You sing the hook then and use the auto tune. You don't have to be a singer for that, but you right, I can't be out here doing that shit," Fendi said.

"Nigga, I don't need any auto tune," I chuckled. Me and Fendi were cool. Matter of fact, he was the only nigga I talked to other than Stacy.

"Go in the booth then," Fendi said.

"Let me see what you got," Stacy said to me. I got up and went inside the booth to play around with my own hook because I wasn't feeling Fendi's hook with the beat.

"Go ahead, youngin'," Stacy said.

"I wanna fuckkkk youuuu until you scream my name. Having those leggggs going insane while you drip bubbly champagne. I know I'm a hustler, baby, but I do it all for you. Put you in designer, especially those Gucci shoes. Buy you that Bentley or that Mercedes coupe…"

I stepped away from the mic and Stacy came into the recording room.

"Why did you stop?" he asked.

"I haven't sang shit in a while so I was ready to mess up," I replied. Fendi came into the recording booth with me.

"Ain't this a bitch. A singing street nigga," Fendi joked.

"Fuck you, nigga," I replied.

"Let's wrap this up. I'm trying to get home before Tuchie today. I can't stay here all day like I used to," Stacy said.

"Put a studio in your crib then so we can come there and Tuchie can still see you," Fendi said.

"Naw, business is separate from home. Let's give this a few more tries with Rush singing the chorus," Stacy replied.

By the time we were done recording, it was three o'clock in the afternoon. Before we went home, Stacy stopped at Maggiano's to pick up dinner. We sat at the bar while waiting for our take-out.

"I'm not trying to get in your business and all that, but how was your relationship with your stepfather? You only mention Thomasine," Stacy said. I waited until the waitress sat our drinks down to tell Stacy about James.

"Mannn that nigga was beating my mother's ass. Beat her ass so bad one time she couldn't walk for a week. That's why she keeps talking about the arthritis in her legs. Nobody knew how much I really hated that nigga. Thomasine thought a nigga was after me when James got merked, but that bullet was meant for his bitch ass. I was beefing with a dude—well, he was beefing with me over a broad I used to fuck with, but he had nothing to do with what happened to James."

"That's deep."

"Yeah, he was on some shady shit. I was smashing his niece but she only came to South Carolina on holidays because she lived in Canada. Anyways, she hasn't visited since the last time we had sex. I came across her profile picture and the bitch got a husband and a little girl, but the baby look like me. She even got my eyes. I hit her inbox up and asked what was really good and she blocked me. James kept in touch with his niece and she was always sending him postcards. I asked that nigga about it because he knew we had a little something going on. Once a month he'd borrow my whip to go to the Western Union. One day he left a slip in my car. She wired him two g's and that's when I realized he was going to the Western Union for a year. My mother was struggling and I was grinding to pay the bills, and this nigga had money and didn't put in on anything. We were taking care of a grown man. I went home and approached him, he was drunk talking crazy so I pulled a gun out on him to get him to talk. The nigga told me everything. He said his niece had been trying to get pregnant because her nigga was shooting blanks. She could've used a sperm donor but she was afraid of the baby coming out with issues so she'd rather have it by someone she knew. She paid James to keep his mouth shut because she doesn't want me to know I have a two-year-old daughter. I hit him with my gun because the nigga betrayed me. I don't give a fuck how old a nigga is, don't take his seed away like that. But the gun went off and killed his bitch ass. I told Thomasine I found him on the floor when she came home."

Stacy sat puzzled for a minute. Honestly, I wasn't trying to tell that nigga all of that but I trusted him. I didn't tell nobody I had a daughter because the situation was embarrassing and I couldn't see her. My daughter was on the side of Canada where you needed a passport. I searched through James's mail and found an address but it wasn't a real one. Kimberly was definitely making sure I couldn't reach out to them.

"Yoooo, I can't believe this shit. What you want to do about it?" Stacy finally asked.

"What can I do?"

"I don't know, bruh. It's crazy because I realized how much me and Tuchie have in common although our situations are different. I guess the apples don't fall too far from the tree," I replied.

"Tuchie will lose her mind knowing she's a grandmother," Stacy chuckled.

"This is between us, though."

"No doubt," he replied and we slapped hands. Stacy ordered another round of drinks for us, but I couldn't stop thinking about Isha's beautiful ass.

She ain't gonna know what to do with a nigga like me.

SOUL Publications

Sadi

Two months later...

It was the beginning of February and I was shopping with Keondra for a few sweaters. She was getting on my nerves about Bogo. She couldn't accept him leaving her. Keondra irritated me but she was the only person my age I could talk to because I didn't have any other friends in Maryland. My salon wasn't getting much business when we first opened, but business was starting to pick up because my IG page was becoming popular. I only had four stylists and three of them just came out of cosmology school. Me and Jay had been getting along great since he left that miserable bitch, Isha, but I couldn't help but to think that he was still in love with her. His daughter moved in with his mother after she was released from the hospital because Jay moved in with me and sold his house. The only reason Hadley wanted to move in with her grandmother was because of Isha. Isha couldn't come to my house to see her so I wasn't complaining about it, but Jay was upset that his daughter didn't want to be with him. Jay's mother, Adele, didn't want to meet me. I heard her tell Jay on speakerphone that I was the devil and she didn't want my bad luck in her house.

"I wonder if Bogo loves his new bitch," Keondra said.

"He'll be back. You know how niggas are."

"Can you get Jay to talk to him for me?"

Bitch, Jay don't like you!

"Yeah, I'll talk to Jay when he comes home," I replied.

My ankles were beginning to swell from doing a lot of walking. I was a little over six months and wanted to hurry up and get it over with. Jay was excited when he found out we were having a boy. He was so loving and caring; I fell in love with him all over again.

We were in Nordstrom's and Keondra was trying on a pair of shoes. I cursed her out in my head because I should've driven to the mall myself. I don't know what I was thinking when I told her to pick me up from the salon. A dark-skinned boy with beautiful curls was looking at a pair of Timberlands. A salesclerk asked him what size he needed. His voice and face were familiar and that's when I realized he was Tuchie's son.

"Bitcchhhh, who is that?" Keondra asked.

She walked to a mirror wearing the heels she was trying on and I shook my head at her. Keondra was a whore and shit wasn't going to change. She was throwing her hips around to catch Tuchie's son's attention, and just like a nigga, he couldn't keep his eyes off her ass. Keondra came back and bent over to take off her shoes when she could've done it sitting down.

"That's Tuchie's son. Remember I told you she claimed she was gang raped and gave up her son because the boys were threatening to kill her?"

"That just happened to a twelve-year-old girl that was walking home from school. Baltimore has a lot going on so it's not hard to believe. You just don't care because you don't like her," Keondra said.

"Anyways, that's her son."

"I'm about to give him some of these goodies. Hell, he looks grown to me and he's tall, too. I know that dick big. Judge me all you want but these young boys can fuck the piss out of someone. Look at him, I bet he's paid, too. Bittchhhhhhhhhh, I know him!" Keondra said, getting loud.

"Would you shut the fuck up!" I whispered.

"Honey, he's a porn star. And matter of fact, I know the girl who did a video with him. I met her at a stripper party in Miami. Tuchie got all that mess going on in her life. Oh well, she better get used to me calling her 'Ma.'" Keondra put her boots back on then walked over to Tuchie's son. I couldn't hear what they were talking about but whatever it was pissed her off because she walked out his face, headed to the cash register.

"What happened?" I asked and she smacked her teeth. She was always getting in her feelings when she couldn't have her way with men.

"I asked him for his number. He had the nerve to tell me I wasn't his type then told me to move on. I bet he's gay anyway because I know I look good," she said.

Girl, please! He probably knows you're a hoe.

She paid for her items then we left the mall—finally.

****

It was nine o'clock at night by the time I made it home. Jay's car was in the driveway and I was surprised he beat me home. A nice aroma breezed past my nose when I walked into the house. Jay was cooking and it made my mouth water. I headed straight to the kitchen and there he was standing at the stove shirtless while stirring something in a pot. I saw the lobster tails on the counter and got excited.

"Have a seat, this sauce is almost done," he said. I sat at the table and my stomach growled. I was happy to have a man that cooked because I wasn't the domesticated type although I tried. There were fresh Gardenias in a vase on the kitchen table, they were my favorite flowers. Jay sat my plate in front of me minutes later and it looked delicious. He made Cajun seafood Alfredo served with a lobster tail, asparagus and garlic rolls.

"This looks sooo goood! What's the occasion?" I asked. He sat across from me and smiled.

"Why can't a nigga just appreciate you? But on the real, I'm just happy to be here. I ain't gotta sneak on the phone or hear Isha's mouth about me being distant. We should've been here already, shorty. But I'm making up for lost time."

"Better late than never," I replied.

"I was driving around while I was taking care of business earlier and all I could think about was making this official, so I bought this," Jay said. He sat a small black box on the table and opened it. The ring was huge! Bigger than the ring I saw Isha wearing when I met her in Hadley's hospital room. Jay picked up the ring and came around the table. He kneeled in front of me.

"I know you might be thinking that I'm bullshitting because I was just engaged to Isha but

I always loved you. I'm serious about this and I'm doing this for me. So, will you be my wife?" he asked.

I held my hand out and he slid the ring on my finger. Tears fell from my eyes because I couldn't believe I was having a baby and marrying the man I waited ten years for. I grabbed his face and kissed his lips. He pulled away from me seconds later then kissed my stomach. We already came up with a name for our baby boy. His name is Haden. Jay wanted it to be similar to Hadley and at first I wasn't feeling the name but it grew on me. I actually wanted our son to be named after his father, so he'd have Jay's first name as his middle name. But who would've thought I was going to be someone's wife? My past made me a little insecure so that was another reason why it took me years to be in a relationship. I was worried about someone leaving me after finding out I was on drugs.

"I can't wait to be your wife."

"I know you can't. Now hurry up and eat that food. I've been thinking about that pussy all day," he smirked. It was time I sat down with his mother to tell my side of the story because it was important for me to have her and his daughter in my corner. Hadley didn't have to like me but she should want to see her father happy since he'd do anything for her. After I ate my food, we took a hot, steamy shower together.

The next day...

I pulled up to Jay's mother's house and my heart was almost beating out of my chest. She lived in a cute ranch-style house with a bird fountain in the middle of the driveway. I fixed my hair in the mirror before I got out of my truck. My hand trembled when I rang the doorbell. Hadley opened the door and she wasn't happy to see me. I wondered if she was jealous of the baby because she wasn't going to be the only child anymore.

"What are you doing here? My father isn't here," she said.

Hadley was a pretty girl but she had a nasty scar under her eye. Jay said it would slowly heal if she took care of it. Her hair was brushed into a high ponytail and she was wearing a FILA sweat suit. Hadley resembled Jay but she was a few shades darker. Her arm was in a sling and she had braces on her legs which made her walk like a robot. I didn't think she was going to make it out of the hospital because of the state she was in, but she improved a lot.

"I came to talk to Ms. Adele. Is she here?"

"NANA! Sadi is here to see you!" Hadley called out.

She opened the door and I stepped into the house. It was a lovely home and jazz was playing throughout the hallways. There was also a strong smell of onions coming from down the hall so I figured she was cooking. Hadley told me to have a seat in the living room until Adele came out of the kitchen. I sat on the couch and stared at the pictures of Jay from when he was younger. There were pictures of him and Isha on the wall and it didn't sit well with me. Jay said he hadn't been happy with her but the picture in front of me told a different story. His arms were wrapped around her and he was kissing on her neck while she was cooking. She had a big smile on her face, probably because he whispered something in her ear. I was jealous and couldn't pretend like their relationship didn't bother me. Isha was perfect according to Jay so there wasn't any bad blood between them to make him not want to go back to her. She was still competition and I couldn't ignore it. She was close to his mother and daughter and I wasn't, so it was easier for him to be with her. I wondered if she was around Jay when she visited Adele.

"The picture bothers you I see," Adele startled me.

"No, it actually doesn't. I think it shows a softer side of Jay." She sat across from me with a tray of cups and a cute tea kettle. She poured me a cup of tea then passed it to me. She leaned into the couch and crossed her arms. Adele didn't look like she was in her early sixties. She was a pretty, thin woman and had a long braid going down her back. She walked with a slight limp and Jay said it was because she had a bad hip. Nonetheless, she was a beautiful woman. Her and Jay had the same complexion and hazel eyes.

"What brings you to my home this afternoon?"

"I want to tell you my side of the story and hopefully it will change the perception you have of me. I love Jay very much and I don't want him to stress about us not being cordial," I replied. Adele sipped her tea with an emotionless expression on her face.

"I don't see a problem with this as long as we respect each other, but I do have my concerns. Something in my gut is telling me that Jay doesn't know you too well. Now, maybe I'm reading too much into this but I don't trust you. I have custody of Hadley and I want to make sure she's in good hands if something happens to me. Jay is all over the place and you were on drugs. Let's keep it real, Sadi. We both know my son still has a hand in the streets. What if he gets locked up? Who will take care of Hadley?" Adele asked.

"I guess Isha fits the bill." Adele shook her head and took another sip from her cup.

"Your soul isn't cleansed and neither is Jay's, so I can see this relationship turning into a disaster. When you do people wrong, it comes back on you. I'm speaking from experience and I know what happens when two people don't belong together. You and Jay would've been happened if it was meant to be. You return home after ten years with his baby? Something in the pot isn't cooked well," Adele said.

"You don't know me. You know nothing about me or Jay. I didn't know he had a woman when we slept together."

"You knew, you just didn't want to believe he loved her. My granddaughter told me what happened."

I thought back to a year ago when I called Jay's phone. Honestly, I was in denial and wanted to believe that Jay wasn't in love with another woman. That's how badly I wanted him. I knew about Jay's girlfriend for over a year, but I didn't know he was engaged.

One year ago...

I dialed Jay's number after I got off from work. I was ready to hang up but Hadley answered the phone.

"Hi, can I speak with Jay?"

"He's helping Isha hang up a picture. I thought this was my phone because we have the same phone," she giggled.

"Isha?"

"My dad's girlfriend. What's your name?" she asked.

"I have the wrong Jay. Can you delete my call?"

"Okay," Hadley said before she hung up the phone...

"Hadley told me your voice sounded familiar when you came into her hospital room. It's one thing to sleep with another's woman man, but it's low down to play the victim! My son bought you all of those expensive things because he felt guilty for dragging you into this mess."

"That's not true at all. Maybe Isha wants Hadley to dislike me so they're brewing up a story about me. I guess they'd do anything to make me seem like the bad guy. This was a bad idea," I replied. I grabbed my purse off the floor and stood up to leave. Adele walked me to the door.

"It will backfire, Sadi. It always does," Adele called out to me while I was getting in my car.

Old bitch!

****

An hour later, I walked into my shop. We were somewhat crowded. As soon as I spotted my client, I told her to have a seat in my chair.

"What do you want today?" I asked while putting the cape around her neck.

"I want finger waves. My man just came home so I want to look good. Honey, I can't wait until we go on a date later. He's been locked up for ten years but I've only known him for three. My homegirl hooked me up with him because her man was locked up with him. Anyways, he's treating me today since I was holding him down," she rambled. People in the shop looked at her and shook their heads. She was extremely loud, wanting everyone to know she hooked up with a jailbird. But then again, she was very unattractive so I assumed it meant a lot to her. She didn't have much hair so after two minutes I was done perming it. I placed a plastic cap over her head and told her to have a seat. The door to my shop opened and everything paused. It had been eleven years since I saw him and all I could remember was him shoving drugs in my face while I was pregnant. I tried to get clean for my baby, but Tae wasn't having it. After I realized he didn't care for me, I called the police on him because he had illegal firearms in his home. I couldn't believe I ruined myself behind him. He was the reason for everything that happened to me in the past. I wasn't expecting to run into him in the area I lived in because Tae was a hood nigga and didn't know any other place outside of the hood. He gave me an evil smirk then winked at me.

"There he goes! I was just telling her about you," my client bragged.

"What's up, Sadi? Long time no see. I see life has been treating you good. Seeing you pregnant again is like déjà vu," Tae said.

Tae used to be so handsome, but now he looked like a bum. His once pretty hair looked matted and his teeth were rotting at the top. He wasn't muscular like he used to be. Now he looked like he weighed one-hundred and sixty pounds. I figured he was still getting high in jail because he looked that bad.

"I have been great. How about you?"

"I don't know. I have been locked up for a very long time. Some bitch snitched on me so you know I won't let it slide. I'll see you again," Tae said. He handed his woman a fifty-dollar bill before he walked out my shop. That dirty-ass nigga had the nerve to threaten me after he ruined my life. Spending all of those years in jail should've changed him.

"You know my man?" my client asked.

"We went to school together, but anyways, let's wash your hair out."

"Already?" she asked.

"Yeah, you don't want it to sit long."

I washed and styled her hair in thirty minutes. I wanted her and Tae far from my shop. After she left, I went into my small office in the back and locked the door. I called Jay and I couldn't stop crying. Seeing Tae looking like a crackhead scared me.

What if I'm not strong enough to face him? What if he drags me back into that life? What if he brings me drugs and I get hungry for it?

My thoughts were running wild while I cried to Jay. I wished I stayed in Atlanta and didn't go to his mother's house.

"Shorty, calm down. I'm going to see what's up with him. Don't trip about that. You want to move your shop somewhere else?"

"No, Jay, I don't want to do that. I just started building up my clientele. Why did he have to find me? What if he brings drugs to me because he can't stand to see me happy? He was checking me out and noticed my ring and baby bump. Tae wants me to be miserable like him. He hates me for what I did to him," I said.

"What did you do?"

"I was the one who got him locked up. I snitched on him," I admitted. The line grew quiet and I called out to Jay.

"I'm here. I was just thinking about something. Listen, I'll handle it. Matter of fact, I'm going to come up there and sit with you until you close. I'm twenty minutes away," he said. I sat behind my desk after Jay hung up the phone and buried my face in my hands. There were a few things Jay didn't know about me and I wondered if he'd still love me if he knew I was the one who set Tuchie up to get robbed. I could either come clean or wait until it blows over. I feared ending up dead for not asking for forgiveness and righting my wrongs. I really wanted to be a good person and get rid of my past but I wasn't doing anything about it. I couldn't lose Jay.

Is love more important than telling the truth? I wondered.

Yes, and with love, the truth isn't needed. Why destroy what you have over something you're not anymore?

Jay

Sadi hadn't been herself for the past few days. I had niggas looking for Tae but it's like the nigga disappeared. The only thing I could come up with is that the nigga didn't live in Maryland. Either way, the nigga was going to get merked when I saw him. Sadi wasn't eating. All she did was cry about being scared for her life. She needed all of my time so I let Bogo deal with our connect. Hadley had a doctor's appointment so I called my mother to see if she could take her while I kept an eye on Sadi.

"What is it, Jadiah?" she answered the phone.

"Can you take Hadley to her appointment? Sadi isn't feeling too good."

"Neither am I. You know my hip acts up when it's raining. I'll call Isha," she said.

"No, I'll do it."

"Okay," my mother replied and hung up.

"Get dressed, shorty. We have to take Hadley for her check-up."

She sat up on the couch and looked at me in confusion.

"Why can't Isha do it? I need you here with me," she said. I loved shorty to death but the bitch had been getting on my nerves the past few days. I did everything to console her and she was still complaining. We had more good days than bad, but I wasn't trying to have those at all especially since Isha had never given me any bad days. I left the situation to be happier, not stressed.

"Yo, I have been cooped up in this house with you crying and shit and you got the nerve to ask me why Isha can't do it?"

"She does everything else, so why can't she take her? I thought Isha was supposed to be her mother or sumthin. That's what you told me, remember?" she asked.

"I'll be back!" I went upstairs and took a quick shower. After I got dressed, I grabbed my car keys and headed out the door. Sadi must've forgotten that Hadley is my daughter. I hoped it was just her hormones because shorty was already making me regret proposing to her.

****

I pulled up next to Isha's car and cursed myself because I wasn't trying to see her. It had been three weeks since I last saw her. My mother was tripping because I told her not tell Isha shit. When I walked into the house, laughter was coming from the kitchen. Isha, Hadley and my mother were cracking up. I stood in the entryway and watched them. It had been a long time since I saw the three of them happy but I had a lot to do with that. My mother blamed me for Hadley's accident. I was betraying Sadi by staring at Isha's pretty face. The fucked-up thing about it, shorty was never pretty to me. She was just cute. Her ass wasn't that big but for some odd reason it looked shapelier. Isha had on a hooded, army green, stretch sweater dress and on her feet was a pair of black logo Chanel boots. Her hair was brushed into a high bushy ponytail with baby hairs framing her soft face. The pink lip gloss on her lips made my dick hard because I imagined them wrapped around me. Maybe Isha always looked that good but I was blinded by the love I had for Sadi. I didn't appreciate what I had, but now I was that nigga on the outside looking in and wanting her.

"JAY!" my mother called out.

"Huh?"

"You don't hear me talking to you?" she asked.

"Naw, I was thinking about something," I replied.

"I hope you two enjoy the brownies. I'm going to use the bathroom before I go," Isha said to Hadley and my mother. She squeezed past me without looking at me and walked down the hall. My eyes couldn't pull away from her.

"Looks like you are regretting it already," my mother teased.

"Naw, I'm happy where I'm at. I was just checking out her little style. She didn't dress like that when we were together. What Isha got a man or sumthin?"

"She's going on a lunch date," Hadley replied while stuffing her mouth with brownies.

"With who?" I asked and Hadley shrugged her shoulders. I left the kitchen, headed towards the hallway bathroom. Isha was wiping herself when I walked in on her.

"Get the fuck out, Jay!"

"What nigga you seeing? And did you introduce him to my daughter?" I asked. Isha stood up and flushed the toilet. I was talking to her but she ignored me while she washed her hands. Something pulled me towards her and I couldn't decide if I missed her or just wanted some pussy. I pressed my body into her; she was trapped between me and the sink.

"What are you doing?" she asked, looking at my reflection in the mirror. I kissed her neck and she pulled away from me.

"Get the hell away from me!"

She wasn't trying to give in but I knew Isha's body. She wanted it but she was still hurt from what I did to her. I turned her around and grabbed her face so I could kiss her. She slapped me when I lifted up her dress and sat her on the sink. Isha kicked me in the stomach and I backed away from her. She slid off the sink to fix her dress.

"Your dick isn't that good for me to forget how much you hurt me. You made your choice. Congrats on your engagement. Act like you don't know me when you see me," she said.

"What nigga you fuckin'? You set this up, didn't you? You came over here bringing brownies and shit with this tight ass dress on. The fuck is you teasing me for?"

"Muthafucka you must be sniffing what that bitch was smoking. And who I'm fuckin' isn't your business anymore. You made your choice so deal with it! How about I call your hoe up right now and tell her that her nigga won't let me piss in peace. Get the hell out of my face!" she screamed.

I grabbed her face and squeezed it as hard as I could. Tears fell from her eyes but it didn't matter to me. I don't know why I was so jealous of Isha moving on. That shit burned me badly.

"Bitch, I'll kill you! Who are you talking to like that? What, you let Tuchie get into your head because you sound just like her. Better yet, I'll merk your nigga if I find out he was around my daughter. Go cry about that to yah friends!" Isha sat on the toilet seat and sobbed while holding her face after I released her. I walked out the bathroom and closed the door. Hadley was waiting for me by the front door.

"Your cheek is red. Were you and Isha fighting?" she asked. My mother knocked on the bathroom door because she heard Isha's sobs in the hallway.

"What did you do to her? Did you hit her?" my mother yelled at me.

"No, she's just being dramatic like always."

My mother slit her eyes at me because she didn't believe me.

"Isha, open the door!" my mother banged.

"I'm fine, Ms. Adele!" Isha yelled back.

"Don't you ever come to my house again with this mess! Everything was fine until you showed up!" my mother yelled at me.

"Why are you always taking her side? She ain't your blood! I am! Her brownies ain't that good!"

"I'm taking her side because you're WRONG! Look at yourself, Jadiah. When have you ever disrespected women and used them like toys? You were a better man when you were with Hadley's mother and y'all were teenagers! I watched you cater to that girl and love her. What happened to that Jadiah? That Sadi woman is making you go backwards and soon you're going to be nothing! She preyed on and you don't see it. She tricked you into believing she didn't know about Isha but that's a lie! I wasn't going to say anything because I wanted you to see it for yourself but some blind dogs can't find a bone. That girl got you down to Atlanta to sleep with you knowing you had a woman. You turned around and gave her EVERYTHING! Isha was the one who financially helped you because you didn't know anything about investing! You took from her nest and gave it to a woman you know nothing about! A person can be who you want them to be over the phone, just remember that. Don't come back to my house until you get your life together for yourself and your daughter. It hurts me to my heart to see you turn into a no-good man," my mother said.

"I wasn't planning on coming back anyway," I replied.

"Good, now get out of my house."

Me and Hadley left the house with the screen door slamming behind us. Hadley got into the car then burst into tears. My daughter had been experiencing deep depression and she had to see a therapist about it. The car accident traumatized her and losing all her friends made it worse. She was very emotional. I got into the driver's seat of my whip and closed the door in frustration.

"I only told you she had a date so you could get jealous and want her back. I didn't think you were going to hurt her, Daddy," Hadley said.

"Why would you do that?"

"Because I miss you! I saw you more when you were with Isha! I was happy when we were all living together but that was my fault, too. Maybe I was too young to understand what relationships were when I told you I wanted Isha to be my mother. Now I regret it all. Nothing is the same anymore. I have an ugly scar on my face, my friends are dead and my father wants to forget about me because of a new baby. I wish I was dead! Maybe then I could finally meet my real mother," Hadley sobbed. My eyes watered from hearing all the pain I caused my daughter. I hadn't shown her much love lately because of Sadi's sudden move to Maryland.

"Baby girl, nothing is your fault. The accident is my fault and I was the one who hurt Isha. We love you but people grow apart and you will experience this more often as you get older. I was your age when you were born. Your mother was my heart. People thought I was too young to be in love but I loved her and still do. She was beautiful, smart, intelligent—she was perfect. Long story short, I still can't let her go and that's why I fell for Sadi because she resembles your mother. It's wrong of me but I have been hurt for a very long time and it seems like this is the only way it'll go away."

Hadley wiped my eyes and I remembered her doing that when she was five years old. Every time we visited her mother's gravesite, she said, "Don't cry, Daddy," in the sweetest voice.

"I'm sorry, Daddy. I didn't know. But let's make a deal, you get over my mother and I'll stop blaming myself. We can pinky swear on it," she said.

"Don't tell nobody your father be pinky swearing. It might mess up my G-code. Sike naw, baby girl. I love you and I messed up. Now, let's make this appointment then I can take you to get some ice cream," I replied. Hadley frowned her nose up then giggled.

"I'm too old for that. I'll be sixteen soon, but can you do me a favor?"

"What's that?"

"Apologize to Isha so I can know it's really over. I'm sorry for being nasty to Sadi and I promise I'll do better."

"Okay, I can do that," I said.

"But I still want that ice cream, though," Hadley responded.

My relationship, the streets and everything else I had going on didn't matter to me much. All I was worried about was Hadley. I could accept being an ain't-shit nigga, but a no-good father was something I couldn't grasp. Truthfully, I couldn't say I lost myself because I didn't get a chance to figure out what I really wanted. All the decisions I made were based off what seemed right when it should've been what felt right. So, I decided to hand my connect over to Bogo. He was my partner but I was the one who was responsible for the shipments and re-uping. All Bogo did was move the weight through the DMV area. I was financially set but making more money wouldn't hurt. A nigga just had to find a proper way of hustling.

Three days later...

It was Valentine's Day and I decided to go to Hadley's mother's grave alone. Another reason why I couldn't let her go was because it was my fault she was killed. I accused her of being pregnant for this nigga I saw her talking to in school. She told me he was just helping her with her science, the one subject I failed. But I didn't believe Joy. I waited after school for him and beat him up. He said he didn't sleep with Joy but I was so jealous that I was blinded by the truth. His brother and cousins caught me and her walking from her house and shot at me but the bullets hit Joy instead. Joy was a good girl despite the type of household she came from. She had good grades and didn't come outside much. She was pretty like Sadi and had Isha's angel-like ways. But I had to let her go. I laid the pretty roses on her grave and hugged her tombstone.

"I know you'll hate me after this but I gotta let you go now. It's hurting a nigga's soul and I'm getting worse. I let our daughter down and left a good woman because another woman had your smile, eyes and lips. She looks so much like you, but I don't know if she's good for me. I can't go on like this so please don't stop looking down at me because I need you more than ever. I'm damaged, Joy. I'm so fucked up that I can't even be a good father. I'll come back when I'm not sick anymore 'cause every time I leave here, I leave a piece of me behind. I'll always love you because you gave me the best gift a man could have."

A sense of relief came over me when I kissed her grave and walked away. After sixteen years of having a dark cloud over my head, I was finally able to see everything I'd done wrong. When I got into my whip, Usher's song, "U Got It Bad," was playing on the road and I turned it up. I wasn't the type of nigga who listened to slow music but it reminded me of Isha. It was ten o'clock in the morning so I decided to swing by Isha's crib to apologize to her. I knew where she lived because I picked Hadley up from her home one day. She didn't live too far from my mother, only ten minutes away. Her car was in the driveway of her single-family home along with another car I'd seen before. The whip had South Carolina tags. I remembered that lil' nigga, Rush, driving that kind of whip.

"Tuchie must have her son's whip," I said to myself when I got out of my car. I reached out to ring the doorbell but the door opened. Rush stepped out the crib with a breakfast sandwich and a homemade smoothie. Isha used to make the same thing for me in the morning.

She ain't fucking that lil' nigga. Ain't no way! He can't do shit for her but fuck up her good credit.

"Yo, what's good?" I asked.

"Shit, what's good witchu?"

"Tuchie here or sumthin?" I asked.

"Naw, what you looking for her?" he asked, slurping his smoothie.

"ISHA!" I called out.

She came to the door wearing tight jeans and a V-cut tight sweater. Her hair was styled in skinny cornrows going into a bun. She had a little make-up on her face and I should've appreciated her smile but I was furious because I wondered if Rush was the cause of it. He was young but he wasn't that young for her to dismiss him.

"Oh, good morning, Jay. What brings you by here?" she asked.

"Yo, I'll holla at you when I leave the studio. Stay beautiful," Rush said to Isha. She blushed when he walked away, getting into his whip.

"Care to explain that?" I asked when Rush backed out of her driveway.

"Explain what exactly? He's not the only one who stops by in the morning for my breakfast and smoothies. But fuck all of that, why are you at my house?" she asked. She leaned against the doorway and crossed her arms.

Damn, she's sexy when she's mad.

"Can I come in?"

"No, unlike Sadi, I do respect your engagement. And to make things easier for you, I will not go to your mother's house anymore. The last thing I want to do is get between you and your mother's relationship."

"Why do you always have to be the bigger person, huh? I'm standing out here trying to apologize but you gotta be all extra and shit," I replied.

"No, you were trying to come in. Why wouldn't I be the bigger person when I'm trying to move on with my life? What do you want from me? You get mad when I come around and get mad when I don't! I'm tired of this back and forth with you. Enjoy your woman and new bundle of joy. You keep apologizing and I'm tired of it. Apologies don't erase the embarrassment and heartache you gave me. Why is this apology any different than the last ten times?"

"I went to Joy's gravesite today to get closure. I've been holding on to a lot and I failed when I didn't share that with you. This time is different because I know I fucked up. All those other times I fucked up but still made an excuse for why I did. Truth is, I don't have an excuse for what I did to you. This is coming from a man who is trying to do better, Isha. I'm really sorry for hurting you. I don't think you should stop seeing my mother. You nursed her back from surgery and took care of my daughter while I roamed the streets. You're superwoman, any man you get with will give you more than I ever did," I said.

"I don't know what to say. I want to accept your apology but every day I tell myself how much I hate you for treating me so bad. This is still fresh."

"I don't care if you don't forgive me. I just want you to know how fucked up I was," I replied.

"Have a good day," she said. Isha stepped into her house and was ready to close the door but I stopped her.

"I love you."

293

Damaged: Damages Spinoff   Natavia

"Goodbye, Jadiah," she said and closed the door.

I went back to my car feeling worse than I did when I woke up. Something about that Rush nigga coming around was rubbing me the wrong way. He was trying to take advantage of my shorty because she was vulnerable. All he wanted was the pussy.

I'll merk that lil' broke ass nigga if he's fucking Isha.

Tuchie

Stacy was on his way home and I wanted to make the night special for him. He wanted to take me out to a fancy dinner but we had been doing things outside the house for years. We went on vacations, romantic dates on boats and one year we had a picnic in a hot air balloon. This Valentine's Day was going to be a memorable one. I cooked red snapper, collard greens with smoked ham, baked macaroni and cheese and potato salad. I also made him a heart-shaped red velvet cake. Niji was with my mother and Rush wasn't home. I wanted to have a talk with Rush because I had a feeling he had more going on with his life than what he told me. He was quiet, almost like he had a lot on his mind and he wasn't home much. I was only seeing Rush once or twice or week. I even asked Stacy about it but he told me Rush was still trying to adapt to me. All I could do was pray on it because I wanted to be there for him and help him with whatever he was going through. Once the dinner table was set, I lit candles around the house. I synced my music from my phone to the wireless speaker and old school music played. Back in the day, my mother used to play old school music and I hated it. But back then they sang about real love. It wasn't just about sex and money.

I wanted to make sure Stacy's jaw dropped when he saw me. My see-through pink and red teddy hugged my body like spandex. On my feet were a pair of pink stacked fur heels. My robe was see-through, too, and the back dragged the floor like the train on a wedding dress. My hair was styled in big loose curls that framed my forehead. Stacy loved the look on me; and to top it off, I wore pink lipstick. I stood in the hallway mirror checking out my look and I almost didn't recognize myself—I looked that good. I heard the door unlock so I greeted him in the foyer. His eyes lit up when he came into the house and I turned around for him. I wanted to make sure he peeped how my ass cheeks swallowed my thong. Stacy grabbed me into his arms and kissed my neck.

"You feel that?" he asked with his dick poking me in the backside.

"Come on, I got something waiting for you at the dinner table."

"Fuck dinner, Tuch. We can eat that later. I need some right now," he said, grabbing my pussy. I pushed him away and led him to the dinner table. Stacy rubbed his hands together when he saw his plate and the cake sitting in the middle of the table. He grabbed my face and tongue kissed me. His hands gripped my buttocks and I wanted it just as bad as he did but we hadn't had alone time lately because he was working on something new with his artists.

"Have a seat," I said. He sat in the chair and I brought him a bottle of Henny in a bucket of ice. Stacy was still hood at heart so I had three blunts of kush rolled up for him.

"I'm tryna come home like this every day," he said.

"I'll see what I can do."

I sat in the chair at the other end of the table, nervous about telling Stacy that he was going to be a dad again. He finally got what he wanted and it happened right at Asayi's house in the bathroom. We said our grace before we dug into our food.

"Yo, Tuch. You gotta hear your son sing. He's on this song with Fendi and the video drops tomorrow. I wanted to surprise you but I'm excited about this," he said.

"It runs in the family. Niji can sing, too. That's my good genes."

"What if I sign him to my label instead of having him just as a feature? Would you be cool with that?" he replied.

"Rush will be twenty years old soon, he can make his own decisions. I'm happy just as long as he's happy and staying out of trouble. I'm going to be in the front row of all his concerts. I just hope he'll let me support him. Rush acts like he hates me."

"I think you're putting too much into it, Tuch. His mentality is something that can't change so you gotta accept it as long as he's not disrespecting you. I'm gonna be real with you, when I saw how grown he was I thought it would be very hard with him living here. But he just be chilling and doesn't cause any problems," Stacy said.

"I guess you're right. I just want to make up for all the years I missed," I replied.

"But it's many more years to come, so focus on the present and he'll come around," he said.

"Maybe I can be more of his friend so me and him can have the same relationship you two have."

It had been weeks since me and Stacy sat down and talked for hours. It brought back memories of when I used to cornrow his hair. He would sit on the floor while smoking a blunt and tell me about the problems he was having with Sadi. I know she thought I took Stacy from her but that wasn't true. Stacy was beginning to realize she wasn't the woman for him before he admitted his feelings for me. Sadi was already doing drugs and fucking his best friend before me and him became serious so it was pretty messed up how she blamed me. It was ten o'clock at night when I cleared the table. I sat a small gift bag in front of Stacy and watched him open it. I told him to open the card last.

"A diamond Cuban link chain, huh? I must've put it on you last night," he cheesed. Stacy didn't wear much jewelry but I thought it would look good on him. Nothing was sexier than a man wearing a nice thick diamond necklace.

"Now open the card," I said. He opened the card and my due date was written in bold letters.

"September the 20th? What's this date for?" he asked.

"What do you think?" I smiled.

He thought for a few seconds before he figured it out. Stacy was grinning from east to west.

"Yoooo, you pregnant? It happened in the bathroom when we were over Trayon's crib." He got up from his chair and walked over to me. He kissed my stomach and it was already poking out because all I ate was a bunch of soul food.

"Okay, where is my gift?" I asked in excitement. Stacy gives the best gifts. One year he bought me an old school car. It was a black 1969 impala with pink and black rims and leather seats. The car was still parked in the garage and I only drove it in the summertime with the top down. I had been hinting to him that I wanted a slingshot so I assumed he was ready to give me the key. But when he pulled out a big diamond ring I lost it.

"Remember I told you I was going to make you my wife the second time around? You thought I was just saying that so I could get back with you but I was serious, Tuch. I want you to be my wife," he said. He slid the ring on my finger and I was mute. The rock was huge and so were the baguettes in the band.

"Tuchie! Answer me, shorty!" Stacy shouted at me. All I could do was hug him because I thought he was just telling me that so we could get back together. I should've listened to him when he said he wanted a bigger family and for me to be his wife.

"Of course, I want to be your wife but I feel horrible for not believing you. I promise I'll do anything to keep you happy this time around. I'm about to get emotional right now. I love you so much," I replied and he wiped my tears away.

"I love you more, shorty. I'm going to be a better man this time around too. I promise you that. But here is my other gift to you."

Stacy pulled a key out of his back pocket and placed it in the palm of my hand.

"Is this what I think it is?" I asked.

"Go look in the driveway," he said. I grabbed my winter coat before I walked outside. Stacy bought me a slingshot car. It was all white with matching Forgiato rims. I grew to love white-on-white cars because of Stacy.

"I love it! Ohhhh, baby. I'm going to be cruising in the summertime, pregnant and all!"

"That's what you think. I wouldn't have bought it if I knew you was knocked up. Matter of fact, you don't need this right now." Stacy took the key away from me but he couldn't tell me "no" for long.

"We gonna need a bigger house. I want something exclusive with a pool in the inside and outside. With eight bedrooms and all that," Stacy said as he walked into the house.

"My house is a nice size," I replied.

"Yeah, but since we're getting married and expanding our family, we don't need this. Don't worry yourself, I'll handle everything," he said. Stacy had a big house but it was three hours away so he rented it out when we got back together. I couldn't move that far away from my job so he moved in with us. I hung up my coat in the hall closet and Stacy took off my robe. He kneeled behind me and kissed my backside as he massaged my cheeks. He pulled my thong to the side to kiss my moist lips. His tongue parted my slit and curved into my pussy. Stacy always moaned while eating me out and it made me wetter. My walls tightened and my clit throbbed from the movements of Stacy's tongue. Maybe my ass was in the way but he laid on the floor and pulled me towards his face. He tapped my leg, letting me know that he wanted me to ride his face. I pulled off my heels so I wouldn't slip on the glossy hardwood floor. My feet were planted firmly on the side of his face. A moan escaped my lips when my pussy lips French kissed his mouth. I rode his face, making sure he didn't miss a spot. When his lips pulled at my clit, my wetness smeared his face. I pulled away from him to part my lips with my first and middle finger. When I lowered myself back onto his face, I felt everything! I was skeptical about riding his face in the beginning because of my size, but Stacy handled my thickness as if I weighed ninety pounds. He flipped me, pinned me and picked me up. Let's just say we had the best sex.

"Wait, Stacy!" I screamed when his tongue plucked at my clit. My nipples hardened, poking through the thin material of my lingerie. He caused my body temperature to rise and sweat beads formed on my breasts. I was on the verge of exploding. The head he was giving me sounded sloppy, like a big dog drinking water while it splashed outside of the bowl. Sloppy head was the best head and it made me squirt.

"ARRGGHHHHHHHHHHHH!" I came in his mouth. He didn't pull away when I squirted—he buried his face in my slit and pulled my clit between his lips. I begged him to stop but he held me down and use his tongue like a dick. It curved against my walls and I cried out from cumming again. He slid from underneath me then took his clothes off. I prayed Rush didn't come home while we were fucking in the hallway. There was something about having sex outside the bedroom that excited me. I was ready to get up but Stacy told me to bend over and arch my back until my breasts were smashed against the floor. He also told me to spread my legs and bend my knees more. That position was how I got pregnant with

Niji. My essence was dripping down my inner-thighs. He placed his hand on my lower back and told me to arch a little more. I scratched at the floor when I felt the tip of his dick rub against my entrance. He eased himself in, getting in a few slow strokes so he could get his dick wet before he started fucking me.

"You want me fuck you, baby?" he asked.

"UMMMMMMM!"

"Answer me, Tuchie. Can I put it all in?"

"Yesssssssss," I hissed when he went balls-deep inside me. Stacy had my body sprawled out while spreading my ass cheeks so he could drill me. My mouth went dry from moaning so loud.

"Fuckkkkkk, Tuchie! Ummmm, baby!" he groaned. He leaned in to pull my hair and that was it for my vagina. He used his thumb to smear my wetness around my anus before he stuck two fingers in.

"BABBBBYYYYYYYYYYYY!" I screamed when he sped up. My head hit the small table in the hallway where the house phone sat and it fell over.

"Tighten up, shorty. Squeeze this dick and hold it, baby. I'm ready to nut!"

I tightened around Stacy and he almost snatched the sew-in out of my head. It was feeling too good for me to think about my scalp being on fire, so I threw my ass back and he went deeper, pushing my face against the wall. He jerked inside me, he was on the verge of exploding but I beat him to it. My clit throbbed uncontrollably as I came. Stacy fell into me and we laid in the hallway for a few seconds trying to catch our breath.

"We ain't done, Stacy. Go ahead and take a shot of Henny and I'll meet you upstairs," I said when he helped me up.

"Oh, yeah? I'm fittin' to tear that lil' pussy up, shorty. Go ahead and go to the bedroom," he said. I grabbed my clothes off the floor and jogged up the stairs. When I got into our bedroom, I went to the bathroom to take a shower. While I was in the shower, I admired my ring.

I finally have everything I want.

****

SOUL Publications

The next day, I walked into work with a sore body and scalp. I was drained and only had four hours of sleep. Me and Stacy sexed all night until he couldn't get hard anymore. My lips were swollen and I had a rug burn on my knees and back. I buzzed Myisha when I sat at my desk and asked her if she could bring me a cup of coffee. Minutes later, she came into my office with a hot cup of coffee. She sat across from me and crossed her legs.

"So, Mrs. Stacy. How was your day yesterday?" she asked, eyeing my ring.

"It was great. How about your day?"

"It was good, could've been better. Are you engaged? That ring is soooooooo damn pretty. But anyways, congrats. Oh, and you have a meeting in an hour," Myisha said. Her desk phone rang and she excused herself out of my office. I got up and locked the door so I could call everyone to tell them about my engagement. They already knew I was pregnant but I told them not to tell their guys until I surprised Stacy. The phone on my desk rang as soon as I went into my purse to get my cell-phone.

"Hello, Stacy Cook, speaking."

"You and your son are going to die, bitch!" a man said then hung up. The first thing that came to mind was Lucas but I hadn't talked to him since that night I met his parents. State troopers were always in the building so I called the main reception area to see if one could come up to trace my phone. After I handled that, I called Stacy and told him someone just called my work phone and threatened me and Rush.

"Quit your job. I make mad money and I can take care of you. We can figure out something else but somebody knows where you work and that ain't good. The shit is personal and you're carrying my seed. Fuck that, I'm ready come to get you," he said and hung up.

I wasn't that wild hood girl anymore that used to shoot at niggas. My mindset had changed and all I wanted to do was enjoy motherhood and the married life. I had a lot to lose, so I packed my things while waiting for an officer to come to my office.

What did Rush get himself into? I hope he isn't out here selling drugs.

****

A few hours later....

The person called from an unknown on a prepaid phone. The only way they could probably trace it was if he called again. It crushed me when I quit my job. I worked my ass off to get my position. I sat on my couch in the den in tears while Stacy consoled me.

"Fuck that job, Tuchie. Death threats ain't to be taken lightly. I called Rush and he's on his way home. Maybe he knows sumthin," Stacy said.

"What if someone is after him and they know where we live? I can't believe Niji is exposed to this shit. I want to make things right but this is too much. What if he brings the same drama he brought to Thomasine's home?"

"Wait until he comes home and ask him, but I don't think it has anything to do with South Carolina," Stacy replied. The front door opened and Stacy called out to Rush and told him we were in the den. Rush came into the room with bloodshot red eyes and he smelled like weed.

"What's good? Everything straight?" he asked.

"Someone called my work phone and said that me and you are going to die. I want to know what you be up to when you leave this house. This has never happened before. What mess are you involved in this time?" I asked. He looked at Stacy then back at me.

"So, what you saying is that I'm involved in something? Why it gotta be me, Tuchie? Weren't you involved in the streets, too? I haven't sold nothing since I been here and I didn't leave a beef behind in South Carolina. You trying to pin this on me?" he asked.

"No, but I had to quit my fucking job today, Rush! So, I need to know what the fuck you're up to when you leave the house!"

"I got my own crib. The only reason why I show face is because of Niji. I had my own spot for two months now. But before you tell me to stop coming around, how about I tell you I'm not coming back. I have my own problems and nobody is going to make me feel guilty about some bullshit I don't know about. I never been wanted anyway so I'm not surprised you blaming me. Appreciate you for coming to get me but I'm out!" he said then left. Stacy brushed his hand down his waves in frustration.

"How did Rush get an apartment without an income, Stacy?"

"How the fuck am I supposed to know? And he does have an income. I didn't know he had his own crib. I just thought he met a broad and was chilling with her. Look, I'll talk to him later but right now I need to figure out what nigga you got beef with," he said.

"How soon can we move into a new house?" I asked.

"Give me a week and I'll have something for us, but don't stress about anything."

"I think I hurt Rush's feelings. I didn't mean to but this is serious. He should at least alert us if he's involved in something," I replied.

"Go upstairs and take a nap. I'm going to call a realtor and take care of a few things." Stacy kissed my lips before I left the room. It was the first time in years that I felt useless. Life had a funny way of taking away your happiness. I was more worried about Rush than myself. I couldn't get through the thought of someone trying to kill him. I called Thomasine's phone to figure out how I could get through to Rush but my number was blocked.

Ain't that a bitch!

Isha

Someone rang my doorbell at two o'clock in the morning. I was packing for an event in New York. I was doing events all over and I didn't mind because it was helping me to get over Jay. I walked to the monitor on the kitchen wall to see who was at my door. After seeing his face, I opened the door for him. Rush stepped into my loft and I closed the door behind him. Since the day I tried to kill myself, we became friends. I had to keep reminding myself that he was only a teenager. Even though he was legal I couldn't avoid that age gap. I also couldn't get over how good he made me feel by opening me up to different things. Rush hadn't touched me since the day he made me have an orgasm. I wasn't expecting my body to respond to his since he wasn't Jay.

"What's the matter with you? You never stop by this late," I said. He went into my kitchen and poured himself a shot of Tequila. I talked to Tuchie hours ago and she was concerned about Rush. She didn't go into detail but I figured she would to tell me more once she got herself together because she sounded stressed.

"Tuchie was tripping on me earlier. She tried to accuse me of having some nigga threaten her. I haven't been doing shit but chilling with Fendi and the crew. I know she don't want nothing to do with my black ass. I'm a troubled seed to her and Thomasine. Thomasine got her number changed on me. That shit hurts, Isha. That's the only mother I know and she cut me off," he said. Tears fell from his eyes and I felt so sorry for him. The feeling of abandonment never gets old. I hugged him and he wrapped his arms around me. Rush held me like he was protecting me and he was the one who needed to be consoled. He pulled away from me and leaned against the counter.

"I didn't mean to hug you like that. I won't do it again," he said. He spotted my bags on the couch and asked me where I was going.

"I'm leaving for New York at six o'clock in the morning and I'm going to stay for two days," I replied.

"Take me with you. I can drive," he said.

"That might be a bad idea."

"Yo, stop trippin' about this age shit, damn. Besides, I can get my own hotel room. We ain't got to be all up under each other. It'll be my first time going to New York so I'm trying to explore the big apple. I know you ain't driving by yourself."

"Maybe I'm catching a plane," I replied.

"I can get my own ticket."

"Okay, fine. Only because you need some fresh air," I replied.

I went into the fridge to get a bottle of water and I could feel him staring at me. There was something about the way he stared at me. Rush was unique in his own way. He had the knowledge of an older man but sometimes his age was revealed when he did certain things. Whatever it was, he was perfect—inside and out. I turned around and just like I thought, he was staring at me.

"Yo, you got the cutest nose," he said.

SOUL Publications

"Really?" I giggled.

"Yeah."

"Why do you always have to compliment me?" I asked, heading out the kitchen.

"'Cause you're sexy as shit. Stop acting like you don't want me to say sweet shit to you."

I wanted his attitude. He was sad moments ago, but a few minutes later he was back to himself.

I took my things off the couch and placed them on the floor. Rush turned on the TV and I got comfortable on the couch. Jay was always too busy to watch TV with me. Every day I thought about Jay and how he did me. It was hard not to, but I was accepting to the idea of us being over for good. Him proposing to Sadi showed me that he really didn't give a damn about me. Rush pulled me into him so I could lay on his shoulder.

"What did that nigga Jay want yesterday?" Rush asked.

"To apologize. It's crazy because I was somewhat in denial about us being over, but I'm really relieved that we're over for good and I can move on."

He scrolled through Netflix to find a movie and my eyes deceived me. I caught the bulge in his pants and prayed it wasn't a gun. He put on a movie called, *Deuces.* His closeness was comforting and I found myself dozing off.

Why couldn't I have this with Jay?

****

Rush woke me up at five o'clock and told me to look out the window. It snowed the day before but it wasn't much. I thought it was going to stop but it was practically a blizzard outside and the snow was high.

"There is no way I can go to New York. I have to check my email to see if they canceled me." I checked my email but I didn't see anything yet. Being pissed off was an understatement. I was going to get paid thirteen thousand dollars serving a party of two-hundred and twenty people. My name was already out there so I knew there would be more big events in the future. I had a YouTube channel for when I cooked inside my kitchen at home. My videos were shared on Facebook and Instagram. I checked the weather for New York on the internet and it was worse than Maryland. A lot of places lost electricity and I even saw where the mayor's party was canceled, the event I was going to cater.

"It was drivable on my way here but now I can't even see my whip. This is my first time experiencing snow," Rush said, looking out the window. Rush's cell-phone rang on the coffee table. He picked it up then turned it on silent.

"That's Tuchie calling me. I don't know what she wants," he said.

"Call her back. Tell her you're okay. The weather is bad so I'm sure she just wants to make sure you're safe."

"Naw, I'm good. She doesn't feel safe around me so she doesn't need to worry about me. She blamed me over some dumb shit because of something that happened back at home," he said.

"I've known Tuchie since I was eighteen. She started out doing my hair then over the years we became close. I'm the only child just like her so I looked at her as a big sister. But what I'm saying is I've known her for a long time and sometimes she overreacts but she does it out of love. You'll see once you let your guard down and get used to her."

"I know it might sound fucked up but I don't look at her as my mother, more so as a long-distance sister. But I'm not trying to get into that right now. I want to take a shower and go to sleep," he said.

"What bed are you getting in?"

"Yours," he smiled. He took his shirt off and I covered my eyes.

"Go in the bathroom!"

"Why? You've seen a dick before, haven't you?" he asked. He pulled my hands from over eyes and he was standing in front of me naked. I couldn't hide the expression on my face when I caught a glimpse of his thick chocolate masterpiece.

"You gonna take a shower with me?"

"No, I'm cool," I replied. He walked towards me and I backed away from him until my back was against the wall. Rush's hand slid underneath my over-sized lounging sweatshirt and he cupped my breasts. Damn him for making my body feel so good.

"Nooooo, this isn't right!" I tried to get away from him but he cupped my face then kissed me. He picked me and placed me against the wall with his dick pressed against my center.

"You scared?" he asked and I nodded my head.

"Focus on us right now, not our age, Tuchie or that nigga you were with. Pretend that I'm everything you want and give me everything you got," he said. He carried me to my bedroom and sat me on the bed. He pulled my sweatshirt over my head. Rush laid me on my back then slid my thong down my leg. It felt like it was my first time because everything was so different. Usually, I'd have sex after dating for months but with Rush there was a mysterious vibe. I was being the bad girl I wanted to be where I didn't have to live by any rules. It was all about me at the moment. He climbed on top of me then kissed my breasts. My legs wrapped around him when he hungrily attacked my nipple. His hand slid down my torso and landed on my mound. He parted my lips then used his thumb to play with my clit while suckling my nipple. My nails dug into his shoulders and my lower body raised off the bed. He pulled away from my breasts to kiss my neck with his tongue. My neck was a sensitive spot and my pussy gushed on his fingers. My breathing could be heard throughout the bedroom. I wanted him to hurry up and shove his grown dick into my tightness. He slid onto the floor then pinned my legs back. For the life of me I couldn't figure out what he was trying to do.

Do teenagers perform oral sex? Maybe I should tell him to stop. He doesn't know what he's do—

I moaned the moment he gently kissed my clit. He pressed his tongue flat on my slit then pulled my clit between his lips. I sat up to push his head away from between my legs but he stood up and pressed me into the bed. Rush was eating my pussy like a pack of Starburst. He managed to curve his tongue like a hook and the tip was dipping into my entrance as I cried. My legs shook and my moans grew louder when he used his two fingers to fuck my pussy as he licked my bud. I don't know what he was digging for but when he found it, I creamed on his tongue. There was a puddle underneath my bottom.

"UHHHH!" I groaned. His cucumber-sized dick entered me and it wasn't a pleasant feeling.

"Relax. Damn you're tight," he said.

Once he was inside me, that was it. He fucked me so good my orgasms were coming back-to-back. Whomever taught Rush how to get nasty should be locked up because I was sure the bitch was way older than me. Jay was thirty-one and his stamina wasn't like Rush's. As Rush dug into me, he arched his lower-back with each thrust so he could dig deeper into my pussy. He threw my leg over his shoulder then slammed into my G-spot. My hand rested on his abdomen, pushing him back because it was too much but he smacked my hand away.

"Don't touch me!" he said.

"WAITTTTTTTT!" I screamed out when he sped up.

"Yo, what I say? Huh?" he asked. He wrapped his hand around my throat and gave it to me deep. I felt him in my stomach. My mouth was gaped open and my eyes were rolling into my head.

"You wanna cum, Ish?" he asked.

This lil' nigga is so disrespectful in my pussy!

"RUSSHHHHHHHHHHHH! UMMMMMMMMMM!" I came on his pretty chocolate piece. He pulled out of me and laid me on my side in the spooning position. He slipped his leg between mine and slid back in. He gripped my bun while kissing the back of my neck. I felt every inch of him in that position and it was painful but that didn't stop me from coming one more time. Rush pulled out and spilled his seeds onto my ass cheeks. I don't care how good his dick is, I wasn't going to tell him it was the best dick I ever had. He climbed off the bed and pulled me up. I hauled ass to the shower to get his semen off my butt. When I got into the shower, he stepped in with me.

"You regret it?" he asked.

"To my surprise, I don't regret anything that we've done. You make me happy."

"You make me forget a lot things," he said.

"Do you think we're using each other?"

Rush turned me around so I could face him. His gray eyes stared into mine and SWV's song, "Weak," played inside my head. Rush was making me weak in the knees.

"You can do whatever you want. It's your call, but if I fall deeply for you, it's a wrap," he said.

Damn, Lil' Daddy. Wait! What did I just call him? Oh, whatever bitch. That boy laid more dick than a plumber laying pipe.

Staying home from, New York worked out better than I expected. I wasn't sure how things were going to between us afterwards, but he was mine while we were snowed in.

****

We were stuck in the house for three days and I had a blast. I cooked for him, we watched movies and took long naps together. I wasn't looking for a man but I enjoyed the company. And I couldn't get enough of the sex. Tuchie would kill me if she knew I slept with her son but I saw it in a different way. I wouldn't have done anything with Rush if Tuchie raised him and I watched him grow up the same way I watched Niji. It didn't justify my actions but it wouldn't have gone anywhere if it happened that way.

"What are you thinking about?" I asked him.

"About this music and signing a contract with Stacy. He hit me up while you were in the shower. I kinda like the freedom I have now, but I also know I can get far with this music shit. It used to be something I wanted when I was younger but I don't know, Ish."

"I think you should do it. That video you have with Fendi is bomb!" I said in excitement. Rush showed me the video when I woke up and I was blown away. The only thing about it that was distasteful was the shower scene he had with a video vixen.

"I'm shy. It took a lot for me to sing in front of those niggas at the studio," he smirked.

"Awww, really?"

"Yeah, when it comes to that," he said.

"Sing for me. Anything."

"Why you putting me on the spot?" he chuckled.

Rush sang a few verses of Bryson Tiller's song, "Don't." He had a sexy voice, a little old school mixed with new school.

"WOW! You should do it! Don't be shy, you sound so good," I replied.

"You just saying that 'cause of this dick," he joked

"I'm serious, though. I really want you to do this and maybe you can express your feelings through your own songs. Singers sound so good when they sing from all the hurt and pain they endured. Can you do it for me?"

"Yeah, I'll do it for you but can you make me some weed brownies?" he asked.

"Are you serious?"

"Hell yeah. I got an ounce in my coat pocket," he replied.

"Clean up this mess and we have a deal."

I went into the kitchen and my phone was sitting on the counter. Something told me to check the messages since I hadn't in a few hours. I had five text messages from Jay asking me if I was okay and if I had electricity. Instead of responding, I deleted his messages. I had a feeling he wasn't happy with the choice he made.

****

"ISHA!" Tuchie called out to me. I was at her home after spending four days with Rush. The snow was still deep but the roads were clear enough to drive. She asked me to come over so we could talk about everything that had been happening. Tuchie was overwhelmed, pregnant and worried about Rush.

"I'm sorry, Tuchie. I'm just tired." I was zoned out while she was talking about her son. The mention of him made me think of us being snowed in together. I needed someone to talk to about my situation so I could stop overthinking it.

"Rush isn't answering my phone calls or texts," she stressed while sprinkling sprinkles over Niji's sugar cookies.

"I think you overreacted. You practically accused him of doing something based off his past. You said it yourself, you were in the streets so maybe it has something to do with his father. What if one of the guys who raped you is out to get you? I pray to God that isn't the reason but there is a strong possibility that this isn't about Rush."

"The boys who raped me are dead but two of them are serving life sentences for other crimes," she replied.

"What if someone else was in the room that you didn't know about?"

"There were six of them. I really hate thinking about it but the only good thing is that I was too drunk to feel anything. I'm just realizing how much it ruined my life over the years. It's like I don't trust men, not even my own son. I keep thinking they are going to hurt me and even though I forgive Stacy, I still have to worry about him hurting me again. Do you think I should get help? Would that mean I'm crazy?" she asked.

"No, there is nothing wrong with getting help. I think I need it, too, because the things that have been on my mind are driving me crazy."

"Do you want to talk about it?" she asked.

"No, I'll be okay. Your issues are way more important than mine," I replied.

We chatted for a few more hours until Stacy came home with Niji.

"Where is Hadley? Why doesn't she come around anymore?" Niji asked.

"Hadley isn't one-hundred percent better yet, but she'll come around soon," I replied.

"Jay just hit me and told me to tell you call him. Hit him up, Ish," Stacy chuckled because he knew darn well I wasn't going to.

"He can wait on it. Anyways, I gotta get going. Call me later, Tuchie." I hugged Niji and Stacy before I left their home. Bogo texted me as soon as I got into my car and told me he was waiting for me outside my home.

Twenty minutes later, I pulled up into the driveway next to Bogo's Maserati. He stepped out of his car wearing jeans, Timbs and a Moncler jacket with fur on the hood. Bogo was a chocolate brother, too, and very handsome. He reminded me of the actor, Chadwick Boseman. He had a charm about him but I couldn't understand why he loved hoodrats. He hugged me when I met him at my front door and as always, he smelled good. Bogo took off his shoes at the front door and I hung my coat up in the closet. He headed straight to my kitchen to see if I had any leftovers. I sat at my kitchen island and watched him.

"So, where is it?" I asked. He went inside his pocket and pulled out a roll of money and placed it on the island. I'd been helping Bogo out for a while, even before me and Jay started dating. I was pretty much his accountant and I helped him purchase properties and buildings. Bogo was damn near a millionaire and nobody knew, not even Jay. He also did a lot of illegal things which is why he didn't want me to tell anyone I was helping him wash his money. He even made me sign a non-disclosure form. I tried to do the same for Jay but he used a lot of his money for his street business when Bogo did the opposite.

"I'll deposit it tomorrow," I said. He sat across from me with a plate of cheesecake I made the night before.

"How you holding up, Ish? Everything good witchu? You look better than before. The bags around your eyes are gone which is a plus. Yo, I'm really sorry how that nigga did you. That's my man and all but I'm sad for you," he said.

"I'm fine. I had an event to go to but the weather messed it up for me. Maybe it was a sign or something. I need to take a month off and relax. Being snowed in was fun for me. Wish I could tell you more but I wouldn't feel right being as though you and Jay are best friends," I replied. Bogo pushed his plate to the side then crossed his arms on the table.

"Naw, shorty. You my homey, too, so spill it. I know you want some advice. You ain't slick, that's why you threw it out there," he said and I blushed.

"Fine, I slept with Rush." Bogo burst into laughter with tears falling out his eyes.

"Yo, just when I thought that lil' nigga was going to be flirting with Hadley or some shit. You know how everyone in this circle is connected," he said. It didn't dawn on me that Hadley and Rush were close in age, they were only three and a half years apart. Bogo stopped laughing when he saw how pissed off I was.

"My bad, Ish. But I ain't surprised at all. The little nigga is different. He'll be dangerous to someone like Hadley. Damn, shorty, he got you smiling? Yooo, Jay would have a heart attack if he knew Rush was banging you. How you feel, though?"

"Like a slut, but I also feel good. This is very different for me and although sometimes it feels desperate, Rush makes me smile and he notices everything about me. We can't be in a relationship but this is getting us through a tough time. He's dealing with some stuff, too. We just clicked but Tuchie will hate me if she knew," I replied.

"Naw, I don't think so. It ain't like they have that mother-son bond. I still don't believe he's Tuchie son, though. But if it gets serious, tell her before she finds out from someone else. If y'all just fucking, take it to your grave, baby girl. Anyways, I gotta bounce. My shorty got something in the oven for me," he said.

"When am I going to meet her? You tell me everything else."

"In due time, but she's a good woman. I feel fucked up for wasting my time with Keondra. I don't know what it was about her because it took me years to leave shorty. We were toxic to each other, she gave me an STD and I almost killed her. I gave her two black eyes and broke her wrist. It was my first time putting my hands on a woman so I should've bounced afterwards but I stayed an extra five years. The shit is tough but once you let go, shorty, you will feel better. I promise you will," he replied. In so many words, Bogo was telling that I needed to move on and be happy. I walked him to the door and he told me he'd see me the following week.

An hour later, I was in bed watching TV and with nothing else to do, I called Rush. He answered on the third ring and there was a lot noise in the background.

"Yo, Ish, what's up? Hold on, let me step outside," he answered.

Bitch, hang up! He might be at a house party doing what young niggas do!

But...I'm bored and don't have nothing to do. A little company won't hurt, will it?

"ISHA!"

"Oh, um, I'm sorry. If you're busy I can call back," I replied.

"Naw, I'm not busy. What's up? Everything straight?"

"I was wondering if you could help me put a lightbulb in the hallway mirror," I replied.

"You don't have a hallway mirror, Ish, but I can put a lightbulb somewhere else," he chuckled. I hung up in embarrassment then turned the phone off. Rush was making me do childish shit. I searched for a movie to watch On Demand. Nothing really caught my attention, so I put it on *Jumanji*. An hour into the movie, my doorbell rang. Without looking on the screen in the kitchen, I opened the door. Rush stepped into my house and closed the door behind him.

"You funny as shit. Call then hang up on me while I was talking. Yo, that was whack. You want something, ask for it," he said. He took off his Nike boots then threw his coat on the couch. Why did he have to be so damn fine?

"I wanted you to watch this movie with me," I replied shyly. Rush placed his hands between my legs. I was only wearing a night shirt with nothing underneath. He felt my wetness and knew what I wanted. And just like that, he bent me over the arm of the couch and gave it to me, long and deep. Rush was my addiction and as long as it stayed between us, things would be just fine because we were just getting started.

Sadi

Three months later...

I was lying in bed, listening to the front door close. My life was like a rollercoaster. Tae practically disappeared off the face of the Earth so I got comfortable again going to my salon. All I could was wait for the baby to come. My ankles were swollen and I gained about twenty pounds. Jay was paying for me to have liposuction right after I gave birth because I wanted my wedding dress to fit perfectly. I was also planning on opening a shop in Atlanta and having Shelley run it. It was four o'clock in the morning when Jay walked into our bedroom. Something wasn't right with him, he seemed distant. One minute he was in love and the next minute he would shut me out. I wondered if he missed that bitch, Isha. He thinks I don't know about the ten or more calls he made to her on a daily basis. She was the real reason why I wanted to get married sooner. If Jay decided to cheat, I'd be taking everything he owned. I came from a peaceful life to be with him so the level of disrespect was not going to be tolerated. Jay sat on the bed and took his shoes off; his back was facing me.

"Where have you been?" I asked.

"Out," he replied.

"Where?" I asked.

"With my homeboys," he said.

"You stopped hustling! There is no reason why you should be out in the streets at this time of night!" I yelled at him. Jay didn't respond, he went into the bathroom and closed the door. He made my blood boil when I heard him lock it. I got out of bed and banged on the door.

"Open this damn door!" I yelled.

I thought everything was going to be better when Jay moved in with me, but it only lasted a few months. All I could think about was him and Isha messing around behind my back. I saw her a few times and she looked peaceful; the hoe even had the audacity to tell me I was carrying the baby well. Being insecure while pregnant was a horrible feeling that I wouldn't wish on anyone. It was better when Isha was on the other side of fence. She was the one who had to wait up for him at night, calling his phone every hour while we were in bed making love. But here I was, begging for my fiancé to talk to me.

"Jay! Open this fucking door, now!" I screamed as I kicked at the door. A stream of fluid ran down my legs and onto the carpet. I knew I wasn't peeing because it was coming from my vagina. A second later, I started cramping.

"Jay, call 911!"

"I'm on the toilet! Can I shit in peace? My phone is on the nightstand if you think I'm talking to a bitch. Yo, you are getting on my damn nerves! We had a party for Stacy at the studio because he's getting married and I told you that earlier," Jay complained while I sat on the floor trying to catch my breath. He came out the bathroom minutes later and saw me crying. He rushed to me and asked me what was wrong.

"I'm going into labor," I replied. He grabbed the house phone on the dresser and called 911.

"Baby, I'm so sorry. I thought you was bullshitting," he pleaded.

"Grab my bag and call my mother. Hurry up!"

Jay ran to get my hospital bag. The contractions were coming every two minutes. Ten minutes later, there was a knock on the door. Jay went downstairs to get the door. He came back upstairs with the EMT's.

"Hurry up and get me out of here!" I yelled at everyone.

****

I was in labor for twelve hours. The medication the doctor gave me slowed my baby's heart rate so they gave me a C-section. I couldn't hold him because I was heavily sedated from the surgery but Jay held him. My mother and a few other family members were inside my room. Jay's mother didn't say anything to me. Matter of fact, she didn't hold the baby. Me and Adele still weren't on good terms. She couldn't stand to be around me and the feeling was mutual. My father was excited about his grandson. We were slowly building a relationship but there was still tension between us. Stacy's mom, Deborah, came to visit me, too. Keondra was taking pictures to post them on the internet. Jay was putting on a show in front of everyone as if we hadn't been bumping heads the past few months. My heart almost stopped when Trayon walked through the door with balloons and shopping bags. I hadn't seen him in eleven years and I couldn't believe how young he looked. He still had the same nice physique that he had when he was twenty-two. Trayon's watch probably cost more than my house. I also noticed the wedding band around his finger. There was something about Trayon that was alluring. I wasn't lusting after him, but his presence oozed sex appeal and intimidation. Asayi was a regular hood girl but the minute she met Trayon, she turned her back on me. A part of me hated Trayon because he took Asayi away from me. A tear fell from my eye when Asayi stepped into my hospital room carrying my favorite flowers. I was so caught up in watching Trayon and Asayi that I didn't notice Stacy in the room.

"The old gang is here," Deborah said.

"Oh, my heavens. Come over here and give me a hug!" my mother said when she saw Asayi. Asayi hugged my mother and it brought back many memories from when we were best friends. Why did I have to get on drugs and ruin everything I had?

"Hi, Sadi. Congrats on the bundle of joy. He's soooo cute," Asayi said.

"Thanks," I said dryly.

Stacy came over to me and kissed my forehead. He grabbed a tissue and wiped my eyes. Stacy was always a caring person. I often wondered how my life would've turned out if our daughter had survived.

"I'm proud of you, Sadi. You really grew up on us," Stacy said. I looked out the corner of my eye to see if Jay was getting jealous because my ex-boyfriend was in the room. But the nigga was smiling in Trayon and Asayi's face. It pissed me off so much that I wanted them to leave. It was my moment and there they were stealing my happiness once again.

"Thank you two for the gifts but y'all can leave. Let's not pretend that y'all came here to congratulate me on my success," I said. Everyone looked at me, probably thinking I lost my mind.

"Come again?" Asayi asked.

"Bitch, you heard me! You weren't here for me when I was on drugs but now you want to be my friend because I have a lot going for myself?"

"Let's bounce, shorty. Not every bird heals from broken wings," Trayon said to his wife.

"Nigga, fuck you, too! You locked me in a basement for days while I was carrying my daughter, Aja. You tortured me and made me sick! You also turned my friend against me!" I said.

"What is she talking about, Tray?" Asayi asked her husband. Jay wasn't surprised because he knew everything about it. He worked for Trayon at the time and he was the one who took me home after being kidnapped.

"I forgot about that. But, yeah, I kidnapped her to scare her into getting clean because she was hurting you and Stacy. It was done out of the love I have for y'all and the baby she was carrying. It ain't that deep," Trayon said nonchalantly to his wife.

"Yo, Sadi, chill the fuck out!" Jay yelled at me.

"Fuck you, Jay! All of y'all kiss that nigga's ass like he's God or something. I need you by my side and you over there smiling in their faces. They don't give a damn about Haden!" I yelled back.

"Wow, Sadi. You really have some issues. We came here to support Jay because whether you like it or not, he still belongs to this family. This has nothing to do with you, so don't even make it about you! We love Haden, too, and Trayon is his godfather so get over it. And watch how you talk to my husband," Asayi said. Everyone thought she was sweet and loveable but Asayi was just as ghetto as Tuchie. My mother told everyone else to leave the room because I was getting upset.

"You kidnapped my daughter?" my father asked Trayon. Trayon grilled my father and Jay stood between them. Haden was in his bassinet sleeping peacefully through the mess.

"Yeah, I did. The fuck you wanna do about it, nigga?" Trayon asked.

"Get the hell away from my father, Trayon!" I yelled.

"Come on, baby. This is miserable folks' problems. Isha would never behave like this,"

Asayi threw in there to piss me off. Trayon grabbed Asayi's hand and pulled her out of the room.

"I'm calling the police," my father said.

"No offense, Larenz, but I don't think you wanna do that. I was there when Sadi was kidnapped and we didn't hurt her. We only had her best interest at heart because she was going down the wrong path," Jay said, taking Trayon's side. Jay's mother was staring at me, probably trying to put voodoo on me. She was an evil witch.

"Nothing but misery surrounds you. Cleanse your soul before it's too late. A damaged heart ruins lives. You and Jay both need healing," Adele said. She grabbed her purse and walked out the room. My mother stood in the corner with her arms crossed; she was disappointed.

"I'm going home. I'll be back tomorrow and hopefully everyone can act like adults." My mother kissed my son on his cheek before she left. My father walked out behind her without saying anything to me. The most important thing was that he stood up to Trayon for me. The only people in the room were me, Jay and Haden.

"You're a real bitch, Sadi. Trayon and Asayi came here on the strength of me! But you got jealous because I wasn't kissing your dumb ass? Do you see how childish you act? And you wonder why I don't like talking to you anymore. Yo, I thought me and you could start over when I moved in with you, but I realized why nobody fucks with you. Yo, I can't believe you was just on some snitching shit. You must've forgotten that I was a part of your kidnapping and we damn sure didn't hurt you. You were hurting yourself. Trayon did a lot for me and that nigga is like my blood brother. I'll co-parent witchu if you ever in your stupid-ass life disrespect my family again! That goes for all of them! They let that shit go and you still holding on to the past. You BETRAYED them! Our son is a part of their family as well. Get over all that shit before you lose me," he said.

"Oh, I get it. You wanna fuck Asayi? Is that it? You are sticking up for that bitch more than you stick up for me!" Hadley came into the room and told her father she was leaving with Adele. She didn't say anything to me, but I didn't care about that, neither. Fuck all of them.

"Who are you cheating on me with, Jay? Just tell me so I won't be so angry and disrespected."

"I'm not cheating on you for the last damn time!" he said. The nurse came into my room to get Haden for his circumcision and Jay left with them. I hated everyone and I thought giving birth would be the happiest day of my life but it went from sugar to shit.

****

Nine days later...

Since the incident in my hospital room, the only person who visited and took care of me was my mother. Stacy's mother was ignoring me and I wondered if Stacy told her not to visit me anymore. I had to sleep in the bedroom downstairs in my home because of my incision. I wasn't allowed to take the stairs yet. Jay was doing most of the work with Haden because I was in terrible pain. I had to use a walker because my legs swelled up badly. Jay had to help me shower because my mother was at her part-time job. Shelley and her husband was flying in to see me and the baby, so I wanted to look decent.

"Hurry up, please. They'll be arriving soon."

"Yo, shut up. I gotta make sure I get rid of this funny smell. No offense but that coochie must got an infection," Jay said. The nigga had the nerve to talk about my vagina as if I could properly wash it. My body ached and I refused to take the pain pills I was given because they were narcotics. When I was in rehab, I remembered a girl relapsing because she got a tooth pulled and the dentist put her on Percocet. I was literally suffering from the pain I was in and Jay was getting frustrated instead of feeling sorry for me. He didn't understand my concerns since I'd been clean for eleven years.

"Get the hell away from me!" I snatched the rag from him to wash myself but my muscles ached.

"Shorty, you must don't trust yourself with taking the pain pills. This ain't good at all. At least take the ibuprofen. I gotta tend to the baby and you being selfish about it. The doctor said you can get a blood clot if you don't walk around but all you do is sit in a recliner chair all day. I'm tired as fuck, Sadi. You're stiff because you don't move around," Jay said. Haden's cries came through the monitor on Jay's hip and he ran out the bathroom. I stepped out the shower and sat on the toilet seat to dry off. Moments later, Jay, came into the bathroom with my clothes while I was moisturizing my skin.

"My friends are coming and you want me to wear this?" I asked. Jay handed me a pair of leggings and one if his T-shirts with a pair of mix-match socks. He was getting on my nerves so bad that I wanted to kill him.

"The laundry is piled up, shorty. Besides, I like when you walk around the house like this. Anyways, I'm ready to take a nap before Haden wakes back up for his bottle."

"Fine, just unlock the front door so I won't have to get out of my chair when they come," I replied. Jay leaned against the wall by the door and stared at me.

"What is it?"

"You're gonna be my wife soon. Our wedding isn't far away and you think everything is going to go back to normal by sitting on your ass? Shorty, you can't even wash your pussy. I'm in this muthafucka with sweaty balls and a dirty house because you can't even hold Haden or keep an eye on him while I clean up. This is the most I've seen you move around and that's because your friends are coming. You wanna impress them so bad with this big house and the fancy cars in the driveway but you don't care about how the house looks on the inside," he said.

"Well, can you at least straighten up then? I carried Haden for nine months and was in labor for hours! You're complaining about taking care of Haden until I heal? You wouldn't give two fucks about doing all of this if it was for Hadley. Didn't you take care of her and nurture her back to health when she got into that car accident?"

"Yo, shorty. I'll kill you in this house if you mention my daughter again. That's my fucking daughter! I'll give my life for her. You don't compare to that, dummy," he replied. I waited until he left the bathroom to shed a few tears. Jay has always been mean and blunt but for him to be that way towards me after all we had been through cut me like a knife. He did a lot for his daughter like having a thirty-thousand-dollar sweet sixteen birthday bash for her. He even bought the little bitch a two-door Mercedes coupe right after I told him how much I loved those cars. I was hinting for him to buy it for me, not her. She was sixteen, what did she need with a car, especially after she was in an accident? Jay had been spoiling me since I came back to Maryland then suddenly it stopped. I never thought I was materialistic but you can't spoil a person then leave them to fend for themselves. The bell ring after I struggled putting my socks on. I couldn't believe how long it took me to get dressed in house clothes. I grabbed my walker by the bathroom door and pushed it into the hallway.

"COME IN!" I shouted.

The door opened and Hadley walked in with grocery bags. She walked past me and headed straight to the kitchen. I walked down the hallway and into the kitchen where she was putting groceries away.

"So, you just come into my house and don't speak?" I asked. Hadley turned away from the fridge to face me.

"My bad, I didn't know that was you with the walker and poor people clothes. No Fendi or Balenciaga today? How are you feeling?" she asked.

"Great, but your father didn't tell you I was having company today?"

"Yes, that's why I came so I can straighten up around here. I'll stay out of the way. Where is the vacuum?" she asked.

Good question. Jay has been the one cleaning up and cooking dinner.

"Ask your father, but anyways, I'm going in the living room to wait for my company," I replied. Hadley rolled her eyes at me and I returned the gesture. I thought she'd be a sweet girl but she was a spoiled brat. The living room had baby things everywhere so I tried my best to straighten up and almost fell over my walker. I got frustrated with it and tossed it in the corner. The doorbell rang and Hadley came down the hall.

"I'll get it. I'm here for a week to help out so relax," Hadley said.

"What about school?"

"Home school this year," she said.

Great, now I gotta be around her! Knowing her, she probably offered to help out so she could report back to Isha. That's exactly why she's here and I'm going to show them that I can handle my household. I bet Isha is laughing at me knowing I need a walker. Jay's mother is enjoying it all.

"Go back in the kitchen. I can handle this. I need to move around more anyway," I replied. Hadley shrugged her shoulders and went back to the kitchen. Sweat dripped down my face and I was out of breath as I made my way to the door without the walker. I opened the door to great Shelley and Arnold.

"Awwww, look at you! Give me a hug!" Shelley screamed. She hugged me and I wanted to tell her she was hurting me but I didn't want anyone else feeling sorry for me. Arnold stepped in and hugged me, too. I wasn't too fond of her husband but I tolerated him because Shelley loved him. Arnold was older, around forty, and he was a school teacher. Shelley could do better because he wasn't attractive. Arnold reminded me of Anthony Anderson.

"Girrllll, this home is lovely. I feel like I'm in a celebrity's house. I've never seen a townhome this big before," Shelley said.

"It sure is a nice home. Definitely a reason to run away from Atlanta," Arnold said with sarcasm and Shelley elbowed him. Hadley came into the foyer and introduced herself.

"Awww, she's pretty, Sadi. How old are you?" Shelley asked.

"I'm sixteen. Sorry for the mess, but I'll go upstairs and get Haden. My father is asleep," Hadley replied.

"She's a polite young lady," Arnold said when she walked upstairs.

I showed them to the living room and they sat on the couch across from me.

"I'm so happy for you. You always wanted Jay and now he's about to be your husband," Shelley gloated.

"We have a few things to discuss alone before you leave," I replied.

"Have you contacted Kareem?" Arnold asked.

"What has gotten into you?" Shelley replied.

"She knows what happened. I gotta sit here and be in denial like the both of you? We all know why she really left," Arnold said. I was ready to butt in when Hadley came downstairs with the baby in her arms. Shelley held her arms out to hold him.

"Awww, he looks just like you, Sadi," Shelley beamed.

"Anyone want something to drink?" Hadley asked.

"No, thanks, we stopped for lunch before we came," Shelley replied. Arnold was staring at my son's face and I wanted to punch the shit out of him.

"I'll be in the kitchen," Hadley said.

"Hold him, Arnold. I need to go to the bathroom. I've been holding it for a while," Shelley said.

"I'll show you where it's at," Hadley replied and they left the room.

"Hand me my damn baby. I know what you're doing and it's not what you think it is," I said to Arnold.

"You know I thought you'd be a good woman for Kareem but you used him after that nigga upstairs told you he was engaged. Me and Shelley know you went to Kareem's house the night of our wedding. He told me you came crying to him because Jay dogged you out. He fucked you the same night and suddenly you want to move to Maryland. This baby looks just like him. But I guess the salary of a car salesman doesn't fit your bill," Arnold said.

"You don't know what you're talking about! Kareem has been a creep and he'll do anything to get me. I didn't sleep with him."

Arnold got up to give me my baby. He sat back on the couch and crossed his legs with a grin on his face.

"I want twenty thousand dollars in my hand before I leave town. We're trying to buy a house and we're short so that will help, plus put furniture in our new home. I'll go home and not mention a word to Kareem about this. Do we have a deal?"

"This is not his damn baby!" I said.

Damaged: Damages Spinoff   Natavia

"Looks just like him and he's only an infant. What will happen once he gets older and Jay realizes that's not his son? Your dreams will be gone, Sadi. Twenty g's before I leave town or else I'm going to tell Kareem he has a son with another man's name. You can't fool everybody," he said.

"Fine, I'll do it," I spat.

I wanted to curse Shelley for not coming back to the living room. She was talking to Hadley about modeling. Shelley saw good in everyone but her conniving-ass husband. She came back into the living room minutes later and brought Arnold something to drink. I asked Shelley to hold the baby so I could use the bathroom.

"Arnold, help Sadi up. She's crouching over," Shelley said.

"Nooo, I'm fine. I've got to make myself walk. I'll be back in a few minutes," I said. The pain was excruciating and I couldn't take it anymore. I headed towards the kitchen to get my pain meds.

"No. I cannot come out right now. I'll text you when everyone's asleep. I'm over my dad's house. Okay, love you, too." Hadley hung up.

So, she's fucking now. Gotta be. I was at her age. Jay thinks Hadley is an innocent virgin. I know she's only over here to spy for Isha.

"Oh, hey. I didn't know you were in the kitchen."

"I came in to take my meds," I replied.

"Want me to take Haden upstairs for his bottle?" she asked, wiping off the counter.

"Yes, thank you," I replied.

My pills were sitting on the counter. I picked up the bottle of ibuprofen and took three pills. I was only supposed to take one but the ache in my lower abdomen was causing me to walk hunched over. Fifteen minutes later, I was back in the living room.

"Are you feeling better?" Shelley asked.

"Yes, thank you. I really hate to cut this short but I'm exhausted. Come by tomorrow evening?"

"Sure, we're tired, too. Thank you for having us and I'll see you tomorrow. I'll cook dinner for everyone because I know y'all have been very busy," Shelley said. She gave me an envelope and told me it was a gift card to Target for the baby.

"Come on, Shelley. We have a forty-minute drive to my cousin's house," Arnold said to her. She rolled her eyes at him and told me she'd see me later. Arnold held the door open for Shelley while mouthing the words, *pay soon.* I gave him the middle finger. The fool licked his tongue at me before he closed the door behind him. I hated Arnold with a passion! He was going to get his money alright. I went into my bedroom downstairs and called Keondra. She answered the phone on the first ring.

"About time you called me. I was getting bored," she said.

"Hey, I need a favor from you," I replied.

"Look, I'm not playing on Tuchie's work phone anymore. Bitch, that's the government phone," she said.

"Girl, who cares. She talks too much, shit. The bitch needs to humble herself."

Keondra disguised her voice and called Tuchie's job. I told her not to mention Niji since she was just a kid. She called back the next day and found out Tuchie left. She was all talk and no bite. All the mouth she had, she let a prank call stop her bag.

"What do you want this time?" she asked.

"Find someone who makes counterfeit money. I'm not talking about the monopoly money, neither. I need something that looks real."

"Oh, bitch, you about to pay a lot of money for that. How much you need?" she asked.

"Twenty thousand."

"Girl, that's like seven thousand dollars," she replied.

"Listen, I'd rather spend that then twenty thousand. I'll tell you about it later."

"Wait! Don't hang up yet," she said.

"What is it, Keondra? I gotta go tend to Haden."

"Tell Jay to tell Bogo to call me or else I'm going to tell his bitch I'm pregnant," she said.

"What?"

"All you do is talk about Jay's yellow ass messing around with Isha. You didn't ask me how I was doing when Bogo left me. I really need a friend right now," she sniffled.

"Okay, what do you want me to do? You and Bogo break up all the time. He'll be back," I said.

"I guess you're right. Anyways, stay by your phone. I know this one nigga in the city that can make it look real. I'll see how long it takes," she said.

"Okay, thanks. We are going to hang out more after I heal, I promise," I replied.

"About time. We had a lot of fun back in the day," she said.

I told Keondra I was going to call her back before she talked my head off about Bogo.

Midnight...

Jay was still asleep and the house was quiet. I was lying in my bed watching TV. Hadley was upstairs with Haden while he slept. The only reason I stayed up was to catch Hadley and that boy she was going to meet outside of my house. I wanted Jay to know how much of a bad influence Isha was on Hadley. After I watched a Lifetime movie, I looked at the clock and it was two o'clock in the morning. The ibuprofen I took made me feel so much better. I was able to walk around with only a slight limp. I heard the front door close.

Bingo.

"Ohhhhh!" I whispered to myself while looking out the living room window. Hadley's arms were wrapped around a boy's neck while he groped her backside.

"JAYYYYY!" I called out and he didn't answer. I yelled his name again and heard him opening the master bedroom door.

"Yo, you going to wake up the baby!" he yelled downstairs.

"Hurry up and get down here!" I called out while peeping out the curtain. Jay came downstairs seconds later still half asleep.

"Yo, what happened? You know I haven't had any sleep," he said with attitude.

"Get your damn daughter before I call the police on the boy she's standing outside with. Don't believe me, look out the window." Jay pushed me out the way and looked out the window. His cheeks turned red from clenching his jaw. Jay rushed to the door only wearing house pants and socks. I didn't feel sorry for him because I wanted him to feel how I'd been feeling since I gave birth. Jay was sensitive when it came to his daughter, so this was the only way I could get through to him.

"Get yah hot ass in the house before I bust a few rounds in that nigga's dome!" Jay shouted as he walked down the steps. I stood in the doorway watching the scene unfold. Jay snatched Hadley from the boy and he stood up in Jay's face.

"Damn, nigga. You didn't have to do all that," he said and Jay pushed him. Hadley tried to get between them and I covered my mouth when Jay punched the boy in his face. The boy was taller than Jay and a little thicker. He had the build of a football player. Hadley screamed at her boyfriend for choke slamming Jay on the hood of his Jaguar.

"Do something, Sadi!" Hadley screamed.

"You shouldn't have bought that grown-ass man to my house! I'm calling the police!" I said.

"He's nineteen, bitch! Do something or I'm going to kick *your* ass!" Hadley yelled at me. She was disrespectful but I didn't think she had it in her. But then again, she was Jay's daughter. Jay and the boy tussled around on the ground punching each other. I grabbed the house phone and called the police.

"DADDY, STOP!" I heard Hadley scream. I hung up the phone after I gave the police my address and rushed back to the door. Jay was arguing with her boyfriend and Hadley was standing in front of him.

"Get in the house or I'm going to shoot this nigga for trespassing!" Jay shouted.

"No, you're not! I love him and you can't do anything about it! Jared is a nice guy and you had no right to put your hands on him. Can we just go in the house and talk?" Hadley asked.

"Get the fuck in the house!" Jay yelled. He grabbed Hadley by her shirt and snatched her away from her boyfriend. She was screaming and crying because her father was dragging her on the concrete.

"You want to be a teen mom? Is that it? You want to go through the same shit I went through when I had you?" Jay yelled at his daughter while dragging her up the stairs.

"Stop fucking dragging her like that! Nigga, you gotta a problem with me, not her!" Jared yelled.

"This ain't over, muthafucka! You'll see about me soon!" Jay replied back.

What did I do? I wasn't expecting things to get out of hand like this. Jay is hurting her by dragging her up the steps.

Jay slung Hadley into the house and she fell into a lamp.

"Wait a minute, Jay!" I yelled out. I grabbed at his arm and he pushed me into the wall.

"Stay the fuck out of it!" he yelled at me. Hadley was lying on the floor crying while holding her arm.

"Stay away from that boy, Hadley! Why was you letting him touch on you like that? Are you having sex now?" he asked, grabbing her face.

"I'm a virgin!" she yelled and snatched from him.

The police was outside and I opened the door. They were telling Jared to put his hands behind his head while they had guns pointed at him. Hadley ran outside and begged for the police to put their guns down. Jay ran outside behind her and I was nervous, afraid someone was going to get shot and it was all my fault. Maybe I should've told Jay when I heard Hadley on the phone instead of waiting until she snuck out.

"Get on the ground now!" an officer yelled at Jared. He got down on the ground and an officer patted him down.

"He didn't do anything! I told him to come over here! Daddy, tell them it was a big misunderstanding, please," Hadley cried. Jay watched the officers handcuff her boyfriend and wrestle him to a police car. There were four officers on the teenager. My eyes watered while thinking about all the black men whose lives were taken from police brutality. I reported him trespassing when in actuality, Hadley invited him over. We stood on the sidewalk and watched them take the young man away.

Jay

"**Y**ou could've told the truth! That bitch told them he was trying to break into our house and that's why they had their guns drawn!" Hadley yelled. She was getting out of hand. I never put hands on my daughter before but she was throwing away her life. First, she was getting drunk with her friends which led to a car accident. It hadn't even been a year yet and she was getting herself into something else. The thought of a lil' nigga touching on my daughter was heartbreaking. She was more than that and was throwing her life away.

"Watch your mouth and apologize to Sadi! Talk to me, Hadley. What's up with you, baby girl? Where did this nigga come from?" I asked.

"Rehab. I met him there when he was visiting a friend who got injured on his team. We've been talking since and I love him. Jared is not that type of boy. He never asked me for sex!"

"Why was he feeling on your ass then?" I replied.

"Because we love each other," she said.

"He doesn't love you. He wants to fuck you then dump you for another girl. I was a teenager and that's what they do!"

"Oh, cut the crap, Dad. Men your age dog women out, too, so why are you telling me this? I watched you treat Isha like a dog but Jared never treated me that way. Don't worry, Father. I'd never date a man like you. You still love my mother and you were younger than me when y'all were together, so why can't I have that with someone I love? We are not having sex! Jared is a virgin, too. He plays football and he's on the Dean's list. Might I add, his parents are rich! You should've talked to him instead of putting your hands on him. He defended himself and tried to defend me, too," Hadley sobbed. Sadi reached out to hug her but Hadley pulled away from her.

"Don't touch me. I really hate you. At first, I tried to get along with you and even help you out.

You wanted my father to see this. Now that I think about it, you heard me talking to Jared in the kitchen earlier. You set me up!" Hadley yelled at Sadi.

"Seriously, Sadi? You knew about this and didn't tell me?"

Sadi rolled her eyes at us then sat on the couch unbothered. Her true colors were showing. I cursed myself every day when I heard the sound of her voice. Living with Sadi wasn't how I imagined. I knew she didn't cook but I had it in my mind that she was going to learn since I paid all the bills. She was a spoiled brat and sometimes acted younger than Hadley. They argued like sisters and Sadi seemed to be jealous of her.

"Yes, I knew but I didn't think she was going to go through with it. I overheard her talking on the phone and I forgot about it. I had a busy day with Shelley and her husband. Can we just go to bed and talk about this later? It was an honest mistake," Sadi said. She was sincere about the situation. Sadi had a lot going on and it probably slipped her mind.

"Get some rest so I can talk to my daughter," I replied. Sadi walked out the living room to her bedroom.

"Have a seat so we can talk." Hadley wiped the tears away from her eyes.

"I don't want to talk. Sadi is lying to you. I tried to accept her but I can't. Sorry, Daddy. I'm over the both of you. Jared could've gotten killed by the police and nobody stuck up for him. Why didn't you stick up for him? He did nothing wrong."

"I only care about you. That nigga isn't my concern. Go to bed, we can talk about this when we wake up."

Hadley walked up the stairs to the guest bedroom and slammed the door. I went to the master bedroom and Haden was still asleep. Feeling defeated, I called Isha. It was three o'clock in the morning but I took a chance anyway, hoping she answered the phone.

"Hello," she answered wide awake. Slow music was playing in the background and I heard a nigga's voice.

"Is that Rush in the background? Yo, Isha, you fucking that lil' nigga? He's Hadley's boyfriend's age."

"He's twenty now. Anyway, what happened? Is Hadley alright? You never call this late," she said.

"Can we talk tomorrow? We can meet up at a deli or something. Hadley and Sadi can't get along and she snuck a boy over here."

"Who, Jared?" she asked.

"You knew she had a fucking boyfriend and didn't tell me?"

"I thought you knew but I honestly didn't know it was serious. He called her phone and she told me to answer while she was in the bathroom. Look, Jay. I gotta go. I'll see you later and we can talk about this," she moaned in my ear.

"Yo, you fuckin' or sumthin?"

"Gotta go, Jay," she said and hung up.

I laid on the bed and stared at the ceiling. The women in my life were breaking a nigga. The last person I wanted to talk to was my mother. I swear I didn't need any more, "I told you so's."

****

It was around two o'clock in the afternoon by the time I got dressed for the day. Hadley locked herself in the room. Teenage girls weren't easy to deal with because of the mood swings.

Sadi was at the kitchen table feeding Haden a bottle. We didn't say anything to each other. I opened the fridge to grab a carton of milk for my cereal. The doorbell rang and Sadi raised her eyebrow.

"We having company?"

"You tell me. It ain't your Atlanta friends?" I asked.

"Can you get the door? I forgot they were coming."

I was taken by surprise when I answered the door.

"Yo, what's good? Is Bogo alright?" I asked my old connect which was now Bogo's connect. For him to show up meant something happened. I didn't tell the nigga where I lived.

"This ain't about that nigga. I heard you had an altercation with my baby brother," Hamisi said. He stepped into the house and I closed the door. I wasn't a bitch nigga but my daughter and son were in the house. One dumb move could've had me pushing up daises.

"Your brother came to my crib and was feeling on my daughter. Besides, I didn't know that was your peoples." Hamisi walked into the living room and made himself comfortable. Trayon put me on to him when he got out the drug game. Around that time, Hamisi was starting to make a name for himself. Hamisi's father ran a billion-dollar drug ring in the eighties to the late-nineties. Hamisi Jr. wasn't a hood nigga, but he had a way about him that let niggas know he wasn't scared to merk a nigga. I sat on the couch across from him and he grilled me.

"My brother was charged with robbery and sexual assault. Nigga, let me ask you something. What would you do if that was your blood?" Sadi came into the living room and paused when Hamisi pointed a gun at her.

"Sadi? Is that you?" he grinned.

"Who are you?" she asked.

"Crackheads always forget shit when they get clean. You let me smut you out in the back seat of my pop's Maybach when I was a young nigga. I've been meaning to ask for a refund," he said.

"I don't know you."

"Don't worry, shorty. Come have a seat," Hamisi replied with the gun on his lap. I realized he had gloves on and shit wasn't looking good for us.

"Yo, this shit is uncalled for. My girl and kids are in the crib and you trippin'. We can discuss this somewhere else."

"I want to discuss it now, muthafucka. You think this is a fucking game. They are throwing mad charges against my brother to destroy our family name. Do you know how many football teams want him off the field because he's unstoppable? Niggas been trying to tarnish my baby brother's name and you gave them what they wanted. This shit here will hit the news, the newspaper, the internet and his school. Nigga, I don't give a fuck what you got going on, but you and that dirty nose bitch is going to erase this shit and I mean ASAP. I'll murder anything attached to you if my brother loses his image. He ain't fucking your daughter, neither. The lil' nigga is still a virgin," Hamisi said.

"I'm so sorry about what happened this morning. It was a big misunderstanding. I'll give them my statement and tell them the truth but you need to leave my house," Sadi said. I wanted to knock that bitch's head off for making decisions. Hamisi stood up with the gun still pointed at us, walking backwards towards the door to make sure we didn't try anything. My fingers were itching to put a bullet in that nigga's skull.

"You got one hour to fix this bullshit. Fuck me over and I'll turn this city into a warzone. I'll get up with y'all later because I will be back," Hamisi said. He turned the doorknob the stepped out of the house. Sadi was still shaken up and started panicking.

"He's going to kill us!" she panicked.

"Go handle that and I'll sit here with the kids. Sorry, shorty, I don't fuck with the police." Sadi stormed out the living room and slammed the door to her temporary bedroom. While Sadi was getting dressed, I called Trayon and told him to swing by because it was important.

This gotta be the karma my mother was telling me about. I have nothing but bad luck on my side.

What killed my spirit was Hamisi calling Sadi out for selling her pussy to get high. I knew shorty was out there but her turning tricks for it was new to me. Sadi had me thinking Tae supplied her for all those years, and when he couldn't, she stole money from her parents. Thirty minutes later, Sadi headed out the house wearing leggings and an oversized jean shirt with crocs on her feet. She told me Haden was in her room sleeping in his bassinet before she walked out the door. I went into the kitchen and grabbed a bottle of cognac out the cabinet. It was almost time for me to meet Isha but it was pointless. Hadley was in love with some lil' nigga and there wasn't nothing I could do about it except talk to her so she could make the right choices.

The front door opened while I guzzled the smooth brown liquor as it soothed its way down my throat.

"Yo, Jay! Where you at?" Trayon called out. I told him I was down the hall in the kitchen. He shook his head when he saw me sitting at the table with a bottle in front me. Trayon pulled out a chair and grilled me. He told me a while back that Sadi wasn't no good for me. Matter of fact, Trayon knew about me and Sadi before Bogo. He was the only nigga I could talk to about that mushy shit because he was in a faithful marriage for years.

"Sadi got you out here looking like a chump, huh? Come on, my nigga, I told you to get over this obsession shit you have with Hadley's mother, now look at you, bruh. Shorty still don't know why you with her?" he asked.

Seventeen years ago...

"That's my father," Joy said to me while we were standing in the Wetzel Pretzel line at the mall. I had a little job at a fast food restaurant and managed to save sixty dollars so Joy could buy larger tops because her stomach was getting bigger.

"How do you know?" I asked, looking at the man who was standing with a girl who looked a few years older than Joy. They were only a few feet away from us at the soda fountain machine.

"My mother took me to his job when I was six years old. She begged him to give her money because I needed new shoes and he told her I wasn't his daughter because he already had one. I'll never forget his face. I know he's my father because I resemble him and my sister. Me and her look a lot alike but he still denies me. Look at them...that's the only daughter he claims. I bet he bought her all the bags she has in her hands. I hate them," Joy said.

Joy was Sadi's younger sister, but those weren't my real intentions when I met Sadi. It didn't come about until we started talking on the phone and her sending me pictures which reminded me of Joy. Sadi's father didn't know anything about Hadley and I wanted it to remain that way. Basically, I had some deep-rooted issues that I couldn't let go. Being with Sadi was the closest I'd ever be to Joy. Hadley came into the kitchen and her eyes were swollen, her hair all over her head.

"Hi, Uncle Tray."

"What's good witchu? Who fuckin' with you?" he replied.

"Jared broke up with me."

"Who is that nigga?"

"It's a long story," she replied.

"You hungry?" I asked her but she ignored me. She went into the fridge to get a soda before she left the kitchen.

"I don't know what to tell you anymore, fam. You got a lot of shit on your hands. Maybe you don't want to hear this but maybe you need to call that engagement off until you get better. Find a shorty that you can talk to without giving judgement," Trayon said.

"I had that but I messed it up."

"Make it right then 'cause shorty is never going to amount to what you had with Hadley's mother. Stop by my crib later and I'll give you this book my wife got for me before we got married. In the meantime, just do what you gotta do for your kids and say fuck everything else. Grind harder so your kids won't have to work for another muthafucka when they get older and stop stressing about old shit. All I'm saying is I would still be a fucked-up empty-hearted nigga without a future if I stay dwelling on old shit. Let it go, bruh, because nobody knows this nigga I'm sitting across from," he said. Trayon slapped hands with me and told me he'd get up with me later, and just like that he was gone. I was on my way upstairs to have a talk with Hadley but Sadi's cell-phone vibrated on the counter.

I know she feels lost without that thing.

The vibration stopped and I shrugged it off until it vibrated again. I thought maybe she was calling from another number because she was looking for her phone but it was a text message from a nigga named Arnold.

Have my money before I leave town or else I'm gonna tell Kareem why you really left Atlanta! I'll expose you for the gold digger you are if you tell my wife about this...

Come and get the money now while Jay is gone, I texted back.

I scrolled the message thread and he harassed her all morning.

"Hadley, open the door! I need you to do me a favor," I yelled while knocking. She opened the door after I knocked five times.

"Pack Haden up for me and take him to Nana's house. It's an emergency."

"I don't have a carrier," she replied with an attitude.

"Look, baby girl. I know you're tripping because of what happened earlier but we will talk about that later. In the meantime, I need you to get your baby brother and leave this house. Someone is getting ready to come over and I don't want y'all around. Don't argue with me, just do it."

"Okay, I'll do it," she replied and I kissed her forehead.

I went downstairs and grabbed Haden to buckle him in his carrier. Hadley was dressed in three minutes. She grabbed his diaper bag and I carried him outside to her car to strap him in.

"He's awake so he might cry soon. As soon as you get to Nana's house, make him a bottle. Let me know when you get there and don't take him anywhere else. Go straight there and do not speed," I replied.

"Okay, I won't. Goodbye," she said.

While Hadley was pulling off, Sadi was parking in the driveway. She got out of the car without a care in the world and even cracked a smile at me.

"They are going to drop the charges on Jared," she said in excitement but that was the least of my worries.

"Let's go in the house," I replied.

We went inside the house and I locked the door. Sadi was stepping out of her shoes when I pushed her cell-phone into her face.

"Why is Shelley's husband asking you for money and what does Kareem have to do with it? I didn't tell you how that nigga approached me in the men's bathroom at Shelley's wedding reception. In so many words, the nigga was feeling me out to see how much I was involved with you. You put on this innocent role so I didn't stop to think that maybe you were entertaining another nigga."

"It's not that serious. I cheated a bet and he's going to tell Kareem if I don't pay him. I owed him since I lived in Atlanta," she lied.

"Read the fucking message! He said he's going to expose you for the gold digger you are if you tell his wife on him! Bitch, you think I'm fucking stupid? How much money does this nigga want from you? Lie to me and I'll break your neck!"

"Stop yelling at me before you wake Haden up," she said.

"He's with Hadley. Somebody is getting merked today and possibly in this house if yah hoe ass don't tell me what the fuck is going on!" Sadi started crying, apologizing to me for not being honest.

"It's not what you think! Just listen to me, please. I was going to tell you but you were so tired yesterday," she replied.

"How much money does this nigga want from you or should I ask him when he gets here?"

"Nooooooooo! Why were you going through my phone?" she asked and swung at me. Sadi's actions showed me she was guilty of something, but I was done. That was the last sign I needed to get away from her. I couldn't focus, my car wash and corner stores were going out of business and my money wasn't the same as it used to be. Arnold called her a gold digger for a reason. Shorty saw me as a meal ticket and I saw her as a replacement of Joy. We used each other, but at one point, I really loved her. She scratched my face and accused me of looking for an argument.

"You just want to fuck Isha! You're looking for shit to have a reason to leave me! That crazy-ass daughter of yours is the problem! She has been nothing but trouble since you brought her here. Stay out of my business and worry about Hadley not having the same fate as her mother because she keeps going down that path!" Sadi said while hitting me. I forgot who she was as my mind went blank. Hearing her talk about my daughter that way made me snap. I jabbed her in the face and she fell over the coffee table.

"SAY THAT SHIT AGAIN! You jealous of my daughter because she ain't gotta fuck for the things she has? You a broke bitch! I upgraded you so don't forget that!"

The doorbell rang and Sadi got up. I was beginning to think she was overexaggerating about the pain she was in because she was moving around. Sadi threw a lamp at me when I reached for the doorknob.

"Please, don't let him come in!" she sobbed. I opened the door and Arnold was surprised to see me. He tried to make a dash down the steps but I grabbed him by the collar of his shirt and pulled him into the house.

"Move again, bitch!" I said with my gun pointed at him. He had his hands up and begged me to let him go.

"I didn't do nothing!" Arnold said.

"Tell me about this money she owes you and why!"

"Please tell him it was about a bet," Sadi screamed at Arnold. I smashed the gun to his forehead, threatening to pull the trigger if he lied to me.

"You gonna listen to her when I'm the one with the gun?" I asked him.

"I wanted twenty thousand dollars to keep my mouth shut about her sleeping with Kareem. The baby might not be yours and she knows it! He looks just like Kareem. I needed the money because all my wife talks about is having her own salon, living in a big house and driving these cars that I don't have the money for. Sadi put that shit in my wife's head and it's messing up our marriage because I don't have what you have. Come on, man. What would you do to please your wife?" Arnold asked. I lowered my gun and Sadi grabbed the gun out my hand, pointing it at Arnold.

"I never liked you and Shelley deserves better!" she said and shot Arnold in the head. She dropped the gun on the floor and her hands were shaking. Sadi killed him.

"What in the fuck did you do?" I yelled at her.

"I—I—I wasn't thinking," she stuttered. Arnold's blood was seeping through the cracks in the hardwood floors and flowing down the hall.

"We can go to jail behind this! Why would you kill a nigga in your fucking house?"

"You were going to kill him," she said.

"I was bluffing, dummy! I planned on pistol-whipping him. Shorty, you on your own. Clean this shit up."

I snatched the gun from her then jogged upstairs to grab my things out the safe then tossed them into a duffel bag. When I went back downstairs, Sadi was sitting on the floor by the door crying and asking me to help her. Arnold was sprawled out on the floor with his eyes open.

"Jay, please help me. I can go to jail for this! Shelley is my only friend and she'll kill me if she finds out what I did. I swear I didn't mean to do it, he made me so angry," she sobbed.

"I'll contact you soon for a DNA test. Don't call me for shit until then because I'm not taking care of another nigga's baby. Peace and blessings, shorty," I replied and stormed out of the house. I was done with Sadi for good. Adele was right about one thing—a person can be whomever you want them to be over the phone. Sadi probably felt the same way about me, but it is what it is.

Isha

A week later...

Rush was performing at Fendi's concert. My baby became a star overnight after he gave in and signed to Stacy's label. We were officially dating but it was still a secret. I woke up every morning, thanking God for sending me someone who was able to heal me. My recipes were even better because I was cooking from the heart. Jay, on the other hand, was going through a lot with Sadi. I heard from Asayi that he moved out of Sadi's house because he wasn't sure if the baby belonged to him. As for Sadi, I heard her house burned down and she went back to her parents' house. At one point, I wanted their relationship to suffer, but I sorta felt sorry for them. Having to wait for someone for ten years just to find out it wasn't meant to be is a bummer.

Rush was singing his new single, "Sex and Henny." The lyrics were very sexual and explicit.

"This song is so hot," Tuchie said.

The song was definitely hot. He wrote the song while we were lying in bed one night. We sexed for three hours and it was mind-blowing. I couldn't get enough of him and even got over the thought of moving on too fast.

"Yes, it is. I love it. These girls are screaming their asses off in here," Asayi replied. Asayi and Tuchie were talking loudly over the music while I watched Rush bring a girl on stage who looked to be around eighteen years old. Most artists interacted with their fans at concerts and shows but I was slightly jealous. Rush was young and very attractive so the girls were surrounding him. The crowd went crazy when the little hotbox twerked on him and he was enjoying it.

"Are you okay?" Asayi shouted at me.

"Yes! I'm just a little tired!" I shouted back.

Fendi came out on stage to perform the song they had together. Someone grabbed my hand from behind and it was Jay. He called me days ago because he wanted to talk about Hadley. Jay being at the show wasn't unusual because he went to all of Fendi's shows.

"You look good," he whispered in my ear.

"Thank you. How have you been?" I asked.

"Sick, I miss you. Can we go outside to talk?"

Rush wasn't performing anymore so I joined Jay outside so we could talk in peace. I needed fresh air anyway because the building smelled of weed and cigarettes.

"How are you really doing?"

"I'm straight, I guess. I know you heard about what happened between me and Sadi. I deserved it because I was chasing a fantasy all this time and ended up losing my reality. Six and a half months I spent with her and it seems like forever. That's how much shit has been happening between us," he said.

"Things happen. You just gotta bounce back."

"How did you get over me so easily, Ish?" he asked.

I wasn't ready to tell Jay that I still cared for him. It wasn't as easy as he thought. I'd learned to hide my feelings from people who could do whatever they wanted with them.

"That's too personal."

"Answer me so I can know where to go from here. Should I keep my distance or can we still be cordial? I thought I didn't love you but I thought about you every day when I was with Sadi. It's hard not thinking about you," he said.

I stepped away from Jay because he was getting too close. The last thing I wanted to do was give someone the wrong impression.

"I'm sorry, Jay. Some things we shouldn't discuss anymore. I don't want to confuse you."

"I feel you," he said.

My phone beeped and it was a message from Rush telling me to come backstage.

"I'll see you around," I said.

I turned to walk away but Jay grabbed my hand so I could face him. It had been months since he touched me and I didn't know how to feel about it because another man was touching me in all the right places.

"Can you help me start over? I let a few of my businesses go down the drain because I lost focus. I stopped hustling so this is nothing but clean money I need to flip," he said. Jay's eyes weren't the same, they had so much sadness in them. He was no longer that confident man anymore but there was nothing I could do.

"Call me tomorrow at three o'clock and we'll go from there. I hope to God you stay focused because this is my last time helping you. You've got to put your heart in it so you won't fail again. I gotta go so I'll talk to you soon," I replied. He released my hand so I could go back to the building.

Backstage was filled with so many groupies and they all looked no older than twenty years old. A security guard let me inside of Rush's dressing room. Rush was sitting on the couch smoking a blunt.

"Yo, why you keep breaking your neck to speak to that nigga?" he asked.

"What are you talking about?"

"Didn't you go outside with Jay? And didn't he call you days ago, asking you to meet him for lunch? Why do you keep entertaining that bullshit?" he asked.

"Where is this coming from?"

Me and Rush didn't argue much and if we did, it was always a small argument. He was really upset with me because of Jay.

"Yo, don't disrespect me like that again. I let all that other shit slide but not tonight. Come sit down so we can talk," he said. He knocked a few shirts off the couch so I could sit next to him. Rush picked up my leg and laid it across his lap so he could massage it. He was gentle but had a mean streak. Rush wasn't disrespectful but he didn't hide his feelings which was another thing I loved about him.

"I think we should be us around everyone else. I'm at your crib more than I'm home and if I'm not at the studio, I'm with you. It's been more than four months since we hooked up. Don't think about it now but let me know soon how it's going to be so I can focus more on this music shit instead of chasing something that's running from me. I'm not talking about a serious relationship and I don't want to be that nigga that's only in the picture because of good dick, you feel me? I'm just tired of hiding and shit. We gotta sneak off and kiss like little kids. The shit old now, Ish."

"But what about Tuchie? I don't want to ruin my friendship with her," I replied.

"Real friends will be happy as long as you're happy. Tuchie will have to accept it. She's happy, ain't she? She's ready to get married and she's pregnant. Don't forget that big-ass house Stacy copped for them. All I'm saying is your friends are living their life but you gotta put yours on pause to please them. We above that."

"I don't think I'm ready for that," I replied.

"Cool," he said and scooted away from me. I was getting a bad vibe from him like he wanted to be done with me. He wasn't asking for much, he wanted me to treat him the same way I treated him behind closed doors.

"I'm confused. Are you doing this because I went outside and talked to Jay?" I asked.

"Naw, I'm doing this so niggas won't feel too comfortable calling you all hours of the fucking night while we're in bed. They don't know I'm in the picture so they won't give a fuck. I'll holla at you later, Ish. Hit me up when that nigga knows his place," he said.

Rush opened the door so I could leave his room. I snatched my purse off the couch and headed for the door.

"That lil' bitch on stage must've really got your dick hard. Suddenly you have a problem with us being a secret. I'm not buying your excuse. You just want to fuck all these groupies," I spat and he chuckled.

"I don't have to make up an excuse for that, but you do. I'll get up wit' you later," he said.

I stormed out of his room and walked through the crowd in the hallway. Rush wanted to be with different women like his friend Fendi and there was nothing I could do about that.

"Everything okay?" Asayi asked when I met back up with them.

"Sure, I was talking to Jay about something. Everything is fine but I'm getting tired. I have to wake up early so I'll see y'all later," I replied. Chika looked at her watch.

"Girl, it's only nine o'clock," Chika said.

"I have a headache," I replied.

"Did Jay say something to you? You seem a little off like you're upset," Asayi said.

"We'll walk you to your car. It's really crowded now," Tuchie said to me.

We walked out the building and I saw Jay talking to Bogo. Our eyes locked and something sparked in me. I still loved him. Tuchie, Asayi and Chika were chatting about something and giggling. All I wanted to do was go home and get in bed to think about my life. Maybe I was better off without anyone.

"Why is Jay staring over here? We don't like him," Chika said.

"He is staring because he realized Shady Sadi was a fraud. Some people don't change. I knew the bitch was still the same person when she told Niji about the daughter she had with Stacy. I still don't get what was the point of that. The bitch is evil," Tuchie said.

"Sadi was spoiled since she was a baby so that's her mentality. She's a Daddy's Girl and feels like every man she meets is supposed to spoil her and let her do what she wants. It's her father's fault for that. I remember we all had summer jobs when we were fourteen. Her father told her she didn't need it and thought she was too above packing groceries for homeless shelters. I know y'all don't want to hear this but she just has a bad case of being a brat," Asayi said.

"She's too damn old to be a brat," Chika said and we all agreed.

I had flowers on my windshield. Jay smiled at me when I turned around. I read the card attached and it was a small note from him. I read the note out loud.

"Can we start over again? How about we take Hadley to get her nails done tomorrow? Remember that day?"

"Awwww," Asayi said and Tuchie rolled her eyes.

"Awww, shit. Jay is ignorant for this. He only wants her back because his baby mama didn't turn out the way he wanted her to. If it was genuine, he would've left her before him and Sadi broke up. Fuck Jay's yellow ass," Chika said.

"You stayed with Lim after he had a baby on you. Let their love heal on its own, damn. Nobody is perfect," Asayi said.

"Okay, first of all. Lim cheated on me because I cheated on him first. Secondly, he didn't use me the same way Jay used Isha. That nigga didn't want Isha to be his wife, he wanted her to be his daughter's mother so he can fuck another bitch. Those are facts, sis. I bet you Sadi didn't like Hadley so now he's running back to Isha to use her again. Let that nigga parent his own child, but what do I know. Isha is too nice and Jay is taking advantage of her again," Chika said.

"Let's just drop the subject. I'm going home to go to bed. I'll talk to you all later," I said, getting in my car.

I burst into tears once I pulled out the parking lot. Jay was using his old tricks to win me over. Rush was also on my mind; the thought of losing him made me sick. We hadn't been dating long but it was long enough for me to fall for him which wasn't my intentions. I thought we were using each other until I couldn't go a day without being with him. Fifty minutes later, I pulled up to my house and noticed a small black car parked on the street. A woman got out the car and slammed the door. She walked across my yard and I froze.

"Are you Isha?" she asked.

"Who are you?" I replied.

"Can I come in?" she asked, looking around.

"Who are you and what are you doing at my house?" I replied.

"I followed you from Rush's concert. The security wouldn't let me through but I saw that you were able to go to his room. I figured you had to be special to him. Anyways, I need to get in contact with him. It's very important, I'll even pay you," she said.

"What is your name?" I asked.

"Kimberly, please let me in before he finds me," she said.

"Before who finds you?" I asked.

"My husband!" she cried.

Something was very strange about Kimberly but I couldn't ignore the bruises on her face. She also had a few teeth missing and her right eye was swollen. I didn't know who she was to Rush but she needed my help.

"Come on," I said.

Kimberly followed me into my house after I unlocked the door.

"You have a beautiful home. You're that chef that has a cooking show on YouTube?" she asked.

"Yup, that's me. Come have a seat. Do you need anything?"

"No, thank you. I don't have much time. So, are you and Rush dating or something?" she asked when I sat on the other end of the couch.

"Yes, we're dating. How are you two connected?" I asked.

"We had a daughter together. I came here to tell him she passed away two weeks ago. She was born with complications," she said.

"Wait a damn minute. Rush didn't tell me about a child," I replied.

"He doesn't know she belonged to him. I cheated on my boyfriend with Rush and instead of leaving me, he took on the role as a father. I lived in Canada but we lost our home because of the high medical bills we had for Kara. We're staying with a family member in Pennsylvania. My husband has been beating me since I was pregnant but he really loved Kara. The final straw was when she died and I begged him to let Rush spend her final days with her. I think he's going to kill me so I want Rush to know about Kara before it's too late. Tell him I'm very sorry for everything I've done. I took advantage of him when I should've known better but Rush is very easy to talk to. My husband was shooting blanks and I wanted a baby so bad that I slept with a seventeen-year-old. I was twenty-eight at the time. My uncle threatened to tell Rush about Kara because she needed a blood transfusion but my husband didn't want Rush involved in anything. My husband made me pay my uncle James money whenever he asked for it so he wouldn't tell anyone. I know you think I'm an evil person, maybe even sick, but I wanted to please my husband so much that I seduced a teenager. Funny how life turns out because my daughter was born with a very weak heart and her lungs weren't fully developed so she needed an oxygen machine. Her immune system was weak so she always had pneumonia. She had so many surgeries and the last one killed her. I blamed God for giving me a sick baby but it was my fault," she said.

Kimberly appeared to be sincere in the beginning but something was odd about her story. I believed what she said about Kara but I doubted she wanted Rush to know about the child before she died. Kimberly was looking for something else.

"I'll be sure to tell him. Do you have a number where we can contact you?" I replied.

"I don't have nothing. I'm poor and this is the only outfit I have. Rush is the only person who can help me. All I need is five thousand dollars," she said.

Oh, wait a minute, bitch. You saw his fine ass in that video and now you know he is getting paid!

"I'll be sure to tell him you stopped by," I replied.

"Tell him to message Ebony Carlson but her name is Pudding Cake on Instagram. She's my cousin and she'll give me the message," she said.

"Okay, I'll be sure to tell him."

I walked her to the door and she thanked me again before I closed and locked it. Kimberly and her husband were probably in on it together after he beat her into milking Rush's pockets. I texted his phone, telling him to call me because it was an emergency.

Two days later...

"Add the flour into the mixer," I said to Hadley. We were making a double layer chocolate and coconut cake.

"Ugh, I don't like cooking," Hadley complained.

"A way to a man's heart is through his stomach but wait until you're thirty," I replied.

"Right, because Daddy will ruin it."

"You still haven't talked to Jared?"

"No, but we loved each other. I miss him and he was my best friend. All we ever did was kiss," she said.

"I hope you and Jared work it out so I can meet him."

"Daddy wants to get back with you. All he does is talk about you and how wonderful you are. He still loves you," she replied.

I picked up my phone off the counter to see if I had any messages or calls. Rush hadn't responded to any of my texts or even visited me.

I wonder if he ran into Kimberly and they're trying to reconcile.

The doorbell rang and Hadley went to answer the door. Jay walked into the kitchen moments later with Pepper in his arms.

"You missed Daddy, didn't you?" Jay asked Pepper.

"What are you doing here?" I asked.

"I didn't have shit to do so I stopped by. Is that okay with you?" he said.

"I'll be back. I have to get something from my car," Hadley said. She left me and Jay alone on purpose.

"How are things with you and Hadley? She's still upset about Jared."

"She'll have to get over that nigga. His family got a bad history and I don't want my daughter to be a part of that. Is protecting my daughter a problem?" he asked.

"No, but you need to find a better way of doing it. Accusing her of being sexually active because you saw her hugging a boy isn't the right way to handle the situation. You cannot base her life off your past. I trust her and maybe you should, too."

"I apologized to her for reacting that way but I don't regret letting that lil' nigga know that my daughter is off-limits. The situation is dead and Hadley isn't talking to him anymore so it is what it is," he said.

Jay's phone rang and he walked out the kitchen to answer the call.

"Yo, why do you keep calling me? I don't give a fuck about that shop! Call someone so they can fix the pipe or call that nigga Kareem up," Jay said. He hung up the phone and slammed it on the counter.

"That bitch keeps calling me about everything," he complained.

"That's what you deal with when you think with your dick. Pass me that milk over there, please." He handed me the cartoon of milk and I added it to the mixture.

"Who is the cake for?" Jay asked.

"For a football banquet. They'll pick it up tomorrow morning," I replied.

"You should get your own building so people won't know where you live," he said.

"I thought about it but I kinda like doing business from home. It's peaceful and I can function better," I replied.

"Tell me the truth, shorty. Were you and Rush fucking?" he asked. Jay asked me about Rush every day. I didn't deny it nor did I admit to it. I found ways to change the subject.

"Why do you want to know?"

"Because he's in this circle and I gotta see him when he comes around. It's embarrassing that a young nigga can make you happy when I couldn't. It's a slap in the face," he said.

"Hadley hasn't returned. Go check on her and see if she is okay."

"I texted her and told her to take Nana to the grocery store so we can talk," he replied.

"We talked already so I don't understand what's left to say. I'm only dealing with you to help you build your business back up again, that's it. There is nothing else to discuss if it isn't about that or Hadley."

Jay wrapped his arms around me and kissed my neck.

"How about I help you finish this up while we talk about that," he said. Jay changed the subject so we could discuss his new business plans. He expressed how much he wanted to open a restaurant and I thought that was a big step for him because he wasn't consistent.

Five hours later....

Hadley hadn't returned and Jay was still at my home. He was lying on the couch while drinking a beer. I asked myself how could I be content with him in my home after he betrayed me, but having him there reminded me of the good times we had in our relationship. It was eleven o'clock at night when I left Jay in the living room to take a shower. While I was in the shower, I thought about Rush. For the past few days I tried to make myself believe that I couldn't be with him in that way. Jay stepped into the shower and pinned me against the wall. He lifted my leg and licked the nape of my neck. It had been months since he'd been inside me and I wanted to feel him again. The body reacts how the mind thinks.

"I missed you so much," he said while kissing me. His hands groped my breasts and my nipples hardened for him. My pussy throbbed when he slipped my nipple into his mouth. He picked me up and my legs wrapped around him as we fervently kissed. Moments later, his dick poked at my entrance, squeezing to slide in. His fingers sank into the flesh of my buttocks when he pumped into me. He was slow and gentle. He kissed my tears away while I sobbed. Jay was deep inside of me, and even though my body craved him, he could no longer please me. I cried because I had the answer I'd been searching for. I was completely over Jay. In those months we were a part, I fell deeply in love with another man. Someone who paid attention to every detail on my body and always gave me his attention when I vented about the smallest thing. It was unexpected and I wasn't ashamed of him anymore. Jay moaned he was coming while his body jerked. After he was finished, he rested his chin on my shoulders, breathing heavily against neck.

"We can move slow. No rush," he said.

Nigga, you think there is no Rush.

We took a shower in silence then got out to dry off. Afterwards, I got in bed and Jay slid in beside me, wrapping his arm around my waist. He kissed me again before he went to sleep. I, on the other hand, was wide awake and staring at the ceiling.

What have I done? How can I tell Jay I'm completely over him without him thinking I'm bluffing?

****

Jay woke me up the next morning by placing kisses all over my face. I looked at the clock on my nightstand and it was almost ten o'clock. The doorbell rang, startling me.

"Wait, my client is here to pick up the cake. I gotta get that." He rolled off my body and I slid out the bed. I grabbed my robe and rushed to the door without looking at the screen. My jaw dropped when I snatched the door opened. Rush was standing in front of me with a bag of food.

"I bought you breakfast and hopefully we can talk about what happened a few days ago," he said.

"Why didn't you call or text me back?"

"Yoo, the night of the concert was crazy. A big-ass fight broke out. I lost my chain and my phone. I'm working on this new song so I've been in the studio the past few days," he explained.

"Yo, Isha, who is that?" Jay called out. He heard Rush's voice which was the only reason he came out of the bedroom. Rush dropped the food on the ground and pushed me out the way as he stepped into my home. Jay was standing in the hallway only wearing jeans. Jay and Rush stared each other down and I was terrified because Rush looked more than pissed off.

"Yo, why is this clown here?" Rush asked.

"Why are you here, muthafucka?" Jay replied.

"Wait, this is a big misunderstanding. Jay, can you leave so me and Rush can talk?"

"You want me to leave? Damn, what you about to fuck him while my nut still inside you?" Jay asked.

"You fucked this nigga?" Rush asked me.

"It wasn't like that. I wanted to know if I was over him and you weren't answering my calls so I thought we were over. A lot has happened these pasts few days. A chick named Kimberly came here looking for you. I'm so sorry, Rush. It won't happen again. I'm really over him and I love you."

"Oh, so you love this lil' nigga? What the fuck can he do for you, Isha? He's young enough to be with my daughter!" Jay yelled.

Rush charged into Jay and knocked him into the hallway wall. I screamed for them to stop while they threw blows at each other. Rush gave

Jay a mean left hook which made Jay's mouth bleed. They were trying to kill each other. Jay grabbed Rush by the throat and I pulled at his arm to let him go, but Jay pushed me and I tripped, hitting my head on a table. Rush slammed his fist into Jay's face then punched him in the ribs.

"STOP!" I cried.

They were ruining my house. Plants were on the floor and I had a few holes in my walls. I couldn't call the police so I called Tuchie. She answered the phone half-asleep.

"Please tell Stacy to come over here and break up this fight. Rush and Jay are fucking up my house!"

"WHAT? Why are they fighting?" she asked. I could hear her moving around in the background.

"Rush brought me breakfast while Jay was here. Please send someone!"

"Why is Rush bringing you breakfast?" she asked.

"Damn it, Tuchie! It's because I have been sleeping with him so please send someone!" I yelled into the phone. I hung up when I heard glass breaking. They were in my kitchen. I left the cake on the counter inside an electronic cake cover to keep it chilled.

"NOOOOOO!" I yelled when Rush slammed Jay onto the counter and the cake toppled over.

"I'm calling the police!" I lied.

They pulled away from each other with the mention of police. Rush's nose was bleeding and Jay's lips were swollen and bruised. He also had a bruise around his left eye.

"Fuck this, I'm out! I'm not fighting over no old-ass hoe," Rush said and walked past me. I ran after him, pulling at his shirt so I could explain.

"Jay kept coming on to me and it just happened. I swear it didn't mean a thing!"

"Fuck you! You cried about how that punk muthafucka dogged you out then turned around and gave him the pussy. We just fucked a week ago! You out here on some grown thot shit and expect me to listen to your dumb ass? That nigga had you on suicide watch and you go back to him?

Yo, like on some real shit, I don't fuck with hoes. I was just in yah fucking bed!" Rush yelled in my face.

"Pleaseeeee don't do this to me. I wasn't ready to tell Tuchie about us but she knows now. Everybody is going to know," I sobbed.

"Cry all you want because I'm not fucking with you like that. You know where I be if you really wanted to find a nigga. Go on back to your circus and keep fucking with that clown. That nigga stays making you look dumb. You outside barefoot with snot hanging out your nose," Rush said. My client parked on the street to pick up her cake. Rush got into his car and backed out the driveway, running over my mailbox. Jay came out the house fully dressed and told my client her cake was on the floor so the roaches could eat it.

"Roaches?" she asked Jay.

"Yeah, shorty got mad roaches and she licked the spoon while putting icing on your cake," Jay replied. I always knew Jay had petty ways but that was the worst I'd seen him. Not only did he ruin me when it came to relationships, but he was screwing up my business.

"Nigga, you mad because a twenty-year-old was fucking me better than you ever had and he beat your ass! The only roach I know is the one you have in your pants, bitch! And you're going broke. Is that why you caught an Uber over here? Trying to save up on gas?" I said.

"Where is my cake?" my client asked.

"He was mad at me and knocked the cake over. I'm so sorry to upset you but I'll give you your money back."

"You will be getting a low rating from me. This is the most unprofessional business I've dealt with and I will be contacting the health department," she said, peeking over my shoulder. My front door was wide open and it was a mess inside. She thought I had a dirty home.

"Do what you have to do but get the fuck away from my house!" I yelled at her and she ran to her car. Jay was walking down the street and I yelled after him.

"All you do is screw up my life!"

"And you keep letting me!" he yelled back.

I'd fallen for his trap once again. He didn't want me, he wanted me to be miserable like him. Jay also knew Rush was making me feel like myself again and just like that, I helped him take it away. I never wished death on a person, not even my worst enemy, but I wanted Jay dead because I didn't feel comfortable with him alive. Something wicked was inside him and he was finally showing himself.

An hour later...

Stacy and Tuchie came into my home while I was sweeping.

"Damn, they fucked this place up," Stacy said.

Tuchie looked at me and I told her to curse me out and whatever else she had to do later because I couldn't take anything else.

"Why didn't you say anything? And how long has this been going on?" she asked.

"It started the day he came over here to help me unpack. I didn't want to hurt you, but I swear I wasn't expecting it to happen the way it did. In the beginning, I needed an escape from Jay, and Rush had everything I wanted in a man despite his age. I'm so sorry, Tuchie, but I've fallen in love with him," I admitted. Tuchie sat on a chair in disbelief. She was pregnant and I wanted to wait until I told her so she wouldn't be stressed.

"Are you sure you're in love with him or is he just a phase? I need to know before I overreact," she said.

"In the beginning, it was a phase. Jay's situation forced me to move on. I needed comfort and Rush gave it to me. I'm so sorry, Tuchie. My life is so fucked up to the point that I'll understand if you hate me or even beat my ass," I replied. Stacy took the broom away from me and told me he'd sweep the hallway so we could talk in private. We went into the living room to talk.

"I hope Rush whipped his ass," she said.

"He messed up Jay's face pretty bad. You can see everything on Jay's skin."

"I'm not mad at you. I'm just a little concerned for you. I don't want you forcing yourself to do something to get over someone. If Rush is what you really want, I'll respect it. If he's just a piece of dick, then I can't. At the end of the day, he's still my son and I'll feel some type of way if an older woman is taking advantage of his feelings. So, let's carefully think about this," she said.

"I thought about it last night and realized how much I care for him. I'll agree that it's the wrong timing but there is nothing I can do about that. I'm so damn embarrassed. Look at my home."

"Me and Stacy are going to help you clean this up," she said.

Everything seemed like a dream. Tuchie was being too calm about the situation and I didn't know how to take it.

"This isn't like you. You're not going to curse me out?" I asked and she chuckled.

"For what? He has been through a lot, so the last thing I want to do is get involved so he can hate me for it. I know what type of woman you are and I'm not worried. Now, if I raised him since birth and we had that mother-son bond, honey, me and you would've been throwing down. I've known you since you were a teenager. Rush was ten when I met you so imagine you coming around when he was that age. Now that's uncomfortable. I have to accept that all I can do is be his friend at this point because his mind is already made up about me," she said.

"He'll come around. But in the meantime, I have to fix this house up before the health department comes. Jay really tried me today. I seriously can't stand that clear bitch," I replied.

We talked for twenty minutes. I told Tuchie everything and didn't hold anything back. The weight of the world was lifted off my shoulders. My relationship with Rush was no longer a burden on my life or my friendship with Tuchie.

****

Eight days later...

Jay hadn't called me since him and Rush got into it, but it didn't matter to me because he finally saw the picture. What bothered me was Hadley. Jay didn't want her to talk to me; she was the only way he could get to me. Jay needed professional help. I believed he had a few loose screws. As far as my business, my clients still wanted to work with me and even defended me on my YouTube channel in the comments. There were a few comments about me having roaches, but my loyal viewers weren't having it.

"You can do this," I said aloud.

I was sitting outside the studio. Tuchie talked Stacy into letting me in, even though Stacy didn't like visitors when his artists were busy. I checked my make-up in the mirror. There was a lot of sadness behind it. I was wearing a long-sleeve jean distress jumper with a pair of nude pumps. My hair was styled in cornrows—everyone was calling the style Lemonade braids. I stepped out of my car and headed towards the building. I wanted to talk to him days ago, but I had a lot going on. My head had to be clear when I approached Rush because he was difficult to talk to when he was upset. Security let me into the building, and two of them escorted me to the recording room. When the door opened, a cloud of smoke blew into my face. I waved my hand in front of my face to keep the smoke from going down my throat. Rush was sitting on the couch writing in his pad. Fendi was in the recording booth and Stacy was on the computer. Before Stacy and Tuchie got back together, he kept a lot of females in his studio. The only females that were allowed in there now were the ones who was with the label. Rush looked up from his notebook when Stacy tapped him on his leg. I wanted to run back to my car when he grilled me. He saw me as the enemy and I had no one to blame but myself.

God, please get me through this. Just show me the way and I'll follow.

Rush

*D*amn, she's so fucking beautiful.

Isha was standing in front of me with tear-filled eyes. I wasn't the type of nigga to put my hands on a woman, but I wanted to knock her clean the fuck out. She knew what she was doing by coming to the studio and wearing the perfume I liked on her. Isha's outfit hugged her hips and she had a gap between her legs. Just one glimpse of her had me weak and ready to give in and make her mine. I had a feeling she was going to go back and fuck that nigga—it always happens after people break up. But I fell for her and the shit had me about to merk something. That nigga Jay was about to catch a hot one to his dome. His pussy ass kept saying slick shit about me like he knew me. He must've thought I couldn't hear his punk ass begging Isha on the phone while I was in bed with her. Instead of her saying she was with me, she'd pretend like she was alone. I let it slide so many times but that shit was dead.

"RUSH!" she called out while I was thinking.

"Yo, why are you here?" I asked.

"Can we go outside and talk? I promise I'll leave you alone after this. All I want to do is explain what happened," she said.

"I already know what happened, Ish. But the problem is I don't give a fuck. Now, go on about your business and let me work," I replied.

She walked away from me and out the recording room. Honestly, I felt a knife piercing through my chest from degrading her in that way.

"FUCK!" I said aloud. I slammed my notebook on the couch and walked out the recording room. Her heels were clicking down the hallway as she rushed out the building. I jogged out behind her and caught her in the parking lot. I grabbed her around the waist and pulled her into me. She turned around and wrapped her arms around my neck while burying her face in my chest.

"Can we please be friends again? I miss you and I promise I'll do better. I'm not ashamed of you, I was ashamed of myself and didn't want anyone to think I was a whore or had low self-esteem because of how fast I moved on," her voice trembled. I pulled away from her and she wiped her eyes.

"What do you want me to say? Yo, that shit hurt me, especially how easy it was for you to jump in bed with that nigga. I wasn't ready for this, neither, but it happened. I saw how fucked up you were when he left you, and for some reason, I wanted to make you feel better without being your man. Being with you helped me, too, because I saw how hard a woman loves and us niggas don't be appreciating that shit. Females be throwing themselves at me, especially now since Stacy put me on. But I'm not even with that shit because I wanted to prove to you that a nigga my age is capable of being a good nigga."

"What can I do to fix this?" she asked.

"Get that nigga out your system then come holla at me."

"He's out of my system. I'm so done with him," she said.

"You said that so many times, Ish. You're not done with him yet. You might just be mad at him but he'll come back and you'll be right there for him. Holla at me when that nigga stops calling you and coming to your crib whenever he feels like it. Plus, I have a few things to take care of myself. Time ain't on our side right now," I said. She stood on her tippy-toes to kiss me and I hugged her. I pulled away from her and opened her car door.

"I love you," she said.

"Love you, too."

I closed her door after she got in and started the engine. When I headed back to the studio, I almost got choked up because being with Isha was a different experience. She was the type of woman that left a stamp on niggas. Jay knew it, too, which was why he couldn't leave her alone.

"You good?" Stacy asked me when I came back to the recording room.

"Yeah, I'm straight."

"Did you hit up Kimberly?" he asked.

"Yeah, I'm gonna meet up with her tomorrow in South Carolina. I'm not trying to, though, because that bitch is shady," I replied.

Isha mentioned something to me about Kimberly coming to her house. Something told me to check my social media. It took days to go through my messages until I came across a woman stating she was Kimberly's cousin and she was messaging me for her. She told me my daughter passed away and Kimberly wanted to tell me. I didn't know how to feel because I only saw pictures of my daughter. I sent my number to her cousin and Kimberly called me the next day, asking to meet up with me. The messed-up part about it is that I didn't want to meet Kimberly but I wanted to know why she dogged me out that way. I had bad luck with the women in my life.

The next day...

I caught an Uber to Thomasine's house. Being in Maryland made all the houses look small on the small road where she lived. Kimberly told me she moved with her when she called me. She made it known she was getting a divorce from her abusive husband. The Uber pulled off after I stepped out the car. I stood in front the house asking myself why did I come back home. I hadn't talked to my mother in months. I could've gotten merked and she wouldn't have known. The front door opened and Kimberly stepped out. She didn't look anything like she did three years ago. Kimberly ran down the steps and into my arms. She pressed her breasts against my chest, telling me how much she missed me. I pushed her off and she fell on the ground, looking at me in confusion.

"Yo, don't fuckin' touch me. Where is Thomasine?"

"She's in the house, cooking. Today is James's birthday. Did you forget?" she asked. I ignored her and walked into the house. I heard dishes moving around in the kitchen. Thomasine's back was towards me while she was stirring something in the pot.

"Hey, Ma," I called out to her.

She turned around and dropped the spoon on the floor. Thomasine wasn't happy to see me. I wondered what had I done to her for her dislike me.

"What are you doing here? Did anyone follow you here?" she asked and ran to the window.

"Why would someone follow me?"

"The same reason why they followed you here and killed my husband," she said.

"Kimberly wanted me to come here, but I'll leave if you want me to."

"Yes, please go. My home has been so peaceful since you left," she said.

"Why do you hate me so much, Ma? You're the only mother I have and you just turned your back on me. I'm not leaving until you tell me what I've done. You're worried about some nigga that didn't take care of you? He used to get drunk and push you around! I don't matter to you anymore?" I asked.

"You matter to me but I loved my husband and you're the reason he's dead. I sent you home in hopes of not seeing or hearing from you again. I gave you my final goodbye. Let your real mother love you. I can't find it in my body to forgive you. I'll always love you but I'll never forgive you, so please leave my house! I'll pray for you from a distance," she said.

"Cool, I came here to see Kimberly anyway," I replied.

Kimberly came into the kitchen and sat at the table. Thomasine looked at her then looked at me.

"You told him, didn't you?" Thomasine asked.

"Yes, I had to. We don't have any money. We gave it all to you and James to keep y'all's mouths shut," she said.

"You knew about Kara?" I asked Thomasine.

"Yes, she knew. Which is the real reason why she wanted you to leave because I was coming back home. They weren't really broke, my husband took care of them so they wouldn't tell you about Kara. We didn't want you to know because my husband is connected to a wealthy family. The only way my husband could inherit his father's law firm was to have a baby so the company could get passed down. My husband is the only child so it was a must he marry me and start a family. We had a lot of financial problems after she was born. We lost everything and moved to Pennsylvania. Please help me. I don't have nothing," Kimberly said.

"You little bitch!" Thomasine yelled at Kimberly.

"KARA IS DEAD! Why keep hiding the truth? I'm sick of it! I'm homeless because of y'all milking our pockets. We had nothing left after her hospital bills," Kimberly said.

"I offered you a home!" Thomasine said.

"Fuck all this! What did you tell Isha?" I asked Kimberly.

"I told her half the truth. I figured if I sounded pathetic she'd let me into her home and feel sorry enough for her to tell you I visited her. But I wanted you to come here so I could give you her ashes, but it'll cost. I need the money to get away from my husband. He knows where Thomasine lives," she said.

"Yoooo, this shit is too funny. So, all this is about selling me her ashes? All your fake pleas about your husband is to get me feel sorry for you? Why now? Because you saw two videos of me floating around and think I got all this money, right? I haven't got paid yet! I should knock you on your ass for making me waste money for a plane ticket!" I yelled at her.

Money was the root of everything. My mother hid a secret from me so she and her husband could get paid. I sold drugs so she could pay the bills but all along she had money but was afraid to tell me so I wouldn't know where it came from. Kimberly wanted to sell ashes of a person I had never met before. Those ashes weren't sentimental to me.

"It's not what you think and you were better off not knowing. You were a teenager who impregnated an older woman who was already established in her life. What could you have done with a sick baby? Take care of her with drug money? I was protecting you so you wouldn't be a teen parent like your mother. Now look at you. You are going to be a star. A sick baby wouldn't have gotten you this far. Kimberly's husband, Isaac, had the ability to step up to the plate and take that burden off your back," Thomasine said.

"I'm out. I appreciate you for taking care of me, but I'll never come back. My real family is in Maryland. Love comes before money. It took me to leave home to see how fucked up y'all are. I gotta go," I replied.

Kimberly ran out the house after me, begging me to give her twenty dollars.

"You want twenty dollars, huh? Aight, work for it then," I replied. I pulled her behind the tree and told her to get on her knees.

"Yo, suck my dick and hurry up because my Uber about to pull up." She got down on her knees and I pulled my dick out. Kimberly showed signs of being a drug addict. She was ready to put my dick in her mouth but I snatched it back so fast I almost snapped my piece off.

"You a crackhead, huh? Gotta be if you're trying to sell your daughter's ashes. Where is your husband at and tell the truth! You keep lying about everything! Where is that nigga at?" I asked while jacking her up against the tree. Kimberly scratched at my arm so I could let her go, but I tightened the grip I had around her neck.

"I'll kill you if you don't tell me the truth!"

"I—can't—breathe," she gasped.

I released her and she dropped to her knees with tears falling from her eyes.

"I have an addiction and my husband left me! I've been following you so I could get some money. Kara was getting so sick that I couldn't handle it so I started using pain pills. When I could no longer afford it, I began smoking crack. My husband beat my ass because I stole a lot of money. We lost everything because of my addiction. Thomasine offered to help me go to the rehab through her church. I'm so sorry, Rush. I'm sorry! I just want to get high!" she cried.

"Yo, you told so many stories!"

"This is the truth! I'm practically homeless. My cousin paid for a Greyhound ticket so I could come here. I lost everything because of my addiction. So, I've been telling everyone my husband is abusive and people feel sorry for me and give me money, but I can't help it. It's so hard," she cried. I went inside my pocket and gave Kimberly one-hundred dollars.

"Hopefully this will hold you. You shouldn't be out here trying to suck dick for twenty dollars," I replied.

"Thank you so much. I'm going to get clean after I smoke this up," she said. Kimberly ran off to the back of the house like a hyena. I remembered a time when she was beautiful, but her looks and body were gone. She looked around sixty years old in the face and ninety in the body.

My Uber pulled up and I got in the backseat. I was supposed to chill in South Carolina for a few days before I headed back to Maryland, but I told the driver to take me to the airport. I never had a life there, and I didn't start living until I saw my mother, Tuchie for the first time.

Four days later...

I was chilling around in my crib while writing. Since I left South Carolina, I'd been in grind mode. Isha told me music sounded better when the singer poured their true feelings out. I put a little of everything I'd experienced in a song called, "Broken Glass." The title was cheesy as shit, but it meant a lot to me. I wanted to pick up the phone and call Isha to see what she was doing but I couldn't. My doorbell rang while I was dotting down lyrics. I went to the door and looked out the peephole. When I opened the door, Niji ran into my crib and jumped on the couch.

"Yo, get yah ass down!" I yelled and she burst out laughing. Tuchie stepped into my crib with a bag of food.

"You missed family dinner so I brought it to you," she said.

"Appreciate it, can you heat it up for me? I'm starving."

"You don't stay here much?" she asked, looking around.

"Naw, I was always at Isha's crib. I need to fix it up a little better."

"Or you can come live with us. The basement is set up like a condo and it's already furnished," Tuchie replied.

"No, thanks. I'm good. I'll come visit, though."

Niji was walking around my crib playing inspector gadget.

"Everyone knows you were dating Isha," she said. Tuchie yelled at her and told her to stay out of it.

"I love Isha," Niji said.

"Go in the room and watch TV so I can talk to your brother," Tuchie replied.

I turned a movie on for Niji in my bedroom. She whispered she didn't watch cartoons anymore. She wanted to watch *Love and Hip Hop* On Demand.

"Hell no. Why you want to be so grown?"

"Grandma lets me watch it with her and her friends all the time. She even lets me gossip about my stuck-up friends at school. Shut the door and I'll keep quiet," she said.

"Hell no. Which grandmother? Can't be Stacy's mother," I replied.

"Mommy's mother. Don't tell anyone. This is between us," she said.

"No, you're not watching that sh—I mean junk. I don't even watch that. It's a bad influence on young girls," I replied.

"But the tea is hot," she said.

I put it on the Disney channel and took the remotes out the room. Tuchie was sitting at my kitchen table across from my plate. I hadn't had soul food in a minute. Isha cooked a lot but her dishes were fancy and probably cost over a hundred dollars at the restaurant.

On my plate was catfish and gravy over rice, with greens and homemade macaroni. She also bought me over two thick slices of pineapple upside down cake.

"Who made this?"

"Me and Asayi. We're the soul food cooks. If you want something you can't pronounce, Isha steps in," she laughed.

"This is good. Appreciate it."

We sat in silence for a while as I smashed my food. It was too good, I wanted another plate. I gained ten pounds since I moved to Maryland.

"I heard you went to see Thomasine. How did it go?" she asked.

"A lot happened."

"Do you want to talk about it?" she replied.

Tuchie listened while I told her what happened with Kimberly and Thomasine. We even talked about Isha and the situation that happened between me and Jay. It's crazy how so much can happen in a person's life in a short period of time.

"Living is to feel life. The only time you feel nothing is when you're dead. Sometimes you have to remind yourself that whatever you are going through is better than being six feet under," she said.

"I can dig it. I apologize for not understanding your situation when you had to pass me up. Thomasine raised me and I felt like I was betraying her by getting to know you so I held back. I didn't want to discredit her. It took for me to leave in order to figure out all the pieces to the puzzle. I'm thankful you came and pulled me out that situation because I got back in touch with what I wanted to do as far as music."

"I never stopped caring about you," she said.

"No doubt."

"But I'll see you at the wedding Friday. I gotta go home and help clean up. You're always welcome to come home. You don't have to live here by yourself," she replied.

"I'll keep that in mind."

She stood from the table and I walked over to her and hugged her.

"I know I should be minding my business, but Isha is feeling down. Maybe you should call her to see how she's doing," Tuchie said.

"She'll be fine. She'll get over me in no time, but right now I'm focused on this music stuff."

"I know how you really feel. I wasn't a forgiving person myself and made Stacy wait for a long time. You'll regret this because time passes by fast. Me and Stacy could've been married with more kids by now. So, if you care for her, go for it," she said.

"What's the catch?" I chuckled.

"Seeing Jay's bitch-ass suffer."

Tuchie called out to Niji and told her to come on because she was ready to leave. Niji came out the room stomping her feet because she didn't want to go.

"I was watching TV," Niji said.

"You have one at home. Hug your brother goodbye so we can go," Tuchie said. Niji hugged me and I kissed her forehead before they left. I went back to my couch and picked up my notebook to write. Isha's smile penetrated my thoughts and I couldn't concentrate.

Why is she so fucking addictive?

I slammed the notebook on the coffee table in frustration. She wasn't my girl or nothing like that when she fucked that nigga. Tired of thinking about it, I took a shower and got dressed. I grabbed the keys to my new convertible Range Rover and headed out the door.

****

Why am I here? Go back and forget about her! She'll never get over that fuck-nigga.

I was fighting with myself while I stood in front of her door. We had something special and it ended too soon. I wasn't sure how we were going to turn out but that's what kept me coming back. It was the curiosity. My heart almost beat out of my chest when I rang the doorbell. Seconds later, the door opened and it was an older woman. She resembled Isha a lot but she had gray in her hair.

"May I help you?" she asked.

"Umm, I'm looking for Isha," I replied.

"She ran out to the store with her father."

That's why her car is in the driveway.

"Okay, I'll come by tomorrow," I replied.

I turned to leave but the woman called out to me.

"Is your name Rush?" she asked.

"Yes, Ma'am," I replied.

"Boy, get in here," she said. She held the door open for me when I entered the house.

"I'm Isha's mother, Miriam. I've heard a lot about you. Me and her father travel a lot. After we retired, we bought a boat. We travel so much we don't have time to see our little girl. Anyways, come and have a seat," she said. I followed her to the living room. Isha's home was back in tact, even the hole in the wall was fixed.

"So, you're twenty years old?"

"Yes, Ma'am," I replied.

"You don't look it, but anyways, I'm not here to judge. I've always told Isha that the only men who were off-limits are family members and young boys. Other than that, love doesn't pass judgement."

"She gave me a hard time in the beginning," I replied and she giggled.

"Isha has always been cautious when it comes to her heart which is why I'm upset behind Jadiah's actions. I've heard nothing but great things about you. Do you want something to drink? To eat?" she asked.

"No, thank you. I ate before I came."

"I heard you're a singer. We moved back home today so we'll be around. I told Isha I have to see you perform," she said. Isha's mother was the nicest woman I'd ever talked to and Isha had her personality.

"You can come anytime. I just can't give you backstage passes because a lot of things go down after the show."

"Oh, I can party, too. I was a wild peacock in my day," she said.

Isha's mother told me stories about her when she was a little girl. She also went into her purse to show me pictures of Isha when she had missing teeth and glasses.

"Isn't she adorable? I want a granddaughter to look like this. Are you hoping to have any kids?" she asked. The front door opened before I could answer her question.

"Hey, ummm, what's going on?" Isha asked.

"Talking about you to your mother."

Her father came in with grocery bags and I helped him take the bags into the kitchen.

"Nice to meet you, son. My name is David. Did my wife talk your head off?" her father asked. We were in the kitchen putting the bags on the counter.

"Naw, she did put me on the spot though when she asked me about babies," I replied and he roared in laughter.

"I tell Miriam every day that Isha will have a baby when she's ready. I guess we came home right on time," he said.

Isha pulled me out the kitchen and into a bedroom in the hallway so we could talk.

"What are you doing here? I don't think I can take any more of your lashing out," she said.

"I planned on staying away but Tuchie scared my ass after she told me how much time she spent being angry with Stacy. I don't have that type of energy, especially when it comes to something I want. I don't regret fucking that nigga up. He kept bringing up my name on some sucka shit."

"I'm never going back and I mean it. We can take it slow but I know where I want to be," she said.

I pulled her into me and hugged her by gripping her ass cheeks. My face was buried into the crook of her neck and she smelled heavenly. She giggled when I kissed her neck.

"My parents are here," she said.

"I'm not trying to fuck. I just want to feel on my work. Where did this ass come from?" I asked. She pulled my face to hers and licked my lips.

"I want to wait a while before we have sex again. I'm detoxing my body from him," she said.

"Yeah, 'cause it's too soon. But I'm not worried about that right now. Just know I'm fucking those walls up when I do hit it. I'm taking ownership." She playfully punched me in the chest.

"But my mouth still works. I didn't go down on him," she flirted.

"I'll keep that in mind when your parents leave."

"They moved in. I begged them to come and live with me so I wouldn't be alone. This is their bedroom," she said.

"You can get the key to my crib. It needs a touch of life. Tuchie's mouth dropped when she saw how I was living."

"I'm about to be there every day," she said.

"We can finish this conversation later so your parents won't think I'm doing something to their daughter. We have to a lot to talk about, though."

SOUL Publications

She opened the door and we joined her parents in the kitchen. Isha and her mother were preparing dinner while her father was talking me into riding the boat with him one day.

"So, about these babies. We're in our sixties. I want to see grandkids before I turn senile. Just have one for us and the rest can come later. Me and your father need extra excitement in our lives," Miriam said.

"Me and Rush are only dating right now plus I'm on birth control," Isha said.

"Stop taking it then. Problem solved. Rush is a very handsome young man, I can picture a beautiful chocolate baby with fat cheeks. I'm having grandbaby fever. All my friends have grandkids, even great-grandkids. What do I have besides bug-eyed Pepper?" Miriam asked.

"Cut it out, Miriam. Isha is trying to open up her own catering business. A baby will put a stop to it," David said.

"That's where we come in," Miriam replied.

"Enough of this baby talk already," Isha said.

"Okay, fine. All I want to know is if Rush wants some babies and I'll let it go," Miriam said.

"As handsome as he is, I wonder why you're not pregnant now. You better cut this foolishness because you only live once. Go out with a bang," I heard Miriam whisper to Isha. David heard it, too, and told Miriam to lay off the Jack Daniel's.

"Don't mind my mother. She's just excited," Isha said in embarrassment.

"I want one a few years from now," I replied.

"And there you have it," Miriam said.

Isha winked at me while she was making deviled eggs.

I can definitely get used to this.

Sadi

One month later...

My mother walked into my bedroom holding Haden in her arms. She woke up so I could go to my shop. All I did was sleep to escape the deep depression I slipped in. I burned my house down to get rid of any evidence of Arnold, including getting rid of the rental car he was driving. I lost everything except for my expensive jewelry Jay bought me. It was either that or go to jail. Arnold made me snap—he was going to ruin everything I had. For years I'd been on the right track until Jay ruined my life. I was mad at everyone! Shelley called me all day and every day, crying about her missing husband. She couldn't go back home until the police found him. I couldn't sympathize with her because I was the one responsible for his death.

"Ma, I can't go to the shop," I replied.

"Get up, Sadi! You always do this shit when life throws you stones. What are you going to do? Get back on drugs? I have to go to work! I cannot and will not lose my job mothering your child!" my mother yelled at me. She laid Haden on the bed and stormed out my bedroom. Haden screamed at the top of his lungs. It sickened me how much he looked like Kareem's fat ass. I picked Haden up and placed him inside his crib so I could shower. While I was in the bathroom, I called Jay's phone for the hundredth time. I needed some money to get Haden a few things. My shop wasn't doing too good because I was too stressed to wake up and open the door for the stylists. Three of them quit and there was only one left who was the part-time shampoo girl. I cried when he didn't answer the phone. There was only a thousand dollars left to my name which wasn't going to last long. Haden's screams made me cry even harder. It wasn't a secret that I was going through post-partum depression. I'd been going through it since the moment I had him. Maybe because in the back of my mind, I had a feeling he belonged to Kareem. I took a shower and got dressed in leggings with one of my father's old baseball T-shirts. I grabbed my purse, shoes and jean jacket and stormed out the door.

SOUL Publications

The drive to my shop was long from my parents' house. By the time I arrived, two people were standing outside. One girl frowned her nose up at me because of what I had on.

"Is Diamond working this morning?" she asked.

"She quit but I can take you. What are you trying to get done?"

"Never mind. She's the only one who can treat my hair right," she said and walked off.

"I just want a perm and curls," the one left standing said.

I unlocked the door then turned off the alarm. She sat in the chair at my station while I grabbed things to perm her hair.

"Oh shit!" I yelled out.

"What?" she asked.

"I left my baby home," I panicked.

"Who is in the house with your baby?"

"Nobody," I replied.

"Well, honey, I will have to report you. I work for social services," she said.

"You're shitting me," I cried.

She pulled her name tag from behind her blazer so I could see it. I heard Adele's voice in my head, telling me that karma was out for me and Jay.

"Bitch, whatever. I'm out of here," I replied.

I ran out the shop and got in my car so I could get to my baby, but I ran right into traffic on route 50. So much was on my mind I thought my head was going to explode. Maybe I was better off without Haden. Jay wasn't talking to me because I declined his DNA test which was pointless. With no other choice, I called the one person I didn't want to.

"Hello," he answered.

"Hey, this Sadi."

"What are you calling me for?" he spat.

"To talk about Haden. I can't do this anymore. I'm sorry, Kareem, but you have to keep him for a while. I'm not emotionally capable of being a mother. I'm having bad thoughts. He looks just like you. I'm sitting in traffic, trying to get to my parents' house. I rushed out the house to open my shop and left him in his crib. I'm unfit. I thought I was going to love him because I was in a good place when I got pregnant but everything faded away. Please just come and get him. I'll do whatever you want me to do," I cried. It pained me to betray another child of mine but parenting wasn't in me. I thought the feeling would disappear since I was clean but drugs had nothing to do with it.

"Give me the address. I've been in Maryland for two days to help Shelley look for Arnold. I'll be right there!" he said and hung up.

It took me an hour and fifteen minutes to get to my parents' house. My father's pick-up was in the driveway and I breathed a sigh of relief. I got out my car and ran into the house. My father was in the living room feeding Haden his bottle.

"I'm so sorry, Daddy," I said.

"I'm sorry for failing you. I'm not perfect but everything I did was because of how much I loved you. You have my ways, too many of them, which is why it's hard for me to look at you. I tried to keep this secret from you but when I came home to grab my wallet and saw Haden in his crib alone... You abandoned your child, Sadi. You don't want him? Do not be like me," he said.

"What are you talking about?"

"I used to be a functional addict. I was sniffing coke until you were three years old. Your mother found out and told me she'd leave me and take you if I didn't stop, so I got myself together. While I was getting high, I was having an affair with this woman named Melinda. She gave birth to a little girl named Joy. She would be a few years younger than you if she was still living. For years I pretended she didn't exist because she reminded me of the days when I was at my lowest. Her mother had six other kids which she lost to the system because of her addiction, but I was so gone I impregnated her anyway. Joy didn't have new shoes or clothes while I was spending my last dollars to make up for what I'd done to you and your mother. She looked so much like you and so does her daughter," he said.

"Daddy, please don't tell me what I think you're going to tell me! Please don't fucking tell me!" I screamed.

"Hadley is my granddaughter. I knew who she was at the hospital when you gave birth to Haden. She looks so much like her mother. Do not neglect your son, Sadi. Do not be like me. Your son will grow up hating you, and if something happens to him, you'll live in misery for the rest of your life. I'm begging you to be strong and fight this," he said.

"You don't get it! Jay only wanted me because he can't let her go. He never loved me! I was reminding him of her every day. He called you a deadbeat and now I see why. Does Mother know?" I asked.

"Yes, she found out after Joy was killed. A family member knocked on the door and told me to come to her funeral but I couldn't. Me and your mother haven't been happy for years but we hid it from you. We fell in love again when you were getting high, it brought us back together," he said.

"I was born with your karma and for years you said nothing!" I sobbed.

The doorbell rang and I answered the door. Kareem was standing in front of me. He stepped into the house and my father stood up with Haden in his arms.

"Daddy, this is Haden's real father," I introduced them.

Kareem walked past me and took his son out of my father's arms. My father excused himself and went upstairs to give us some alone time. Kareem sat on the couch with Haden, observing him.

"You took this away from me. Ran off to Maryland because you knew there was a possibility of me being his father. I'm not rich but I would've loved the shit out of you. Now I have to explain to my girlfriend that I have a baby," he said.

Nigga, nobody wants you!

"I'm sure it happened before her, so she'll deal with it. I'll sign anything you want me to. A social worker or someone from the state might build a case against me. I don't need all that right now until I get some kind of help. Please, take him and give him the happy family he deserves," I said.

Kareem got up from the couch and sat next to me. He wrapped his arm around me and squeezed me tightly.

"I'll take good care of him. Please just get the help you need. The only person who is holding you back from being a mother is yourself. I need his records. We can worry about changing his last name later. Soon, we will have to settle this in front of a judge so I can have legal custody over him, but in the meantime, I'll keep him," he said. I hugged Kareem like my life depended on it.

"You're a good man, Kareem. I know you might not believe me, but I made myself dislike you because you're too good for me. I needed someone who was just as flawed as I was and I'm so sorry. We would've never worked."

"Yeah, I see that. But we can be friends. In the meantime, are you hungry? We can grab something to eat while you tell me what I need to know. I'm nervous about this," he said.

"You don't want to eat with me, Kareem."

"I'm starving, plus this isn't a date. I would like to know more about my son before I take him to Atlanta with me. You can't send me out there like this," he said.

"Okay."

I ran upstairs to grab Haden's diaper bag and a change of clothes. My father was standing in the doorway of his bedroom.

"Make the right decision, Sadi. I can't control what you do with him, but raise your son the right way," he said.

"Being with a man like Kareem is the right way. He comes from a great home and he's educated."

"Be careful," my father said. He went into his bedroom and closed the door.

****

"How is the search for Arnold coming along?" I asked while chewing my shrimp. We were at a steak house and Kareem ordered a lot of food. I wasn't a heavy eater but I devoured a lot of food.

"It's getting nowhere," he said.

"Maybe he left Shelley to be with someone else."

"Naw, something bad happened to him. They found his rental car in the woods with his bloody shirt inside," he said. I took Arnold's shirt off and threw it in the car before I ditched it. The authorities thought he was kidnapped or had a secret life. It didn't matter what they found, they couldn't blame it on me. My house and my neighbor's house burned to the ground. The fire department couldn't figure out which house started the fire because they were townhomes. I was waiting for my insurance check to get mailed to my parents' house because I definitely needed the money.

"I will keep him in my prayers."

Kareem was a better listener than I thought, so I eventually broke down and told him my life story and how it led to being engaged to Jay. When I look back at it, my life was a fraud. All I did was pretend to be this sane person when deep down I had issues. When I think I figured out how love works, it knocks me on the ass. I thought I loved Stacy, Tae and Jay but they all shitted on me some type of way, but they all had one thing in common—they gave me what I needed. Stacy bought me my first Mercedes, Tae had me hooked on a drug that I couldn't go without and Jay gave me the lavish lifestyle a woman could ask for. I would've never had my own business if Jay didn't offer me a shop. What Kareem could offer me is time, love, passion and everything else a woman needed emotionally.

"So, tell me about this girlfriend."

"She's someone I met at church. We've been dating for five months now. She's nice and we're happy," he said. Haden cried and Kareem took him out his carrier to pat his back.

"You're learning already."

"I'm a fast learner," he replied.

"SADI!" a voice called out. When I turned around, my aunt Kya was standing behind me. I'd been back home for months and was just running into the bitch. Kya was a troublemaker. She was forty years old and looked younger than me. She still had pretty blemish-free dark skin and a bad-ass shape.

"What do you want?"

"Stand up so I can hug you. I've been asking about you for months. I hope you're still not mad at me about what happened a while back. I'm not that person anymore. Your mother told me you weren't ready to see me so I stayed away. Can we hook up one day and talk?" she replied.

"No, we cannot. You were the cause of so many problems. You are the one who made me turn against Asayi and made me believe Stacy was cheating on me so I could be with Tae. You did all of that because you wanted Stacy for yourself. Stay away from me!"

"People change and I thought you did, too. You're still the same spoiled brat that can't survive without her daddy's help. From the looks of your clothes, maybe you're still that same coked-out whore. Good day," she said then strutted off.

"Whoa, she's feisty," Kareem said.

Kya was always a bully and she had beef with all the girls in the hood. I lost my appetite and told Kareem to get the check. Kya had me furious. Kareem placed five twenties on the table and I grabbed Haden and held him against my chest while Kareem carried his carrier. Moments later, Kareem pulled up to my parents' house and we sat for a minute in silence. I looked over my shoulder and stared at Haden's cute little face. He deserved better.

"Well, this is it," I replied.

"I'm going to drive to Atlanta with a rental instead of catching a flight back with him. Listen, you can pack up your things and come to Atlanta with me. Why are you here anyway? With everything you told me, you should've never left. Seems like Maryland is trying to take you back to your old ways. You can get your job back at the shop and we can raise Haden in a two-parent home," he said.

"What about your girlfriend?"

"This is more important, but you have to let go of this past and be a mother to the innocent life in the back seat. The church I go to has a program for people who are still affected by drug use.

Look, I'm going to be a pastor in a few years. I've been going to school for a degree in Christian Ministry for three years. I'll be done in less than a year so I can take the next step to becoming a pastor. I can get you the help you need. Just come back to Atlanta," he said.

"I've been so mean to you. I even used you for sex to get back at Jay."

"I believe underneath those layers is a godly woman. You just need the right man to peel them for you. Come with me so we can get you together," he said.

"Okay, I'll go back but we need to leave now. I can't stay here one more day."

"You don't want to say goodbye to your parents?" he asked.

"No, I'll call them later. All of Haden's belongings are in his diaper bag and I don't have much because of the fire. My important papers are crammed into my purse. Let's just leave, please. My mother can send me what I left behind if there is something I missed."

"Shelley needs us here for a while," he said.

"She's not alone. Arnold has family here. Please, just go before I change my mind."

Kareem pulled off without further questions. Maybe I had been too shallow. There was a good man in my corner but I overlooked him because he wasn't my type. I looked back at my parents' house as he drove down the street. The car Jay bought me was still in the driveway. My mother could keep it. The truck got destroyed in the fire because it was parked in the garage. The money I am getting back from the fire is going to help me build my own shop in Atlanta. Fuck Jay's shop and anything else he paid for. Kareem grabbed my hand and kissed the back of it.

"I forgive you for everything. There will not be any judgment between us from here on out," he said.

Only time would tell if I could fall in love with a man like Kareem, but his kind words and big heart made me see the bigger picture. I could be a good mother and a better person if I pushed myself harder. The only person who was stopping me was myself. I closed my eyes and fell asleep to prepare myself for the thirteen-hour ride.

Jay

Three days later...

"Yo, wake up!" Bogo called out to me. I drank a bottle of D'ussé and passed out on my mother's couch. I was drinking every day so I wouldn't have to think about all the money I threw out to Sadi and Isha moving on with that lil' nigga, Rush. Hadley wasn't saying much to me and my mother was hollering about my soul not being cleansed. I was sick of hearing all that dark and creepy shit she believed. Bogo was checking up on me like I was a little kid. He had my old life, my old connect and more money.

"Naw, I'm good."

"Yo, get yah ass up! What in the fuck are you doing? What, you a bum-ass nigga now or sumthin? Why you on your mother's couch?" he asked. I got up and pushed him into the wall.

"Nigga, you must've forgotten who put you on! You weren't a fuckin' hustla. You were only good for merkin' niggas. I built this shit then handed it to you so who's a bum-ass nigga?"

"Yo, Trayon put you on by getting out the game! I guess you forgot Hamisi only fucked with you because he had respect for Trayon. You ain't put in no fucking work! I was the one who was doing shit and making moves so you could chase that coked-out bitch! Want to know what else? I talked Hamisi out of merking your dumb ass for pulling that shit with his brother! My nigga, don't get on my bad side. I'm trying to look out for you," he said.

"Yo, just go home."

I went into the kitchen, looking for something else to drink so I could go back to sleep.

"I got five-hundred g's in my trunk right now if you need it, bruh. This ain't us. All you have to do is say the word and it's yours. You could go to jail for not paying your business taxes," he said.

"I let go of all my businesses to start over. My landscaping business, car wash, liquor store, beauty supply stores and all that shit is closed. I gave Isha the money I was going to pay my taxes with so she could have something to fall back on. I went broke in a year just like that. I don't have shit else. Isha's new nigga got more than me. I'm sick of hearing his bitch-ass voice on every radio station. Yo, I failed. I failed and I can't come out of this."

"Take the money and start over. It's not hard. Start off with one business then slowly invest into another one. You had so many at one time and couldn't keep up, you let them run themselves and you weren't checking up on shit. Yo, you gotta move smarter or this situation is going to kill you. You used to turn a dollar out of fifty cents when we were young niggas. Bring that nigga back and get to this money. My mother had us living in this old-ass house in the woods like we were back in time. We had to get water from a well and shit in a fucking bucket! All we ate was potatoes and bread. I was six years old and still was the happiest nigga alive because I knew I was going to have a lot of shit. You crying over spilled milk, Jay. Clean yourself up so we can go to Lim and Chika's wedding," he said.

I was wondering why this nigga was wearing a tuxedo.

"Yo, fuck Chika. I hate that bitch."

"Your tuxedo is in my whip. Go upstairs and clean yourself up because we only got two hours," he said. I went upstairs to shower and shave. Sadi was stalling on giving me a DNA test for Haden. Shorty knew that wasn't my son and milked my ass dry. She wanted a secure life before I left her. After I realized how fucked up she was, I believed my mother when she told me Sadi knew I had a woman. She let me feel guilty about the situation even though she seduced me. I bought her nice things 'cause of that guilt and she betrayed me in the worse way. While I was brushing my teeth, I thought of five ways to kill that airhead. But I couldn't stop thinking about Isha. Thoughts of her were eating at my brain cells, clouding my better judgement. I dreamed about her and the scent of her perfume was still in my nose. Letting her go was the only way I could get better but I couldn't. I hadn't thought of Joy since Isha chose Rush over me.

I'll merk that bitch if I have to think about her the same amount of time I thought of Joy. I'm not going down that road again.

****

Lim and Chika's wedding was hood because of Chika's side of the family. One of her family members brought a Pitbull to the wedding reception and it bit her great aunt. Isha was sitting at the table with Tuchie, Asayi and a few other girls. Rush was sitting at the table with us, but he was across from me. Isha was blowing that nigga kisses and winking at him. Shorty never gave me that kind of attention and it was fucking with me because she was flaunting him in my face. She had me wondering if my dick game was whack, but Sadi never complained.

"Yo, you good?" Trayon asked.

"Yeah, I'm straight."

The fellas were talking and clowning around like always, but I couldn't keep my eyes off Isha. She was wearing a long gold and white off-the-shoulder gown. Her curls fell into her face each time she laughed. Loving someone after the relationship is over was the hardest shit known to man. Isha got up from the table after she realized I was staring at her. She headed towards the ladies' room. I waited a few seconds before I excused myself from the table. My boy, Lim, just got married and I couldn't be happy for him the way I wanted to. I'd been drinking since I left the house. I slipped a small bottle of Remy Martin in my tuxedo jacket. Drinking put me in a place where I had money and a loyal bitch. The women's bathroom was empty when I walked in, locking the door behind me. I walked past each stall and they were all empty, except for the last one. The toilet flushed then the stall door opened. Isha closed the door when she saw me and I snatched it away from her. She stood in the corner when I locked the door to the stall.

"You're crazy!" she screamed.

"Talk to me, shorty. Why you keep staring at the nigga and shit in my face? You trying to taunt me, aren't you? You gotta deal with me because we aren't over. We'll never be over!"

"Please get some help. You've lost your mind! I don't know what else is going on in your life but it's not my fault. You don't know how to let go," she replied.

I charged into Isha and she slapped me in the face. Fed up with her denying me, I slammed her face into the wall twice as she screamed for help.

"I'll kill you if you make one sound," I warned her because someone was banging on the door.

"My face is bleeding. Please, let me go. You're drunk," she cried.

I wasn't thinking about any consequences. Isha betrayed me and was purposely flaunting her nigga in my face, but I wasn't having it. Shorty thought I was a bitch nigga.

"Shut the fuck up!"

She punched me and ran out the stall but I caught her by her hair and slammed her head against the counter of the sink. Blood leaked from her head and ran down the cracks of the tile on the floor.

"ISHA! GET UP! I was just playing. Come on, baby, get up," I cried when she didn't move.

"ISHA, OPEN THE DOOR!" Rush yelled, banging on the door. I cradled her in my arms and rocked her back and forth.

"Who you in there with, Isha? Open the fucking door!" Rush banged. I heard other voices coming from outside the door. Maybe I should've sought help after watching bullets rip through my first love's body. I thought I was fine, but something inside of me snapped. My mother warned me, she saw the signs, but I ignored all of them. I just didn't give a fuck about anything and Hadley was better off without me.

"Tell Hadley I'm sorry!"

"Jay, please open the door! Is Isha hurt?" Tuchie asked.

"She's not breathing," I sobbed.

"What did you do? What in the hell did you do?" Tuchie screamed.

"It was an accident."

A single gunshot rang out and the bullet damaged the lock. I pulled my gun out from behind my pants and aimed it at the door when someone kicked it open. The crew was standing there, looking at me in disbelief. Rush charged into me and I fired. The bullet pierced through his shoulder. Stacy pointed his gun at me and Bogo stood beside him.

"You're supposed to be my brother, right? Do something!" I yelled at Bogo.

"Not this time, bruh. Let us get Isha some help," he said.

"Naw, she doesn't need help. She needs me."

"Put the gun down, muthafucka! The fuck is wrong with you?" Trayon asked, reaching for his piece. My family turned against me.

"You, too, huh?"

"Yo, we can't sit here and feel sorry for your bullshit. You gone too damn far!" he said.

Suddenly, I found myself lying next to Isha. I didn't see it coming. Rush slammed his fist into my face, causing my gun to slide across the floor. Stacy and Trayon carried Isha out the bathroom while everyone else stood around and watched that nigga pistol-whip me with my own gun.

"RUSH! That's enough!" Tuchie said. Jew and Lim pulled Rush off me and dragged him out the bathroom.

"I'm gonna merk your bitch ass! Let me go! I'm gonna dead that nigga, bruh!" Rush yelled out.

My jaw was hanging and blood dripped from my mouth; that nigga broke my jaw. Tuchie kicked me in the stomach when I tried to get up.

"Stay down, bitch! I hope your ass rots in jail!" she spat.

Bogo was the only one standing in the bathroom. Everyone else was tending to Isha.

"You a straight bitch, bruh. I don't know this nigga. I'm done, fam. You straight pussy," he said. Bogo walked out the bathroom, leaving me drowning in my own blood. I closed my eyes and I heard Joy's voice.

"You let me down, Jay. Who is going to protect our daughter? If you really loved us, things wouldn't have ended this way."

"Fuck you! It's all your fault. I should be dead, not you!" I sobbed.

"POLICE!" was the last thing I heard before I blacked out.

Tuchie

The reception ended early because of all the commotion. We were all in the waiting room of the hospital. My gown had Isha and Rush's blood splattered across it. They were both being treated but I wasn't too worried about Rush because his wound was non-threatening. Isha, on the other hand, was unconscious from hitting her head. I couldn't stop crying because I somewhat felt sorry for Jay. Who would've known he was suffering from lifelong depression. Something made him snap; we didn't know if it was Sadi's baby not being his or Isha and Rush—it could've been everything.

"We should've helped him. That person in the bathroom was not our Jay," Asayi said.

"We didn't know what he was going through," I replied.

The guys were quiet because they were closer to Jay and didn't see it coming, neither. Jay was in the hospital, too, but he couldn't have any visitors. The police were guarding his room. Two hours passed and the doctors hadn't come out yet. Hadley was sitting next to Adele sobbing on her shoulder. They rushed to the hospital once word got out Jay was trying to kill Isha.

My stomach was growling even though I wasn't in the mood to eat. My pregnancy was going by fast. I was already close to six months and it seemed like yesterday when I found out.

"Finally," Chika said when the doctor walked out.

Isha had a concussion and a small skull fracture. She was still in surgery to stop the swelling. I covered my mouth to keep from getting sick when I learned she hit her head multiple times. Jay was torturing her while we were on the dancefloor. If it wasn't for Rush looking for her, she would've been dead.

"Is she going to be okay?" Isha's mother asked.

"Yes, I've seen worse, but she'll have bad migraines until it heals," he said. He was the same doctor that gave us the news about Hadley when she was in that car accident. I could only imagine what he thought about us. I excused myself to get something from the vending machine.

"Stacy," a voice called out.

Lucas was standing behind me when I turned around. I hadn't seen or heard from him in months. After the incident at his house, he tried to reach out to me a few times to apologize. When someone called my job with a death threat, I told the authorities who it could've came from even though Lucas had no idea about my son.

"How have you been? Is everything okay?" he asked, looking at the blood on my dress.

"Yes, just a family crisis," I replied.

His eyes fell on my swollen stomach which indicated I cheated on him when we were together.

"What are you having?" he asked.

"Don't know yet, we want to be surprised."

"You're engaged?" he replied.

"Yes, to Stacy. It was nice seeing you but I gotta go."

He grabbed my hand when I walked away and I was hoping Stacy didn't see us because we didn't need another episode.

"I'm very sorry for how we ended and I still think about you. I really did love you and I know we can't get back together but at least I can finally move on knowing that you're in a good place," he said.

"Thank you and I'm sorry, too."

"Lucas, are you ready?" a nurse asked from behind us.

Lucas introduced us. She was his girlfriend and he was picking her up from work so they could go out to dinner. He made sure to tell me how they met and how they'd been dating. Even after he apologized, he was trying to make me jealous. I wished them the best of luck before I scurried off. His new woman couldn't have met Lynn yet.

I sat next to Stacy when I went back to the waiting room. He grabbed my hand and told me it would be okay.

"I sure hope so," I replied.

Two days later...

Isha was lying in bed watching TV while Rush was sitting in a chair beside her bed. I brought her flowers and balloons. Her head was wrapped in a bandage and she had bruises on her cheek. Isha needed thirty staples in her head, so one side of it was shaved. She cried about it the day after her surgery because she couldn't get braids for a while.

"How are you feeling?" I asked.

"I have a serious migraine," she said.

"It will go away soon."

"I'll let y'all talk. I got to head to the studio really quick but I'll be right back. Get some rest," Rush said to Isha. He kissed her lips and gave me a head nod before he left the hospital room.

"He's so wonderful," Isha beamed.

"I'm glad to see you smiling."

"It's not easy. Just think, I was in this wing months ago sitting next to Hadley's hospital bed. Now, you're sitting next to my hospital bed. Life is a funny muthafucka," she said.

"Sure is."

"My parents want me to testify against Jay when he goes to court. A detective came in my room earlier asking me what happened. I lied to him and told him I couldn't remember. All I want is to have a restraining order on him and for him to never contact me again," she said.

"Noooo, Isha. We feel sorry for him, too, but you cannot pretend this nigga wasn't trying to kill you. I'm more worried about you than him. Who's to say he won't try to do it again? He's dangerous and nobody knows what's going on inside his head."

Tears fell from her eyes and I handed her a tissue.

"What if he escapes and kills me because I testified against him or what if Hadley will start hating me?"

"Hadley is old enough to understand you are, and was always, the victim. If she faults you, maybe it's a good thing she stays away from you. You are not obligated to make her happy while you have to suffer from a near-death experience. It's okay to be thoughtful but it's not okay to put blame on yourself. Jay needs to realize what he did and suffer the consequences. Jail is better than death. Maybe he'll have time to think."

"I don't want to do it. I'm here and well," she said.

Isha was so traumatized to the point she was scared to put Jay in jail. We weren't in the bathroom with her so there was no telling what he said to her. I decided to let it go and just be there for her to help her heal. Victims of abuse often times thought it was their fault. Hopefully she got past that phase and did what was right.

"We're still here for you regardless."

"I love you, Tuchie. And I'm grateful for all of you," she said.

I sat with Isha for eight hours. It was getting late and I had to pick Niji up from Stacy's mother's house.

"I'll see you first thing tomorrow morning."

"Okay," she replied.

Her parents walked in with a few of her family members. I hugged everyone before I exited her hospital room.

****

Deborah answered the door after I rang her bell. We didn't talk much unless it was about Niji. She held the door open so I could step in. Niji was on the living room floor watching TV and eating popcorn.

"Come sit with me in the kitchen so we could talk," Deborah said.

"I'm in a rush."

"It will only take a second," she said.

I followed her into the kitchen and she gestured for me to have a seat at the table. She poured me a glass of fresh iced-tea and gave me a muffin. I thanked her and she sat next to me.

"How are things holding up with your friend?" she asked.

"Good, she's getting better."

"That's great," she replied.

"So, what's this about Deborah? Our wedding is coming up and I hope you are not trying to talk me out of marrying your son. I love him too much."

"Actually, I want to give you my blessing. After all these years, I finally see how much you and Stacy belong together. I had this impression you were going to bring my son down. I'm very sorry and I couldn't ask for a better mother for my grandkids," she said.

"Thank you. I'm glad we can have a healthy relationship now because it was wearing me down to the point where I thought it was impossible to be with Stacy."

"Stacy said to me one day, 'Ma, I've waited all these years for this woman and I'm going to marry her.' He loves you very much," she said.

Niji came into the kitchen, singing and dancing. Deborah clapped her hands and cheered her on.

"Sing, baby!"

I recorded her on my iPhone so I could post her on my social media. Other than Isha getting better, I wasn't stressed from any drama. I was having another baby, getting married and building a bond with my oldest child. Life couldn't get any better.

Epilogue

Isha

Two years later...

Camera people were setting up their cameras in my kitchen. Before my incident with Jay, the Food network contacted me but I wasn't emotionally ready to take on that responsibility until I was completely healed. After they heard what happened to me, the CEO told me to take all the time I needed. Well, a year and a half later, I made a decision to sign the contract. Me and Rush were also in a serious relationship but it didn't come overnight. We didn't rush it and with the faith of God, it naturally came. We also bought a big house together in Bethesda, Maryland. I had a small make-up station set up in the living room. Tuchie was fixing my hair while Asayi helped me with my make-up.

"I'm so proud of you," Tuchie said.

"Okay, Isha. I hope this works because my feet are swelling up," Asayi said. She was eight months pregnant with twin girls. She paid to have it done because Trayon wanted two more kids so she did it to get over with.

"Nobody told you to have twins," Tuchie joked.

"Who cares. The hubby is happy," Asayi said.

Rush walked downstairs and we bust out laughing at him. He was a guest on the show and he was wearing a chef outfit.

"Babe, you can wear regular clothes," I said.
"But I don't have a regular woman so I wore this. Yo, stop hating on yah man," he said and I blushed.

My make-up came out nicely. The show was starting in twenty minutes and Tuchie pulled out the last rod and teased my natural curls with a pic. After I lost a lot of my hair, I cut it all off and wore wigs so it could grow back evenly. I wore a cute chef jacket with ruffles; the bottom of the jacket was made like a tutu. Stacy came into my house carrying his son who looked identical to him. His name was Declan. He reached out to Rush and he took him out of Stacy's arms.

"You only showed up so you could clown me," Rush said to Stacy.

"You know me well," Stacy chuckled.

After Tuchie and Stacy got married, Rush surprised them when he changed his last name to Cook to get rid of Thomasine's family name. Thomasine contacted Rush every now and then to ask for money. Rush was a hot artist and all his shows sold out. To my surprise, the attention he got from women no longer bothered me because he never gave me a reason to be insecure.

"I'm ready," I told everyone.

Asayi, Tuchie and Stacy stood back and watched. I went into my huge restaurant-style kitchen and waited until the cameras started rolling.

"Welcome to Isha's kitchen. Today, we will be cooking pan seared steak with lemon and dill asparagus and garlic mashed potatoes. I have a surprise guest, R&B singer, Rush, who will be assisting me today." Rush came into the kitchen and stood next to me.

"First, we'll show you how to marinate the steak," I said into the camera.

One thing about cooking shows, you could be yourself. So occasionally I cracked jokes about my food if I made a mistake or dropped something on the floor. One time a crab escaped the pot and I told everyone I should've asked him for the crabby patty recipe before he got out. It was a corny joke, but they loved it.

"I would give Rush a kiss, but I don't want to make the onions cry," I joked while cutting the onions. It wasn't a secret we were together. I was at every one of his shows except when I had to work.

My show was an hour long. In the first half, I made main dishes, and the second half was desserts. It was my seventh show so far and I looked forward to doing more until I couldn't anymore. Traveling the world was still in the plans for the near future, but I wanted to wait until I had all the advertisement I could use.

Three hours later...

The camera people were gone and so were my friends. I was stretched out on the couch drinking a glass of wine. Rush went outside to get the mail. It was only three o'clock in the afternoon. I planned on going swimming in the pool since it was hot outside. Rush came back into the house with a weird look on his face. Something pissed him off.

"What happened?"

"Yo, why is this nigga still writing you?" he asked.

When we moved, my mail was forwarded to my new address. Jay sent a total of one-hundred and ten letters, asking me to forgive me.

"Trash it," I replied.

Rush threw the letter in the trash and pulled a blunt out of his pocket.

"Are you mad at me?"

"No, but he's only writing you because he thinks he still has a chance. You told the judge you don't remember what happened to you. The nigga only got five years because they found a gun on him. He will get out on good behavior soon," he said.

"Why didn't you tell the judge he shot you if that's the case?"

"I can handle shit and, plus, I wasn't fucked up physically or mentally behind it. You, on the other hand, wake up in tears from nightmares of what he did to you. Listen, I'm not trying to attack you. But I'm letting you know right now, we over if you write that nigga back," Rush said.

I went upstairs to get changed into a bathing suit. Jay scared the shit out of me and it seemed like nobody understood. He tried to kill me and showed no remorse in getting me any help. Jay wanted me to suffer even though he brought us to that point. While getting undressed, Rush wrapped his arms around me from behind. He kissed my neck, quickly taking away the thoughts of Jay. I turned around and kissed him. He picked me up and took me to the bed where he lay on top of me, using his skillful tongue to make me soaking wet. I pulled his shirt off and he unzipped his pants. His tongue danced around my nipples while I ran my nails through the silky coils on his head. He flipped me over onto my stomach, as his tongue traveled from the back of my neck to my ass cheeks. He spread my cheeks and kissed my pussy lips. I pushed myself up so I could be in a doggy-style position. With my back arched, Rush slithered his tongue into my opening, making me clutch the seats. His hands were gripping my cheeks as he had me spread open, eating my juicy fruit like a peach. Rush moved my hips to the rhythm of his tongue and I screamed his name as I came. My nectar drizzled down my inner-thighs like thick honey and he ran his tongue along the trail of my essence.

"I can't stop, Ish. Make me stop or I'm going to nut from this juicy pussy," he groaned against my lips. I didn't want him to stop because I knew it was just the beginning. His first and middle fingers separated my pussy lips into a "V". He pressed his tongue against my entrance and slurped.

"I'm ready to come again!" I screamed when my legs shook. He pulled away from me and laid on the bed with his big black dick standing like the Eiffel Tower. Pre-cum oozed from the tip of his mushroom head. Rush said he could nut off eating my box and he wasn't lying. I never understood the infatuation of the veins in a man's dick until I saw Rush's. They reminded me of roots in a tree. I climbed on top, easing my way down on his girth.

"FUCCKKKKKKK!" he groaned when I squeezed him between my walls. He pulled me to his face so we could kiss as I rode him. I loved when he palmed my ass and thrust upwards, hitting my G-spot. He was the true definition of feeling him in my stomach.

"I love your beautiful ass!" he said, smacking my ass cheek. I went harder, riding him faster. I could feel that big wave coming, the explosive orgasm he always gave me. He felt it, too, then rolled me over onto my back, pushed my legs up and gave me nothing but long inches. My essence coated his dick like milk and drizzled between my buttocks. He bit his bottom lip and went deeper, making me come again.

I loved him so much. He made me feel free, wanted, beautiful and safe. He whispered in my ear, he couldn't pull out. I was off birth control so he always pulled out when he was ready to explode. I wrapped my legs around him.

"You're going to get pregnant," he groaned.

"Are you scared?"

"Hell no," he smirked.

You only live once. I tried the old-fashioned way of wanting a baby after marriage, but I realized I could be happy just following what my heart desired. So far, the choices I'd made were for me and Rush helped me with it all. I was never going back!

Sadi

"**S**top running through the church!" I called out to Haden. Kareem kept his word and helped me become a great mother and wife of a pastor. It had only been a year since he became a pastor. I stopped talking to Keondra and even stopped contacting Shelley who was still in Maryland. There was no sense in her coming back since she stayed away from home so long; she was evicted from not paying her bills. I begged God for forgiveness for ruining the life of the only true friend I had. Kareem came out of his office and picked up Haden. Every day I asked myself why would a man like him want to be with me and the only thing I could up with was that he was my blessing. It was meant for him to never give up on me. He married me four months after bringing me back from Maryland. I wasn't in love with him when I married him. I married him because he took care of me and Haden. After a year passed, I fell in love with him. He gave me everything, but the most important thing he offered was faith.

"Let him be, Sadi. The boy is blowing off some steam," Kareem said. He rubbed my stomach and I blushed. He was excited about the little girl I was carrying. I was seven months and carried it well. It was bible study night so Kareem sent Haden to the room downstairs where a sister from the church watched the younger kids.

"A new family is coming tonight. Can you greet them and show them to the study for me?" Kareem asked.

"Of course," I replied and he kissed me on the cheek.

I went to the front door to greet the members as they came in. We spent more time at the church than we did at our home, but I couldn't complain since I was a housewife and had nothing else to do besides tend to Haden. It was six o' clock when the doors of Great Hope opened.

"Good evening sister, Jenkins," the members greeted me as they came inside.

What is Kareem talking about? Everyone who came is a member.

I was ready to close the door because bible study had already started but a cab pulled up.

"Maybe that's them," I said aloud.

The back door of the cab opened and a familiar face stepped out, along with a woman with a baby. He smirked at me and I thought I was going to puke. Tae disappeared after he threatened me at my shop in Maryland. I thought maybe Jay took care of it and didn't tell me but the asshole moved to Atlanta. They say everyone who wants a new life always comes to Georgia. Tae looked cleaned and had gained his weight back. He looked like he did when we were in our early twenties. The woman he was with wasn't the same ugly one he came with to my shop. This woman was drop-dead gorgeous and on the thick side. Her skin was the color of dark chocolate and her hair was styled in a cute cut.

"Hi, Sadi. It's nice to meet you. I finally get to see you in person. I'm Kareem's half-sister, Eva, by the way and this is my fiancé, Tae, and my little girl, Simiya. It's been a long time since I've been back home. We moved from Virginia two weeks ago," she said. I saw pictures of his sister but she was huge. Tae must've pressured her into doing drugs.

"Come right on back. I'll show you the way," I said. Tae was eyeing me while me and his fiancée were talking. I showed them to the study before I rushed to the bathroom.

"This can't be happening! This can't be happening!" I panicked. Someone knocked on the door and startled me.

"Sadi! This is Tae. Let me speak to you!" he called out.

"Please, leave me alone!" I replied.

"I swear I just want to talk to you. What am I going to do to you in a church? I'm saved, too," he said.

I opened the door and stepped out into the hallway. Tae was smelling good and I noticed the Rolex he was wearing.

"Listen, I know you hate me and trust me, it's taken me a long damn time to get over what you did to me. When you saw me at your shop, I wasn't getting high. I'm diabetic and being in jail with poor care made me look like shit. Anyways, I've been clean for a long time. When I got out and saw you for the first time, it made me mad. You were living without a care while I had to do ten years because of you. After I met my fiancée, she introduced me to this church life and I realized I'm the cause of everything that happened to you. I talked you into doing drugs because I was getting high myself and thought it was a good thing to do. I know it's late, but I'm truly sorry, Sadi. I've never stopped loving you. We don't have to tell them that we know each other. Let's start over. I'm Tae Collins and it's nice to meet you," he said, reaching his hand out to me. Tears fell from my eyes because I couldn't figure out if I was sad or happy for Tae. I hugged him and he squeezed me. Me and Tae were both alike—we betrayed our friends and always thought about ourselves. He pulled away from me and wiped his eyes.

"You got your teeth fixed?"

"Yeah, I got implants. But thank you. I wouldn't be here if I hadn't got locked up. It turned out to be a blessing in many ways. I've got to get back to my woman, so I'll see around," he said. He kissed my forehead before he walked down the hall to the study. God worked in mysterious ways and when the day comes, I'm going to write Asayi and Tuchie a letter. It's never too late to change.

Jay

The guards escorted me to the visiting room. My mother was sitting at a table waiting for me. She was calm when I approached her. My mother and my A-1 niggas knew I was in a dark place and eventually started coming back around.

Stacy wasn't feeling me because his loud-mouth wife and bitch-ass stepson wasn't cool with me. I was diagnosed with Obsessive Love Disorder. The counselor in prison told me I had it before Joy was killed. When I thought back to my younger years, all I did was accuse Joy of sleeping with everybody and I damn near stalked her. Being with someone that reminded me of Joy and was connected to her was a part of that obsession. I tried to kill Isha so nobody else could have her, and till this day I still couldn't get her out of my head. One night I had a wet dream, imagining her riding my dick like she used to.

"How are you holding up?" my mother asked.

"I'm okay. Have you talked to Isha?"

"We're not supposed to bring her up, remember? I cannot tell you and it's better this way so you can get better," she said.

"Can you tell her I love her?"

"Let's talk about Hadley. I came here to tell you she's pregnant. She's five months and has been hiding it from me. I don't know what to do. I'm getting old and can't help her raise a baby," she said.

"Who is the boy?"

"Jared. Apparently, they were sneaking around with each other. Listen, Jay, you have to get better while you are in here. Your daughter is going to need you. She's getting older, she'll be nineteen soon. Forget about Isha and focus on your daughter. I'm not going to live long. I have cancer, son. I had it in my hip years ago and I thought it was gone but it came back," she said.

"I thought your hip was bad because you fell. Why did you lie, Ma?"

"I did fall, the cancer was making it difficult for me to move around. I didn't want you to stress because I'm all you have. I'm begging you to build a relationship with Hadley," she replied.

"Hadley doesn't like me. She still hasn't visited me or answered my letters. I can't do nothing while I'm in here. Hadley has a trust fund set up. She'll have access to three hundred thousand dollars. If something happens to you, she'll get it sooner but she can't have it until she's twenty-one. When I was roaming the streets, I wanted to make sure I didn't leave her out here broke and depending on a nigga. Don't tell her, though, she'll find out if the cancer gets worst, but I need you to fight. I want you to be here when me and Isha get married and have kids." Tears fell from my mother's eyes.

"You won't leave well enough alone. Your fate is your karma, son. I have to go and I love you," she said. She grabbed her cane and left the visiting room. Visiting hours were nowhere near over and she just up and left. The guard took me back to my cell. I had two dudes in my cell and they both were locked up for getting caught with drugs.

"Yo, did you see the new C.O.? Shorty is thicker than prison nut and she's fine!" a dude named Jim said.

"Naw, I'm not worried about these bitches," I replied.

"Yo, why Isha never visit you? Ain't that your wife?" he asked.

"Mind yah fuckin' business, nigga!" I yelled at him.

"My bad, damn," he replied.

We were escorted out an hour later for dinner. While I was in line waiting for the cafeteria lady to pack rat meat on my plate, I saw a familiar face. It was Sadi's old friend, Shelley. She was the new C.O. I turned my head when I locked eyes with her. In prison, I didn't say shit to nobody and they didn't say nothing to me because word got around I was connected to Trayon. The only clowns I talked to were the niggas in my cell.

"Jay?" Shelley asked.

"You're not supposed to be over with me. Go back before you get fired," I said. It didn't make a difference because the C. O.'s did what they wanted.

"How is Sadi?" she asked.

"Yo, don't ask me about that bitch," I spat then suddenly something dawned on me. Sadi merked her husband. I wasn't a snitch nigga, but Sadi had been getting away with a bunch of bull. The lies she told and the screwed-up ways she had towards my daughter angered me all over again.

"Sadi killed your husband and burned the house down with his body inside. I know you still looking for his bitch ass. Shorty, he dead dead. When you find that bitch, tell her we all can't get a happy ending," I said.

Shelley's eyes watered but I didn't give a fuck about her feelings. Arnold was still coming up on the news as a missing person with Shelley holding rallies in search of her husband. She walked away and went back to her corner of the cafeteria.

I know Isha miss me and I can't wait to get home so I can pound that juicy pussy. Tuchie better kiss her fake-ass, Johnny Gill-looking son goodbye because I'm going to dead that nigga!

Broken

(A Damaged Spinoff)

Coming 2019

SOUL Publications